THE SHADOW PROJECT

AN URBAN FANTASY THRILLER

CECILIA DOMINIC

When I started writing this novel in 2019, I had no idea that when it would be published in April of 2020, we would be in the midst of a global pandemic.

Therefore, this book is dedicated to the medical professionals and scientists who do their best to keep us safe and who are racing to find a vaccine and effective treatment.

Thank you for all your hard work and sacrifice. We wouldn't be here if it wasn't for you.

ABOUT THE SHADOW PROJECT

Fae Files, Book One

Sometimes even a Fae princess has to agree to an impossible bargain. Unfortunately there's no "fair" in Fae.

Exiled Fae princess Reine has gotten comfortable in the Earth realm, but she'd drop it all in a heartbeat to return home to Faerie. When her scornful mother proposes a pact, Reine knows she better be careful, because Fae bargains are always loaded with tricks...

On the same day she agrees to help smoke out a traitor on a team of scientists, an invisible shifter attacks her in her supposedly ultra-secure home and a teleporting kitten adopts her. She suspects it's all connected, but time is running out for her to figure out how.

After discovering a shadowy manipulator is intent on seeing her fail, Reine must confront a deadly conspiracy that reaches into the Fae realm and could spell the end for her kind.

Can Reine unmask a sinister cabal before she loses her ticket home...or her life?

The Shadow Project is the mesmerizing first book in The Fae Files urban fantasy series. If you like snarky heroines, memorable creatures, and thrilling mysteries, then you'll love Cecilia Dominic's spellbinding story.

Buy *The Shadow Project* to pierce the veil today!

COPYRIGHT

The Shadow Project
© 2020 Cecilia Dominic

Ebook ISBN: 978-1-945074-57-8

Paperback ISBN: 978-1-945074-59-2

Editorial services provided by Evil Eye Editing

Cover design by Ryn Katryn Designs

LOOK FOR THESE TITLES BY CECILIA DOMINIC:

The Aether Psychics
Noble Secrets
Eros Element
Clockwork Phantom
Aether Spirit
Aether Rising

The Inspector Davidson Mysteries
The Art of Piracy
Mission: Nutcracker

1

The breeze tickled my fingers, and my shoulder cramped from leaning over my desk to the open window, but I didn't move. The little intruder cocked its head, its bandit mask giving it an air of insolence. Just another inch or so and it would pluck the seed from my fingertip. It stretched its neck, and—

The phone rang. In a flurry of wings, the Bohemian waxwing took flight, then alighted on the branch of a nearby shrub and gave me a baleful look.

I checked the number, intending to hit *Ignore* but it was the shop.

"What?"

"I have an emergency." Veronica's voice had an uncharacteristic shrillness.

"What sort of emergency?"

"Something magical. I can't say more. You'll have to see when you get here." Then she hung up on me. The nerve. But if something had my normally staid clerk in a tizzy, it must be bad.

Still, I couldn't leave the birdie without any help. It had

sought me out, but I didn't know why. I placed a thimbleful of seeds in the little dish on my desk just inside the windowsill and said, "Fine, help yourself when I'm gone." Then I grabbed my helmet and ran for my bike.

The trek between my cottage and the village had never seemed so long even with a little Fae enhancement to my motorcycle's speed. I grumbled under my breath the entire way. And here I'd thought everything would calm down now that Veronica had returned from the States, where she'd been caring for her ill sister.

Yet one more reason for me to not depend on anyone unless I absolutely had to. Unfortunately, as the silent financier of the crystal shop in Lycan Village, I had to rely on mortals to take care of things for me. It sucked when they didn't. Hades, I didn't need a crisis right now.

I quieted the roar of the bike as I slid through the back streets and rumbled to a halt behind the shop. I'd managed to keep my involvement a secret – the Lycanthrope Council wouldn't approve if they knew a Fae "interfered" with humans by funding their commerce. They had such a picky definition of what constituted "interference."

Whatever happened must have been bad if she needed me there.

The bell over the back door chimed. I saw she'd turned the sign to "Closed."

"Veronica?" I called softly. My senses were alert for an intruder. Or chaos. Or dark magic. Or any magic at all. The only sensations that I could pick up came from the crystals, each ringing with its own little chime in a chorus of stone bells, a new chime with each of my footsteps.

No, there was something. A whiff of Fae magic, but not strong enough for me to tell where it came from. Something had been here, had gotten past my wards. With my heart in my throat, I walked into the front of the converted cottage to find Veronica holding...a kitten?

"What's the problem?" I asked.

"It's this wee moggie," she said and scratched the creature behind one ear. It angled its head into the caress.

Anger flashed through me and burned out the worry. "You called me here for a *cat*? You said it was something magical."

"It's not just any cat," she said. "There's something seriously wrong with it. Look."

She handed it to me, and I had no choice but to take the warm, soft, purring creature and examine it. The kitten's little face already had character and perhaps the shadow of stripes to come under its lead-colored coat. The most charming part—one white mitten on its front left paw. I checked under the tail—a boy. It fit in the palm of my hand, and I guessed its age to be about six weeks.

"I'm a physician, not a vet," I said. When I ran my hand over it, the silly thing purred louder, but I felt what she must have meant—a frisson of something that didn't feel right.

Still, not an emergency.

I handed the gray kitten back. "He's fine. He just needs some peace and quiet away from his littermates, at least as far as I can tell. Did your time in the States addle your brain, Veronica?"

The little creature looked up at me with big blue eyes that already had flecks of gold and green in them. Ugh. I couldn't resist scratching him under his silky chin. And my fickle frozen heart melted just a touch when he started purring. I mean, who could resist a purring kitten? I might be Fae, but I'm not inhuman.

"Are you sure you wouldn't rather watch him for a day? Make sure he's all right?" Veronica's Scottish burr made the words sound innocent enough, but I caught the undertone.

"Wait a minute... Is this one of your tricks to get one of your kittens adopted? Again, not an emergency. Besides, he's too young to be away from his mum." I arched an eyebrow and put my hands behind my back so I wouldn't succumb to the temptation to pet the little charmer again.

"No, I'm truly worried for him." With a sigh, she held the kitten to her ample bosom, where he kneaded one of her, er, mounds, his eyes half-closed in bliss. She didn't flinch from his tiny but sharp claws going through her top. Or maybe her sweater was thick enough to handle it.

Then he disappeared.

"What in Hades...?" I asked. To say I was astonished would be an understatement. "Where did he go?"

"Oh, good, he did it. I was afraid he wouldn't and then how could I explain?"

Well, I wasn't going to apologize for snapping at her. "You could've just said that he randomly disappeared." I looked under the cash register counter in her shop but found nothing. "'Acting odd' is a vague way of putting it."

"Would you have believed me?"

"Probably not." Then a slight weight on my shoulder, the sensation of tiny claws digging into my neck, and the sound of a small motor by my left ear told me he'd reappeared. Wherever he'd been, it was cold, and I untangled him from my long hair and held him close to warm him.

"How long has this been going on?"

"For about a week now. Since his ears grew pointed."

"So he's younger than he looks." I held the little lad away from me, and he licked his nose with a tiny pink tongue. Then he licked me, all sweetness and sandpaper. "I truly don't know what to tell you." I didn't often find myself at a loss for words, at least not when dealing with humans, but she had me there.

"So can you please watch him? See what's up? His mother is beside herself and it's taking its toll on the other babies."

She didn't tell me what I already knew—that this would be

mama cat's last litter since she'd be spayed once they were all grown and adopted out. But Veronica didn't want any unnecessary deaths on her hands should mama cat breed again on the streets, which could be unkind to animals. I didn't blame her, as much as that sympathy shredded my ruthless Fae reputation. Veronica was the only human I allowed to see this softer side and that was only because she knew what I'd do to her if she revealed my secret. I was a big player in the success of her little shop.

"Fine, I'm intrigued. I suppose I could watch him for a couple of days. What's his name?"

"Raleigh, after Sir Walter Raleigh."

"And you're not afraid he'll come back without his head?"

"Not funny."

I still laughed. "All right, then, Sir Raleigh. Let's get you back to my place and see what's going on with you. Have you noticed any pattern about when it happens?"

She pulled a small spiral-bound notebook from beneath her counter. "I've kept notes. Mostly when he seems to be experiencing some sort of strong feeling. Like just now. But not just positive—it's also happened when he's frightened."

I took the notebook and nodded my approval for her neat, handwritten notes regarding dates and time. "Careful record-keeping, as always."

"Speaking of which..." She rubbed her temples. "I'm still catching up from being gone. Your check will be late."

I should have smote her but it was hard to be in a smiting mood with a purring kitten snuggled on my shoulder. Plus, I knew she'd pay me the rent and my share of the shop's profits when she could. I still couldn't believe the Lycanthrope Council hadn't caught on to our little arrangement. I saw it as an act of rebellion, as did she.

"I know you're good for it. Plus, extra for me figuring out the cat."

"Don't worry, you'll earn that. He's got mischief in his eyes."

The disappearance of the cat from my shoulder confirmed her words, especially when he reappeared on my other shoulder just a minute later. Again, that cold air. And again, I untangled him from my curly, white hair, which he batted at with his little kitten paws. She'd sent me off with plenty of kitten food and instructions, but how could I feed him if I didn't even know where he'd be?

Once I held him in my right hand, I sniffed him. Beyond the delightful smell of cat, there was something else, something familiar, but I couldn't place it. I put him on my chest and zipped up my jacket. He snuggled in and didn't dig in too hard, thankfully.

Yes, in spite of his youth, Sir Raleigh had a certain dignity that deserved the honorific.

When I arrived at my house, my haven in the countryside, I found the door open. I placed Sir Raleigh and his food on top of the mail in the basket to the right of the front door and latched the lid shut. Not that it would deter the cat if he really wanted to escape, but I wouldn't knowingly bring him into harm's way.

With a deep breath, I drew from the energy of the ley line that ran beneath the house, the creek behind it, and the trees over it. Then I wove the nature and ley magic into a web around me that would hopefully capture or deflect any dangerous spells that came my way. Unsophisticated compared to what I could previously do in Faerie, but it was my best for now.

And in case of human intruders, I pulled a small but deadly sharp silver knife from my boot. Its wooden hilt kept the metal from harming me—not that silver did much to me, anyway. Now iron—that was a different matter. I hoped that whoever had intruded upon my home didn't know who or what I was. But who could have found me? I'd kept my address in this realm a secret.

I pushed the door open with the toe of my boot—synthetic, not leather—and crept inside. My eyes adjusted immediately. Nothing seemed amiss, although the air eddied with having recently been disturbed. My spells and wards hadn't been triggered, so who or what could have gotten in?

The foyer held no surprises, nor did the parlor to my right. I glanced up the stairway to my left, but I didn't hear anything moving around or breathing above me. That left the living room and the kitchen to the back.

When I walked into the living room, the lights came on. Again, my eyes adjusted immediately, and I spun around, but saw no one. So who had turned on the lights?

Something brushed by me, and a low growl by my left ear told me Sir Raleigh had returned to his perch.

"You feel it, too, huh?" At least the cat helped me to feel less insane. Whoever was in my house was invisible. A ghost? No, my wards should have kept them out. So then what?

The lights went out again, and with an eddy of air that smelled of must and decay, whoever or whatever it was ran out of the house. I heard its footsteps, but still not its breath. What in Hades could it have been? The entire house seemed to sigh with relief.

"We all have enemies, Lady Reine," Veronica had told me once. "And someone like you must have powerful ones."

I'd demurred—no one should care about a cast-out Fae like me, but apparently someone did. I walked through the kitchen to my office, which overlooked the back garden, and found my desk, cabinets, and shelves had been raided. I thought about checking the hiding place under the desk, but what if whatever had intruded still watched by some means? I didn't trust my wards. No, I wouldn't show it my secrets—my treasure—that easily.

With one trembling hand, I attempted to soothe the cat, which had crawled half-down my front, mewing piteously.

With the other, I picked up the phone, cradled the handset between my head and neck, and called the one person I trusted —and that loosely—with a crime of this nature. The best investigator I knew.

"Gabriel?" I asked. "Can you do me a favor? Someone broke into my house."

~

IT DIDN'T TAKE LONG for Gabriel to arrive in his green Jaguar along with a pleasant surprise—Maximilian Fortuna, "Max" for short.

"Well," I said, "I'm honored to have such high-ranking officials visiting me."

Then another car pulled up and I wrinkled my nose.

"You called Inspector Garou, too?"

"He's the new Lycanthrope Council Investigator," Gabriel said. "I'm not in that game anymore." In fact, while he rarely seemed happy to see me, his voice carried the extra weight of irritation.

I snorted. "Like Hades you aren't."

Inspector Garou hadn't registered on my Fae-dar as important, but now that I looked at him, I noticed something interesting. He was a human with no magic or shifting abilities, but his dark eyes sparkled like flint, and there was a hardness to his jaw. No, Garou might not have any current magical abilities, but I'd bet there was gargoyle in his blood.

My indifference hardened, if you'll forgive the pun, into dislike.

"Problem?" Gabriel asked. He'd come to stand beside me, and I suppose he noticed my expression. I could typically hide my emotions, but not when they hearkened to the reason for my exile.

"Garou. He's not one of you, but he's got elemental in him. Water and earth, specifically."

Gabriel's eyebrows lowered as he studied the inspector. I wondered what he saw with his still-burgeoning alpha abilities. "Gargoyle?"

"Yes. I don't want him anywhere near me."

Now Gabriel turned his hazel gaze on me in surprise. "What do you have against gargoyle blood? It must be several generations ago."

"It's a long story, but one was involved in Rhys' mutilation."

"Ah. I'm afraid I can't do anything about him being here. As I said, he's our investigator. You don't want regular humans mucking about, do you?"

Sir Raleigh chose that point to make an appearance on my shoulder with an irked "mew!"

Gabriel turned away and coughed. Or at least that's what he tried to do. I caught his laugh.

"New friend? Or new hair decoration?"

I swear, every time that kitten appeared, he somehow got tangled in my hair. As I yet again disengaged his little claws from my white curls, the almost-stripes on Raleigh's face made him look amused. I caught the same look on Max's face. Garou wore his customary scowl, and he fiddled with an unlit cigarette.

"Don't you dare light that thing around here," I warned, perhaps more harshly than necessary, but I couldn't bear to be laughed at. Never mind that he was the only one—besides me —not laughing.

"You look good with a kitten," Max told me. He walked over and held out a hand. Instead of shaking it, I handed the kitten to him.

"Here, please watch him. Careful—he likes to—" Sir Raleigh disappeared from Max's hands and reappeared on my other shoulder with an indignant squeak. "All right, then, insolent creature." Rather than pulling him from my curls, I left him. He wrapped his little tail around my neck and started a subtle but content rumbling.

"Where did he come from?" Max asked.

"Veronica." A movement caught my peripheral vision, and I looked over to see that Garou had dropped his cigarette when I mentioned the witch. Interesting.

"Oh, from the mother cat and litter she found. Abby has been bugging us for a kitten ever since she heard. She says there's something magical about them."

"She's not wrong." As we all did, I kept a close eye on Max's daughter Abby. Although barely over a year old, she'd shown intelligence far beyond her age. An old soul, that one, and likely to be powerful.

Max shot me a nervous glance, his expression remorseful.

"Don't worry. I'm not in the child-snatching game anymore."

Gabriel cleared his throat. "While all this talk of kittens and children is fascinating, you called me over for a reason."

"Yes, you. Although Max is always welcome."

"We were having lunch," Max explained. "What happened?"

I told them about returning home and finding the office a mess. That I'd felt something, or thought I had, but I couldn't explain what. I left out that the creature was unknown to me and disturbed me more than I could say.

"So there's an invisible intruder?" Garou spoke for the first time. At the sound of his voice, Raleigh stopped purring. I didn't blame him.

"There was."

"Right, then," Gabriel said. "Let's take a look around. Was anything stolen?"

"Not that I can tell, but I haven't looked thoroughly."

The men went inside. I hung back. My cottage looked the same as it always had—a typical "fairy cottage" prototype with its gray brick walls and Flemish tile roof, plenty of plants, cute cutout windows with green wooden shutters... But it didn't feel like home. Not anymore.

Not that it ever should have.

In my long life, I'd learned to trust my instincts. Something was very, very wrong. Without thinking, I reached up to pet the cat. He began to purr, a sound that should have been soothing but didn't do much to calm my nerves.

"Can't find anything," Gabriel told me when they came out. "No signs of forced entry."

"And your wards are strong," Max added. "Nothing should have gotten past them unless you invited it in."

I took a breath to say I didn't invite anything in, but Garou cleared his throat and interrupted me.

"Are you sure you felt something?" he asked, his eyes narrow and suspicious.

I looked at the three of them and kept my mouth from falling open in undignified amazement. Then heat came to my cheeks—they didn't believe me. Well, Max might. He looked uncomfortable. But what had happened with Gabriel? I'd helped him, for Fae's sake.

"I know what I felt," I said. "There was something in there."

"There are lots of strange things in the woods," Gabriel observed. "Maybe you should move closer into town."

"The last thing I need is to be surrounded by people." I made sure to intone the word, *people*, with enough disgust that, paired with a pointed look at Garou, he'd get the hint.

Gabriel rubbed one temple. Right, he got migraines. Was he fighting one now? Could that be at the root of his less than jovial mood? When he spoke, he sounded defeated. "If something managed to find you *and* got past your wards *and* ransacked your office, then it's going to be too powerful for us. We can't protect you."

That made me sputter. "*You* protect *me*? Did you forget that I helped you with the murders at the ILR? Hades, Gabriel, I'm not asking you to..." I shook my head. Why had I asked them to come over? Because I'd hoped they would have a simple explanation, perhaps some being the activities at the ILR had attracted, something we could do a spell for and get rid of easily. But nothing with humans was ever easy. "Never mind. I'll handle it myself."

"Sorry we couldn't be of more help," Garou said, but I refused to thank him. He still sounded too doubtful of my story, and I wouldn't be treated like a hysterical woman. He and Gabriel moved toward the cars, but Max held back.

"Be careful," he said. "I can't tell you too much, but there are things happening. Big things."

"Like what?" I asked.

"Can't say right now. Just...be careful, as I said." He squeezed my upper arm, a rare gesture for him that brought me back to the days when we'd been students together. He turned and left.

I walked back into my cottage and leaned against the door until the rumble of the car engines faded, to be replaced by a fluttering noise.

2

I ran to the office. The little waxwing I'd been coaxing earlier lay on the desk, barely breathing. I cradled the tiny yellow and gray creature in my hands.

"Where did you come from?" I asked. And what had happened to it? It felt like something had drained its life energy.

A feline chirp reminded me of Sir Raleigh on my shoulder, and I felt that he studied the bird out of curiosity, not a predatory instinct. He'd stopped purring, and I'd forgotten he was there. Well, as long as he didn't try to hurt the bird, I would allow him to stay.

I willed healing energy into the waxwing until its breathing and heartbeat returned to normal. After I placed it on the desk, it wobbled to its feet, then flew back to its bush, where it trilled a thank-you. I wished I could ask it what had caused its malady, but birds and Fae didn't share much vocabulary. A glowing wisp connected the bird to my window for a second, then faded. I shivered. That had been a warning from one of my wards marking an intruder. It should have glowed stronger and lasted longer if the bird had entered my house without invitation, but it hadn't—I'd left food for it. None of this made sense.

What in Hades had been in my house? Bird crisis averted, anger blazed through me. I took some deep breaths to calm it down, but found fear underneath. What had been in here that a Fae, a wizard, and an alpha werewolf couldn't detect a trace of? And a gargoyle-descended human, but I dismissed Garou. He'd never impressed me.

Then I found the familiar sting of betrayal and disappointment. Why hadn't I moved closer into town? Well, besides the modern noises, smells, and other things my five-hundred-year-old nervous system couldn't take, it would mean neighbors and conversations and the chance of slipping into the mistake of trusting people. That never ended well.

So I'd manage on my own. As usual. Or, not quite on my own...

"Well, it's just you and me, kitty." With the cat still on my shoulder, I smudged every room, closet, and the basement with a bundle of dried herbs Veronica had made for me "just in case." Then I strengthened my wards, but until I could figure out what the bird had to do with the intruder, I'd have to keep my windows closed. It was probably for the best, considering the cat.

Did I think the bird could be some sort of shifter? Its size argued against the possibility. While the magic of shapeshifting could stretch the conservation of mass to a point, that would have been extreme.

Sir Raleigh hadn't disappeared again, and I hoped he wouldn't get into too much trouble when I let him loose in the house. While I'd never had a pet before, his presence relieved me. Normally Fae and cats didn't get along—they could see us even when we concealed ourselves, and they took a perverse joy in hunting our smaller cousins like pixies—but he could likely also sense creatures such as whatever the intruder had been. A tingle up my spine told me that the cat coming into my life the same day the mysterious being invaded my house had likely not been a coincidence, but I couldn't see the connection.

Once done with the smudging, I peeled the kitten from my neck and set him on the floor. He immediately started to explore, his little, gray nose working. I set up the supplies Veronica had sent me with—litter box, food, and a couple of small blue ceramic bowls. Once satisfied Sir Raleigh wouldn't get into trouble, I went into my office and commenced cleaning, more to have something to do to settle my nerves than anything.

Nothing seemed to be missing, and the hidden door under the desk called to me.

"I'm not calling her," I said. But every little noise startled me now, and Gabriel's words about the powerful intruder echoed in my brain. Fear had been an unfamiliar emotion, and its shaky presence didn't suit me at all.

It had been almost four hundred years, dammit. I deserved to go home where it was safe. But I couldn't beg.

Or could I? They couldn't deny my entrance back to Faerie if I wasn't safe here, could they?

A small spark of hope lit up the gloomy cavern of my thoughts. They'd have to let me return.

When I checked on the kitten once more—more to ensure he didn't sense anything scary—I found him asleep on the middle of the kitchen table in a sunbeam. How had he gotten up there? He was too little to jump. Right, he had likely teleported.

I had a teleporting cat. Had borrowed one, rather. He might be going back to Veronica sooner than either of us had anticipated.

Between the smudging and an extra layer of wards, whatever had ransacked my office shouldn't return. It was time to check on my secret treasure. And there was one person who might know what the creature had been...

I went to the desk, moved the chair back, and pulled back a section of the rug under where my feet would normally go if I'd been sitting. When I whispered the key word, a stone set in the floor elevated and slid out of the way, revealing a hidden compartment from which I brought forth a wooden box. I smoothed the lid with my hand. The contents shifted inside although I hadn't tilted the box, and a tug at the base of my skull told me it had been too long. When I opened the lid, the crystal and jewel talisman inside glowed so brightly the light sparkled through all the gems—ruby for the sunrise in the east and fire, sapphire for the sky and water, amethyst for sunset in the west and air, and emerald for growth and earth. Golden bands affixed them to a six-inch length of pure crystal, which shone. That could only mean one thing.

I'd thought I would be requesting an audience with my mother, but as it turned out, she was summoning me.

RETURNING to the fairy circle always hurt. In spite of the beauty of the place—inside a cave with a carpet of green grass year-round and a singing waterfall in the corner—the bad memories crowded in. Mother pronouncing Rhys' inability to return to Faerie because of the imperfection his injury had caused. My banishment for not preventing his stupid actions. Her turning a cold, pointed ear to my pleas.

Humans called the passages we made between Earth and Faerie portals, but we called them doorways. Although I hadn't been able to use my ability to enter in years, I still tried—a reflexive internal gesture of opening the air to walk through. Today, as always, the doorway remained locked.

"You'll never stop trying, will you?" Mother's voice vibrated through the air around me.

I stepped back to allow her room to come through. "Never. My rightful place is there, in Faerie. You can't hold me responsible for Rhys' mistake forever." I hadn't come intending to rehash the old argument, but the events of the day had taken their toll. Now that I no longer felt safe in my home, I wanted—needed—to return to Faerie more than ever. Still, I'd hoped to be more elegant in my petition.

Mother appeared, wearing a gown of green satin, her white-blond hair in an updo. My hair had been the same color as hers when I'd been banished, but it had turned white during my time on Earth. I knew that wouldn't be enough to deem me flawed—many of the older Fae had white hair. At least I'd kept my youthful face and figure, but I wondered how long those would last before I melted like a thin wax candle into a stubby, gnarled shape.

"I suppose you are wondering why I summoned you here, Daughter."

Hmmm, no preamble or criticism. She must have really wanted to talk to me. Hope sparked in my chest—could this be it, my absolution and ticket back home?

"Yes, and I have a question for you as well," I said.

"In a moment. First, I have news for you. I suspect you'll consider it good."

"I'm allowed to come home?" The ache for Faerie never went away, as much as it might diminish while I lived in this realm. Earth beauty, as stunning as it could be, didn't compare.

"Perhaps. Your grandmother has consented to forgive you if you complete a task for her. For us."

Great, a fairy task. Guaranteed to be difficult, if not impossible. I knew this because I'd given out more than a few in my time. And they always came with an agenda.

"What is it?" I asked, trying not to allow my misgivings to show.

"Since you were so helpful in the investigation of the murder at the Institute for Lycanthropic Reversal, the Faerie court has decided to allow you to accompany representatives from the ILR to the Center for Disease Control and Prevention. They will give you the details of what they want to accomplish, something about tracking the spread of lycanthropy and blah, blah." She waved her hand. Typical.

"Isn't that in the United States?"

"Correct, a place called Atlanta."

"But my powers..." Panic welled up in my gut at the thought of leaving my home and the network of caverns beneath it, from which I drew my power. I'd still have some of my magic in a different place, but not as much, and the thought made me feel naked and vulnerable already.

"You won't need them for the task, don't worry." She smiled, and I wish I could say her expression was maternal, but the word that came to mind was calculating.

"What is my task, then?"

"You are to protect our secrets from the scientists there, who are studying paranormal creatures. They know we exist, but not the power that we have. And especially not the elemental nature of our makeup."

"They know we're elementals, Mother."

"Right, but not of what kind. Not that we have all five and hold them in balance." She covered her mouth, took a deep breath, and continued in a quieter tone. "And not that we can manipulate them to change the nature of what they call matter. In this age, that is our most dangerous secret. The humans would weaponize it if they could."

I nodded my agreement to that. The humans would turn the most benign of substances into ways to kill each other if they could. The Fae had considered themselves above that since the last Great War between the Seelie and Unseelie courts, when we'd realized that tipping the balance between light and dark wasn't worth the death and destruction caused by the conflict.

"So I go, keep our secrets away from a bunch of academics, and then what?"

"When the investigation you're a part of is over, and all loose ends tied up, you may return to Faerie."

"All right." No, I needed to *hear* what she said. The assigner of a Faerie task always left loopholes for themselves. "What sort of loose ends?"

"Whatever comes up. You've been in this realm long enough to know."

"It sounds simple enough, although I know it probably isn't." But if Gabriel and Max were part of it, they'd be thorough. I hoped.

"You sound like a petulant child."

If I did, it was because she'd made me that way, but I refrained from saying so. Plus, somehow she'd steamrolled me into agreeing to the task before I could express my concerns. Dammit, she always did that to me. Finally I remembered to ask, "Do you know of a creature that can turn itself completely invisible yet maintain enough form to move objects around?"

"You mean a ghost?"

"It wasn't a ghost. I would have been able to identify that. It was a..." I hoped the word would come, but it didn't. "I don't know. But not a ghost. It didn't have that feeling of being dead. But not alive, either."

"You're not making sense, Daughter."

"Whatever it was, it was dangerous," I told her. "I don't feel safe here."

With a blast of cold air that stirred my hair, a now-familiar sensation started on my shoulder, of kneading and a rumbling purr. *Oh, not now...* But it gave me important information about my little friend—he shouldn't have been able to find me in the fairy circle.

"What in Hades is that?" My mother's tone combined revulsion and curiosity.

"Mother, meet Sir Raleigh." I again extracted the cat from my hair, but I didn't hold him out to my mother. The little creature made me feel more protective of it than I had of anything before, even my brother. I knew she'd try to take him away from me if she suspected I valued him.

"May I see him?"

"No. It's a kitten. There's nothing special about him." *Well, other than the teleportation thing.*

"That's not an ordinary kitten," she said. "Where did you get him?"

"He found me." It wasn't a lie.

"Yes, I'm sure he did."

I raised my eyebrows. The woman didn't waste a word, and this was the second time tonight her tongue had tripped ahead of her. I could tell from the rueful expression that flashed across her stonily beautiful face.

"Do you know something about him I don't?" I had to ask.

"I don't know, dear daughter, considering you haven't told me anything about him, so I don't know what you know, and you won't let me touch him."

She could always see right through me. "He's only a kitten," I repeated. "A strange little chap, assuredly, but I'll figure him out."

She shook her head. "Do yourself a favor and drown him in the nearest stream. He's going to be nothing but trouble. Besides, you can't bring him with you. The United States has an animal quarantine."

"How do you know that? You haven't bothered with silly human laws in a millennium."

She shrugged. "We all have to change with the times, Reine.

Remember your mission—don't let them find out more about us than they already know. We survived the so-called Age of Enlightenment, but this current age..." She held her hands palm-up. "They think they can distill everything into their precious science. But some mysteries are best left unsolved."

"Right, I can handle it. And then I'll come home. My *real* home."

"Gods' speed, Daughter."

With that, she faded, leaving me alone in a fairy circle with a squirming kitten clutched to my chest and questions swirling around my brain. I held Sir Raleigh up so I could look him straight in his blue eyes.

"Well, that was interesting. You are apparently connected to more than I thought. I wonder what she meant—she was sure you found me?"

Curiouser and curiouser, as Alice said in the Lewis Carroll story. Especially since I had caught an expression on Mother's face when I asked about the creature in my cottage. It had lasted only a fraction of a moment, but it had been there—fear, a reaction I found most unsettling. My mother feared nothing, so what could it mean?

Only that I needed to accomplish this task and get home soon.

3

When I stepped outside of the fairy circle, my phone dinged with a text. I hated the thing from its guts of chemical and twisted metal to its dead plastic exterior, but it had its uses. Only a few people had my number, and when I pulled it from my pocket, I saw the message had come from Max.

"What now?" I asked Sir Raleigh, who had resumed his perch on my shoulder. He was doing something with my hair, but I didn't feel like questioning what.

Max's text surprised me, making my eyebrows rise again. If I wasn't careful, I'd lose my reputation as mischievous but jaded Fae, and worse, get forehead wrinkles.

Have message for you. Meet me at ILR?

I checked the sky—it was about 6:00 p.m., so most of the scientists would have gone home. I wondered if that included Selene Rial, Gabriel's fiancée. I had nothing against the girl—she seemed nice enough and I had to respect her determination to keep her secrets—but I'd always admired Gabriel. He'd been in the running for my next lover before he'd taken up with her, and I hated that he'd been stolen from me. Well, as long as she knew her place, she'd be fine.

Fine, I texted back. I wasn't going to be too cooperative.

There wasn't time for me to drop the kitten by my place, so I stashed him against my chest under my fake leather motorcycle jacket. I'd have preferred a white mare for my transportation, but as my mother had pointed out, we needed to change with the times, so I had. I'd spent good money on a motorcycle with a hybrid motor so it wouldn't burn so much gasoline, which I detested for its smell and its waste and its association with plastic. Like my cat friend, I could travel between dimensions for short distances, but it wore me out, especially if I had to cross metal and stone barriers.

I arrived at the ILR as the moon rose over the trees behind it, giving the Institute a resemblance to the castle it had been modeled after, Wolfsheim's old place. I'd never gotten the chance to ask him what he thought about the ILR's layout being so like his old castle. Gabriel had killed him—justifiably —before I could. And then Gabriel had burned my one chance to influence him by lunging after Rhys, forcing me to use his name to stop him. Ugh, that still peeved me. In fact, my brother had an irksome knack for interfering with my life. It was bad enough he'd been the reason for my banishment from Faerie. Why did he have to continue to thwart me?

But all that was water under the moon—simultaneously silvery and murky. It was no accident that Veronica had modeled the moon card in her Tarot deck after me. The woman was spookily perceptive sometimes.

Once I stopped the bike, I took a deep breath to compose myself and shifted the sleepy cat back to my shoulder. He must have worn himself out following me into the fairy circle.

"Please be quiet and good," I murmured to him. He purred, but I was not sure if he was promising to be agreeable or saying, "Yea, right, lady."

"You know, you're going into the lair of a bunch of dogs."

He burrowed further into my hair.

I walked through the silent lobby, and I swallowed against the upwelling of hope, residual energy from those who'd come to be treated. As far as I knew, the only ones allowed to access the treatment still included those who'd been turned later in life, not those who were born with it, although they'd petitioned for access to the cure, too.

Gabriel opened the door at the end. He wrinkled his nose. "Cat?"

"He won't leave me be," I said with a shrug.

"Please don't hurt him. He's just a baby."

His words stung.

"You think I'd harm an innocent animal? I'm a healer, Gabriel."

"To be honest, I don't know what you're capable of."

Well. I'd done my job, then, of keeping him at arm's length in spite of my feelings, but not exactly as I'd wanted it. Normally, I didn't care what people or lycanthropes thought of me, but this one's opinion mattered. I didn't say anything— only followed him up the central staircases to the hallway upstairs.

There were more people still there than I expected. Max stood at the entrance to one office and beckoned for us to enter. The light shone off his blond hair, giving him the appearance of a beckoning angel. Or sly demon, considering I was here on my mother's behest.

Once I entered the office, I found myself in a space that looked more like an English study. Lonna Marconi, the director of the Institute and Max's wife, stood when I entered, reminding me of her height and statuesque Italian looks. She gave me a wary look, but I grinned at her. Let *her* wonder what I was capable of. I'd known her husband long before she did.

No matter how much I wanted to escape from the past, it

followed me.

"Thank you for coming, Reine," Lonna said.

"I came because Max asked me to," I told her. I wouldn't allow her to think she had any authority over me. She couldn't grant me what I truly wanted. Only my mother or grandmother could.

"Still, thank you."

I looked around at the three—no, four, because Selene had arrived—of them. No one appeared sick or otherwise in need of my Faerie healing abilities.

"What do you need?" I asked.

"Please, have a seat." Lonna gestured to a group of chairs clustered around a fireplace on one side of the room. I shrugged and complied, crossing my legs and shifting the kitten to my lap. I could feel their curiosity about Sir Raleigh, at least the women's, but I didn't say anything. I wanted to be annoyed—it was hard to maintain my badass fairy image with a purring fuzzball in my lap, but I felt that Sir Raleigh acted for my comfort, not his. How ridiculous was that, thinking a cat acted in anything but his own interest?

"I need to get back and feed my cat," I said and gestured to the feline in question. "Why did you call me here? Do you know what that was in my house?"

"No," Gabriel said, "but I suspect it may be connected to the message that I found waiting for me when I returned here. Max, Lonna, and Selene had similar ones." He handed a letter to me.

"'Dear Sir Gabriel McCord, head of the Lycanthrope Council, I was hoping you could help me with a quandary...'"

I read the rest of the letter, then looked up. "Is this real?"

Lonna nodded. "We checked. They're legit."

"So, you're saying the head of a shadow CDC is inviting you to come over to investigate possible leaks for what started the Chronic Lycanthropy Syndrome outbreak before moving forward with their next major project?" I had to act surprised in spite of having gotten a heads-up from my mother. "What does this have to do with me?"

"Yes, they're asking for our help and expertise," Gabriel said. "And I'd like for you to accompany us. Your medical skills and other talents will be invaluable in helping us to flush out whoever is selling their secrets."

"But you don't have to if you don't want to," Selene added. Her words puzzled me almost as much as the looks the others darted to each other and her.

Interesting. I leaned back and stroked Sir Raleigh's soft head. "Well..." I drew out the word. "Why would I want to go? That's a long way for me, and you know how we're tied to the land."

"You can tell things others can't," Max told me. "We have reason to believe this mission could be dangerous."

"Including to you. Maybe to you most of all." Selene nodded in her eagerness, her wide blue eyes and strawberry blonde hair giving her an air of innocence that I knew hid a clever mind. "I'd hate for something to happen to you."

What was she playing at? And what were the others not telling me? I couldn't seem too eager to go, though. They'd sense I'd been tipped off and want to know why.

Raleigh flopped on his back and let me pet his soft belly. His purr resonated through the room, and the others watched him, giving me a chance to attempt to sense what was going on. Ah, right, Selene and Lonna didn't want me to go—they felt strongly enough they had difficulty hiding their discomfort with the idea. Gabriel had a "duty calls" air, and Max was...concerned?

"If it's going to be dangerous..." I let my sentence trail off, and I almost laughed at Selene and Lonna's almost imperceptible leaning forward. Their anxiety over me fed my power and mischievous side. "When do we leave?"

"Day after tomorrow." Gabriel tapped his letter. "They've

made arrangements already. Without asking us." His scowl described exactly what he thought about that level of presumption.

"That's not much time to prepare. I have a cat now." I sighed. "But I'll manage. Fine, I'll go. Email me the itinerary and ticket links."

"You're sure?" Selene practically pouted.

"If I can be of help, I can't refuse." Especially since my return to Faerie hinged on my success. How hard could it be?

MAX CAUGHT up to me as I was about to walk through the lobby door.

"Got a second?" he asked. He'd put on his jacket, so I nodded and gestured for him to follow me out.

"What do you need?" I asked. Typical human-wizard—Max had only called upon me when he needed my help, most recently when he'd required training for use of blood magic, and then when Gabriel had been injured and needed Fae healing. We'd gone to medical school together, and while we'd been close, something had happened to drive a wedge between us. I keenly felt that now.

Sir Raleigh had curled up on my shoulder again, and I stroked his soft head. Max grinned and I stopped. Right, the cat really wasn't helping me maintain my aloof and cold Fae reputation.

"Cute kitten."

"Thanks. He won't leave me alone."

"Perhaps he knows something."

At first I thought Max must be joking, but his grin had vanished, and he was using his "I'm about to give you bad news as gently as possible" doctor voice.

Hades.

"What do you mean?" I asked. We'd reached my motorcycle, which I'd named Heather out of a joke about its purple color.

"Gabriel wasn't telling you everything." Max rubbed his eyes. "We were arguing over it at lunch when you called, and he took the break-in as a sign that something larger is afoot. He wanted time to check it out before telling you. He says you're strong and clever enough to handle whatever comes your way."

"And you don't think I am?" Curiosity over what they were keeping from me warred with my desire to show...what? That Gabriel was right? That was annoying.

"No, I know you're capable. I also know you have vulnerabilities." He gave me a, *I know you're hiding something* look.

I shrugged. "So are you going to tell me or not?"

Max sighed. It must grate on him to keep something from Gabriel, the man who'd become his best friend.

"The person who sent the invitation, a Doctor Cimex, requested you specifically. He mentioned you when Gabriel called to follow up on the invitation."

"Me? How could he even know about me?" That gave me a chill, and Sir Raleigh stirred and sighed.

"Precisely." Max looked down, and I wondered if he thought about taking my hand as he had that night on the beach a decade before. We'd come so close to trying our luck as a couple, but then an incident had happened that had revealed who I truly was to him. Others had known, too, and that was the problem—Max knew he'd not be allowed by the Wizard Tribunal to make our relationship official, and I'd found out who he was—not the friend I'd thought. We'd drifted apart. But the fact remained—my identity wasn't as secret as I would like.

"What exactly did he say?" I asked.

Max returned his sea-blue gaze to me. "'I would be particularly honored if the Fae princess doctor would accompany you as part of your party.'"

For the third time that day, I tasted the unfamiliar and

unwelcome flavor of fear at the back of my throat. I swallowed. "Do they have contact with the sea Fae? Atlanta isn't near the coast, is it?"

"Not particularly, but it's also not a far drive. Reine, you need to be careful. You don't have to go."

But I did have to go. My mother had put me in a position where I had to say yes.

"I'm going, Max. If this involves me—involves the Fae—I'd be turning my back on my people if I were to stay home."

"You're not as invincible as you think you are. Remember how attenuated your powers will be there. There is a large granite monolith that may give you some access to the earth energy you need, but that won't be everything."

His words only reminded me further of my mission. The humans and wizards thought we were primarily earth elementals. I couldn't let them discover otherwise.

"I appreciate the warning, and I will be careful—I promise. But I need to go. Both home to take care of this little guy and to the shadow CDC."

He sighed, then shrugged. "I figured you wouldn't be deterred." He pulled an envelope from the inside pocket of his jacket. "We leave on Thursday. Is two days enough time for you to get ready?"

"Yes," I said and took the packet from him, then tucked it in my own inner pocket. "We Fae pack light."

"Right. Reine, please be careful."

Lonna emerged from the building and waved to us. I waved back, but I didn't want to stick around and make small talk. The humans already thought me rude, so I tucked Sir Raleigh back in my jacket, and with his little motor going against my chest, put on my silver helmet and mounted Heather. I sensed the kitten was fine—indeed, what sort of creature was he, really— and decided to take the long way home. A ride would clear my head, or so I thought.

4

The lights of the Institute faded behind me. Once I was enveloped in the canopy of the trees with nothing but stars twinkling overhead, I could breathe deeply again. Sir Raleigh had fallen asleep, and his heartbeat beat double-time to mine. I would have to figure out what to do with him while abroad. Hopefully Veronica would keep him for me. He hadn't pulled his disappearing trick on me again. No, he had teleported, but only to find me.

"What am I going to do with you, Little Lad?" I asked him. The thought of leaving him, even though I hadn't even had his company for a full day, tugged at my heart. The heart I didn't want to admit to having. Yeah, the kitten needed to go back.

I rounded a bend. The sensation of a dark gaze brushing over me made me slow the bike rather than accelerate and hug into the curves as I typically did. The air smelled wrong, and with a chill, I recognized it as the same odd scent that had been in my house earlier. Rather than the cool green and sharp brown scents of foliage and mulch, the one that came to my nose was more of the electric static that comes with thunderstorms. Not necessarily of electricity, but instability. What could it mean?

Sir Raleigh had quieted, but he dug his little claws into my shirt just before I rounded a curve and bright lights blinded me. I swerved and heard the trees crying in their silent voices for me not to hit them. Even Fae could be gravely injured. A thick branch reached down for me, and in a flash, I leaped off the bike and into its embrace. Heather smashed into the trunk below as the tree pulled me out of danger.

I sat there, clutching Sir Raleigh to my chest and murmuring to him that he was such a clever kitty to hold on when he did. How had he known? The car raced below me, much too fast for the winding woodland road. They didn't even stop to make sure I was all right. Surely they must have seen me.

Or perhaps that had been the point—to ensure I wouldn't be all right. Selene had warned me, and now the danger felt real.

But for now I had a new problem. I had used up a good portion of the energy that I had left from this trying and exhausting day, and as I sat in the tree and trembled, I knew I didn't have it in me to teleport to the ground. The ground lay a good thirty feet below me, and I didn't see any branches I could use to climb down.

"Well, Hades," I said aloud. "Brother Tree, can you help me again?"

With a rustling, the tree tipped the branch downward. It was a long limb, and I managed to scoot along it until I couldn't balance on it anymore. Then I gripped it and lowered myself so I held on with my hands and my feet dangled above the ground. I moved sideways hand-by-hand like a child on a jungle gym. I could feel the tree trembling to hold me, so I dropped the last ten feet, creating a cushion of air thick enough to soften my fall. The tree raised the limb, and I bowed to it.

"Thank you, Brother Tree. I am in your debt."

"'Twas my pleasure, Princess Reine. It has been a long time since I have had the opportunity to serve your kind."

Then I saw the gash on his trunk and the twisted remains of Heather.

"Please allow me to heal you as a gesture of thanks."

"I would be honored."

I held my hand against the trunk and pulled from the energy of the earth and the surrounding forest. His brothers and sisters lent me strength as I knitted the wood and then the bark back together. By the end of it, he was healed, and I lay panting on the ground. Sir Raleigh emerged from my jacket and licked my face, then batted at me with a paw. I suspected the hunger pangs in my belly belonged more to him than to me, although I would need to eat after all the energy I'd expended. I was out of shape, as the humans liked to say. It had been a long time since I'd done more than healing spells.

"Now how to get home?" It was a good five miles, still.

A neigh, then snuffle made me jump. I turned to see—how fairytale can you get?—a wild white horse standing behind me. For a second, the image of a horn flashed on its forehead, then disappeared. Huh. I guess it had been long enough since I'd engaged in carnal pleasure that I could sort of see the unicorn.

"May I offer you a ride, Sister?" The female voice in my head sounded amused, but I didn't take offense at her tone or her addressing me as an equal. I could tell she and I were probably about the same age.

"I would be honored," I said. "Do you mind my passenger?" I held out the cat for her to see. She sniffed, then drew back.

"If I must. However, you assuredly know he is more than he appears."

I looked down at Sir Raleigh, wishing I could see what others saw in this little gray cat with one white paw. He yawned.

"So I've been told, but he's only protected me thus far."

Then if he protects you, he is worthy of being my passenger. She knelt, and I mounted. Sir Raleigh hooked his claws into my shirt, and through it, I felt each of his eighteen needle-sharp appendages. He seemed as comfortable with the horse as she did with him. However, if it would get me home, I'd ride a gargoyle, I was that desperate and tired.

I didn't like desperate and tired. I held on to the unicorn's mane, and she rose. With a smooth gait that I appreciated, she took trails through the forest rather than the road, and soon I saw the lights of my cottage. I sincerely hoped I wouldn't return to any nasty surprises this time. In fact, I had a call to make.

"Thank you for your help," I told the unicorn when she dropped me and Sir Raleigh by the front door. I wanted to ask what she saw when she looked at the little cat, but I couldn't bring myself to admit that I didn't know. It didn't seem to matter.

"You are very welcome. And as for your companion, you will discover his secrets when it is time."

Right, trust a unicorn to be vague. I bowed, and she lowered her head, then vanished into the night. Her magic tingled over my skin, and I remembered the feeling of being surrounded by such old power in Faerie. It was like bathing in a bubbling natural spring, but without the nasty sulfur smell or embarrassing turning pink. I closed my eyes and relished the sensation until the homesickness became too much.

After I fed Sir Raleigh and got him settled, I went out into my back yard and uncovered my obsidian scrying stone. Well, for witches, it served as a scrying stone. For me, it was a communications method, one of the world's oldest such devices, if it could be called that. I much preferred it to the rectangle of plastic, metal, and annoyance that now sat charging on my desk. At least my stone didn't lose power at an alarming rate just by being near me.

No, in fact the surface glowed silver with moonlight, more like mirror than stone, and I took a deep breath.

"I'd like to speak with someone in the vicinity of Atlanta, Georgia, please. Someone connected with the mission I've been given. Someone who can help."

An image like clouds reflected in the blue sky swirled in the stone's surface, and I found myself looking into the face of a young redheaded witch.

"Who the hell are you?" she asked.

IF I'D HAD any doubt that luck, fate, whatever wasn't on my side, this call confirmed it. But I had trusted the magic to connect me with someone who could help, and... Oh, right, the most likely person to be awake at the time would be a teenager. I'd forgotten that it would be very late at night there.

"Who are you?" I asked and put my hands on my hips.

"You first. Why are you in my laptop?" She frowned and clicked on something. The picture went to *Call Paused*, and then she reappeared. "And why won't you go away?"

Lovely. Before I said something that would alienate her completely, I inhaled again and allowed the air to fill my lungs, then released it with a count of ten. Human tricks weren't all bad, after all.

"I am Renee River," I told her, giving her the legal name I used when dealing with humans. "I live in Scotland, and I've been given a task to come meet some people there in Atlanta. Now who are you?" I asked again, hoping she'd at least identify herself so I could know how she'd fit.

"I'm seriously talking to someone in Scotland? And what program is this? It took over my computer. This better not have deleted the movie I down—er—am watching."

I opted to ignore the almost-confession of questionably legal viewing. "You're a witch, correct?"

That got her attention. Her eyebrows popped up. "How did you know?"

"The program. It knows." Not that it would have made sense even a half-century earlier to call the spell a program, but hey, we all had to change with the times, even witches.

She pressed buttons on her keyboard. "This is literally the weirdest thing that has happened to me."

"Literally?" I couldn't resist asking.

"Are you making fun of—oh, hey, is that your cat?"

Sir Raleigh had chosen that moment to make another appearance. His claws dug into my shoulder, and I caught him before he toppled off since I was leaning over the stone. As per usual, I untangled his little tail and paws from my hair.

"He's so cute! What's his name?" Then, with a shocked expression, "Whoa! What's up with your ears?"

In my effort to disentangle the cat from my curls, I'd allowed one of my pointed ears to show. Crap.

"Don't they teach you acceptance or something in school these days?" I snapped and hastily rearranged my hair to cover my Fae-points.

"No, you're thinking of something else. Are you a Fae?"

Her question made me pause and take another look at her. Most young people would have asked if I was a Trekkie or fairy cosplayer, but her use of the term told me she had magical education beyond the average schooling, even for a witch.

"What if I am?"

"Then I shouldn't give you my name, should I?" She crossed her arms and gave me a stern look. Well, tried to. On her young face, the expression made her look embarrassed or constipated rather than intimidating.

I held up a hand like I was doing a spell and hoped the

universe would come through for me. "Do you think I, a powerful Fae, can't find that out?"

Luckily for my intimidation efforts, someone else had figured out she was up.

"Kestrel, are you still awake?" A sleepy voice came from off-camera.

"Shit, shit, shit." Her hand blocked the camera as she tried to close the laptop lid. I shook my head.

"The spell turns it to stone temporarily. Or something like it." My turn to curse, this time internally. This was exactly the type of knowledge my mother did not want getting out.

"She thinks I'm watching a movie," Kestrel hissed. "Yes," she called. "Just finishing up a movie. I've paused it." Then she gave me a significant look.

I put the kitten down by my feet and told him to stay put, then assumed a cross-armed posture. A woman who looked like an older and more tired version of Kestrel came on screen. She had the same rust-colored hair, but it was shorter, and the fine lines of middle-aged worry had started to show on her face, especially around her eyes. She ruffled her daughter's hair, and I shoved down a surge of envy that I'd thought I'd gotten over. My mother had never touched me with tenderness like that—at least not once I'd passed childhood.

"What are you watching?"

"Some stupid movie about a fairy." Kestrel said with a shrug. "What are you doing up?"

"I heard you talking to someone. Or thought I did."

Not blinking was getting harder by the moment.

"Nope."

"Okay, then. I was worried, thought you may be having another nightmare."

"No, you must've heard the movie." Kestrel shrugged, the picture of innocence as she lied through her teeth to her mother. I had to give her some respect for that. Her deviousness could prove useful.

"All right. Ten more minutes, then lights out for you, young lady. And don't forget to take your nighttime vitamins."

Kestrel's eyes widened, but she swallowed and nodded. "Okay."

"Good." Mom planted a kiss on the top of her daughter's head and left. I indulged in a blink with a long squint for good measure. When I opened my eyes, I saw Kestrel looking at me.

"So you have my name," she said in a voice barely louder than a whisper. "What are you going to do to me?"

I should have told her that's not how the name thing worked, but I sensed I'd need her to be cooperative. "I'll have to think about it. I'll be coming to town in a couple of days and I'll need someone to help me. Will you?"

"Yes." She ran her hands through her hair. "Shit, am I agreeing because you've put a glamour on me, or do I really want to help you? I think I do because I've never met a Fae before. I'll be the only one in the coven who has."

"Coven?" I asked, imagining her sneaking off with her friends into the woods to do spells and rituals with sticks and seashells.

"Yes," she said with a sigh. "The White Oak Atlanta Coven, of which my parents are the grand poobah and grander poobah-ess." She rolled her eyes.

I stifled another laugh. "You don't sound like you're that into it."

"Not really, but that's all I'm going to say. You already have my name."

"Right. What's your cell number?"

She gave it to me, and I noted it on the pad of paper I kept in my jacket pocket. "Great. I'll text you when I get there or soon after."

"I suspect I'll meet you sooner than you expect," she said,

and with that, clicked off. I suppose the spell decided I'd gotten the help I would need from her for then.

Sir Raleigh, meanwhile, had made his way inch by painful inch up my jeans, and I peeled him off my left hip. He purred loudly, apparently proud of himself.

"Speaking of troublesome young things, what am I supposed to do with you? You can't come with me."

He licked my nose, and I held him to my chest. Something about his purr made me feel better, and later that night, carried me off to sleep. I hoped that I wouldn't have nightmares, but all too early the following morning, something startled me awake.

5

I opened my door to find a constable and, behind him, a concerned looking-Gabriel and annoyed Selene.

"Can I help you?" I'd pulled a robe around me but felt exposed. The chill of the late winter air blasted away the remainder of my morning grogginess. It had been a late night with the phone call and then my attempts to research what in Hades the creature in my house could have been. And, tangentially, what a scientist in the United States could want with an exiled Fae princess. Not that he knew I was exiled, but still...

"You're Ms. River?" the constable asked. He was a young one. Which, for me, meant anyone less than a hundred, but this one looked like he'd just graduated from constable school.

"Yes, that's me." I didn't require coffee like humans, but I did enjoy a good cup of tea every so often, and at the moment, I really wanted one.

"Did you have an accident along the Farm Well Road last night?"

Oh, right. They must have found Heather, or what was left of her. I wanted to giggle at the bewilderment they must be experiencing—damaged motorcycle, but no marks on any nearby trees. I did love to confuse the humans, especially those who thought they held authority over me.

"I had a mishap, yes. Did you find my bike?"

"Yes, and Mister McCord and Doctor Rial were kind enough to identify it as yours. You do know there's a fine for abandoning vehicles in public forest land?"

"I wasn't aware. If you'll give me a chance, Officer, I'll have it removed today." I gave him my most winning smile with a little something extra behind it.

He grinned back, his eyes just a tad out of focus. "Yes, yes, ah, that would be fine. Just remove it today."

"Reine," Gabriel practically growled. I turned down the intensity of my smile.

"Thank you for your help, Officer," I said. He tipped his hat and walked to his vehicle, where he sat, presumably filling out some sort of reports. Humans couldn't get by without their paperwork. No wonder the trees hated them.

"Was that necessary?" Gabriel asked. "And what the hell happened?"

I surmised I wouldn't be getting rid of him and Selene that quickly, so I stepped aside for them to come in. I'd gone decades without anyone coming into my cottage but me, and now I'd been invaded twice in two days. I couldn't say I liked the new pattern.

Sir Raleigh trotted out from the bedroom, where he'd darted under the bed when the constable had knocked on the door. Brave guard cat, he was not. I half-hoped he'd arch and hiss at the two werewolves—mostly for the adorable humor—but he didn't. He trotted over to them, sniffed their hands, and with a show of true feline snobbery, turned his back on them, lifted his tail, and pranced to me.

"Well, then," Selene said. She sounded amused, not offended. Too bad.

I picked up Sir Raleigh. "I believe it's time for breakfast," I said, hoping they'd take the hint to leave.

"Breakfast sounds excellent," Gabriel said. "What are we having?"

I huffed at him. "Unless you're interested in cat food, nothing." I did glance at my kettle.

"Tea is fine," Gabriel said. "I'll get it started for you."

"You will do no such thing." I fed the cat then put on water for tea. While the electric kettle—a convenience I would miss when I returned to Faerie—heated, I crossed my arms and gave Gabriel and Selene what I hoped would be an effectively stern look. Well, sterner than Kestrel's expression the evening before. That reminded me—Gabriel was keeping something from me. I hated when people deceived me.

"Can we please dispense with the games?" I asked. "I have a lot to do before we leave tomorrow. Why are you here?"

Gabriel started to say something, but Selene placed a gentle hand on his arm. "Because we were worried about you. They found your bike about an hour ago. We thought something terrible might have happened." It should be noted she did not appear to be distressed at the thought.

"*You* were worried about me?" I asked her.

"I was," she asserted. "The bike looks bad, Reine. It looks like you wrapped it around a tree."

Although Heather was just a machine, a pang of remorse stabbed through my chest.

"But no damage to the tree," Gabriel added with an arched eyebrow. "What are you playing at?"

"You have room to talk," I spat back. "What are you keeping from me, Mister Werewolf?"

The kettle beeped, signaling its successful boiling of water. In spite of my typical delight in making situations more complicated, I thought it would be nice if more things could be that simple and straightforward.

Gabriel and Selene exchanged a look, one of those unspoken couple communications that made me feel less connected from the human race than I already did. Fae could do that, although in our case, when needed, we could transfer words to one another's minds. The humans called it telepathy. We referred to it as secret conversation.

I hadn't had a secret conversation in centuries. I busied myself with making tea so I couldn't pay too much attention to the ache of grief and loneliness that welled up in my chest.

"I'm waiting," I said.

A forceful exhale preceded, "All right, who told you? Fucking Max?"

Oooh, Gabriel must be in a snit if he was cursing.

"I have ways of knowing things," I said and handed him a cup. "Tea will be ready in a few minutes."

"Fairies have tea kettles and pots?" Selene asked.

"I could wave my hand and make it appear," I replied, "but this uses less of my energy. Cream and sugar?"

"Yes, please," she said, and the politeness of her response made me recall she came from the American South. Interesting.

"So what do you need to tell me?" I tried again. I didn't compel him like I had the constable—probably couldn't considering he was a lycanthrope and therefore had a stubborn mind—but I wasn't about to reveal his advantage to him.

"Fine," Gabriel said with a sigh—resigned, this time. "The head of the Shadow Project—that's what they're calling the effort to root out the leak—asked for you specifically to come. He said your unique talents and training would be invaluable, although he didn't give any more detail than that."

Good doggie. "And why didn't you want to tell me this?"

Gabriel ran a hand through his curly brown hair. "Because I didn't want you to get in the way of our investigation. You're not exactly known for subtlety."

"Sheesh, a couple of rough healing spells—necessarily rough, I should add—and a girl gets a reputation." I blew across the top of the tea's steaming surface. I drank mine black so I could watch for any signs and symbols that might appear. This morning some murky figures floated in and out of view, but nothing firm. Nothing to satisfy my curiosity. "Why do you think he wants me there?"

"That's the other thing," Gabriel said. "I don't know. I don't even know how he knows about you."

"And you're sure?" I asked. "You didn't tell anyone about yours or Max's healing spells last summer, did you?"

Gabriel shook his head. "No, but he may be guessing. The Institute has been reporting the results of its trials to the CPDC —Center for Paranormal Disease Control—and they're aware Max is using blood magic. The risks for that are well-known, as is the necessary training, which only the Fae can provide, for handling it safely."

"So perhaps they know you have a Fae on board, but not whom."

"There's still the princess part," Selene pointed out. "Wait, you're a princess?"

I allowed my shoulders to slump. Not this again. I needed that tea to kick in. "In a sense, yes. I'm a granddaughter of the queen, but not in line for the throne. Well, not first in line. That would be my mother, and my father was a humble warrior, not nobility, so it's a long shot at best." I didn't add that my exile made it nigh impossible. Hopefully after this adventure was over, that wouldn't be an issue. I ignored the squirm of doubt in my chest.

"So that sounds like you," Selene persisted. "Someone must know who you are."

"Others do know about me," I said, thinking back through the years at who had confronted me. Most recently it had been the were-sharks back when Max and I had been in medical school, but Atlanta was way beyond their territory. I had always wondered who had tipped them off.

Instead of solving the problem of why the head of the CPDC wanted me there, I only came up with more problems, more worries, and the sense that a web tightened around me.

"That's all I can tell you for now," Gabriel said and put his half-empty teacup back on its saucer. "What happened to your bike?"

I told them about the accident, but I left out the talking to the tree and the unicorn. Some things didn't need to be common knowledge.

"And how did you get home?" Gabriel persisted. He could always tell when someone omitted information. That's why he'd been such a good Lycanthropy Council investigator.

"Proprietary Fae information." I waved my hand to dismiss his question.

"So someone ran you off the road," Selene said. "But you don't know who?"

I shook my head. "All I saw was the lights. Thankfully Sir Raleigh dug in just before it happened."

The cat, who'd been watching birds from the kitchen windowsill, turned his head.

"So he knew?" Selene asked.

"It seems so. Can either of you detect anything weird about him?"

They both looked at the kitten, who proceeded to jump down to the floor and lick his butthole. Right, cats weren't exactly known for their manners, especially while being observed.

"Looks like a normal cat to me," Gabriel said.

"Yes," Selene agreed, although not as firmly.

"But...?" I prompted.

"I don't know. It's barely there, but there's some sort of shadow around him."

Sir Raleigh looked up at her with eyes more gold than blue today, winked out, and then reappeared on my shoulder. They both gasped.

"And that's why Veronica wanted me to watch him," I said. "He's a strange little chap." I caressed his ears, and he purred.

"He's definitely strange," Selene agreed. "He seems to like you."

Gabriel's cell phone rang with the chorus from the "Were-wolves of London" song. Both Selene and I chuckled, but Gabriel cursed under his breath when he saw the number on the screen.

"I have to get this. Excuse me." He walked out of the room, leaving me with Selene.

I typically didn't feel awkward with human women, but something about Selene made me think twice before I opened my mouth. No matter what I did, she'd take it apart, analyze it, and put it back together in a way that might or might not help the image I wanted to project.

"More tea?" I asked after what seemed to be an uncomfortably long period of quiet. What I really wanted to ask was, "Why are you so eager for me not to go to Atlanta?" She hadn't mentioned anything, but I could feel it in the air between us.

With a shake of her head, she returned her attention to me. She'd been looking in the direction Gabriel had gone. I couldn't hear his side of the conversation in spite of my preternatural Fae abilities. Could she?

"Sure, thanks."

"So..." I said as I poured. "Tell me why you don't want me along on the mission."

She fumbled the cup, and I used my Fae powers to steady it before she dropped boiling hot tea all over my feet and floor.

Once she caught hold of the clattering cup, she said, "Gabriel said you were direct."

I shrugged. "When you're as old as I am, you learn what to be patient for. Spill it, Ginger."

She looked down—*Liar*. "I'm just worried..."

"About...?"

She placed her cup on its saucer on the table. "Look, you've been around long enough to know that things aren't always as they seem."

"Yes." Like her, but I wasn't going to say that.

"It's dangerous, Reine." She looked up and met my gaze with her own. "There are tons of lycanthropes and wizards running around and not many Fae. What if they want to do something to you? Experiment on you?"

A shiver tiptoed down my spine, and I stiffened so I wouldn't show it. "So you really care about me?"

She laughed, but not with mirth. "I don't know you. But I know Gabriel does, and he cares." She looked away. "He'd never forgive himself if something happened to you."

"And would you?" I couldn't help it, I had to poke her.

"I'm afraid he'd be angry with me, although what could I do? You're more powerful than all of us combined, even with your powers attenuated like they'd be over there."

And there was the gulf between us, lycanthrope and Fae. Well, any mortal creature and Fae. Occasionally the isolation I tried so hard not to feel welled to the surface, like ink from the well at the bottom of my heart. All the more reason to get this investigation over with and get my Faerie ass home.

"I can take care of myself, Selene," I said softly and, I hoped, firmly. "I'm going. I'm not some delicate fairy statue that needs to be packed in bubble wrap and protected from shattering."

"No, but you're a creature of interest, and you don't know what you're getting into. Atlanta is...different from here."

I hated being called a creature. And I detested when others assumed I had no experience with cities. But she had information I needed. "How so? You're from there, right?"

"Yes, but I'm sure it's changed. It's like that. A strange mix of old and new, but like they kept the wrong parts of the old."

"What do you mean?"

"It's hard to explain. I'm sure you'll see when we get there since you're so determined to go."

"I am." And since her attention seemed to wander every few minutes toward the direction Gabriel had exited, "Who do you think Gabriel is talking to?"

"I don't know." She looked down, and her shoulders lowered an inch. Interesting.

"It must be hard being with the head of the Lycanthrope Council and a new alpha." I pretended to stir something into my teacup, then tapped the side of the spoon on the rim.

She shrugged. "It has its ups and downs. I'd never intended on dating or being engaged to a politician. Somehow I thought it would be different for us, but people are people no matter what they can turn into."

Hmmm, trouble in fuzzy paradise? My mischievous side perked up.

"But it's okay," she added a little too brightly. "We make it work. I can't tell him most of what happens during my day since my patient confidentiality is so tight, so we're even."

"So what do you talk about?" I didn't have to feign interest.

"Outside politics. How world events will affect the Institute. Our upbringings and childhoods, but not in a weird way."

Gabriel returned, and he smiled, although weariness had crept into his eyes. "I'm afraid I have to get to Lycan Castle. Reine, do you want me to arrange to have your bike picked up and towed back here? Or to a junkyard?"

"Back here is fine." I would see what could be done for her. A couple of dwarves owed me a favor. Then, since I would have to act more human once we arrived in the States, I added, "Thank you."

Gabriel's eyebrows shot up, but he didn't comment on my

sudden attack of politeness. "You're welcome. See you tomorrow at the airport? Flight's at ten."

"I'll be there. I'll drop this little lad by Veronica's on the way."

"How will you keep him from following you?" Selene asked.

"I don't know, but I have the rest of the day to figure it out."

Sir Raleigh, who'd dozed off into a heavy cat-weight on my shoulder stirred and began to purr again. Had he heard and understood?

Yes, I'd have my work cut out for me. Meanwhile, I needed to speak to my mother again to see if she had any ideas about why Dr. Cimex wanted me there specifically. And why she wanted me to go if there was a danger I could be experimented on. Or worse. But when I fetched the talisman from the box, it was dark.

6

M y mother didn't answer the wand summons, and as per usual, it didn't unlock the portal into Faerie for me, no matter how hard I tried. I don't know why I was so desperate. Perhaps I didn't want to leave Sir Raleigh even more than I realized. Indeed, my heart hurt with a twin ache—over my exile and over the thought of abandoning him—when the car dropped me at Veronica's shop the next morning.

Sir Raleigh's eyes had turned fully from blue to yellow with green rings around the irises, and he seemed to have gained a pound and some length. His ears also appeared to have decided to outpace the rest of him. Veronica almost didn't recognize him.

"Is that the same kitten?" she asked. "He's growing much faster than his siblings."

I told her the observations others had made of him as well as the one magical creature's assurance that I'd figure out what he was when it was time. With her typical good nature, Veronica shrugged and said, "You of all creatures should appreciate mystery and the timing of revelations."

"It's more fun when it's not aimed at me," I grumbled. "And don't call me a creature. Here." I handed Sir Raleigh to her, and she cuddled him to her ample bosom.

"There's a good lad. Oh, look, your mommy gave you a pretty necklace."

"I'm not his mommy," I said.

The look she gave me said otherwise, but she wisely did not press the matter. "What is it?"

"An elastic string from a clootie well collection of offerings, some quartz from around here, and silver beads between them. He hasn't pulled his disappearing act since I put it on him." Indeed, he'd followed me around the house on foot, grumbling in his cute kitten way.

"Sorry, wee lad," I'd told him. "Can't have you being lazy and not using your legs to jump and climb like a normal kitty."

He'd responded by clawing his way up my jeans. Again. That stunt had earned him a claw clipping, which he'd tolerated. But his claws were razor-sharp again the next morning.

No, this was not an ordinary cat.

"And you said it's an elastic?" Veronica asked.

"Yes, so there's room for him to grow. Please don't take it off him if you can help it. Or if you do, do so in a heavily warded space." Although I wasn't sure any wards would contain him. "I don't want him hurting himself trying to find me." Deep sorrow over the possibility welled up, and I almost choked on the words. What was happening to me?

"I'll take good care of him, I promise. I've sent the others to a friend's house so I can give him all my attention."

"Thank you." The words came out more easily this time. Of course as a Fae I hated to put myself in debt to someone, especially a human, but the balance with Veronica still weighted heavily in my favor since I'd subsidized and supported our shop. As for Gabriel... He owed me for trying to keep Doctor Cimex's knowledge from me. I had no patience for betrayal.

"One last hug for you," Veronica said and handed the cat back to me. He melted against my chest, purring emphatically.

I scratched his soft head and ears and murmured, "Now stay here and be a good moggie for Miss Veronica. She'll take care of you, and I'll be back soon." He looked up at me with a pitiful expression. With one final scratch behind the ears and tug on the collar to make sure it would stay on, I handed him back, then turned and walked away.

His piteous cries followed me out of the shop and to the waiting car. Each one felt like it shredded my soul.

"Please hurry," I said. The anguished yowls echoed in my head long after I should have been able to hear them. Finally, about five miles away, they quieted, and I released the tension that had overtaken my entire body.

Indeed, what was happening to me? I needed to get myself together and return to being my usual cold Fae self before arriving at the airport. With a final determined sniffle, I wiped my eyes and steeled my expression. Woe to the first human who crossed me—they'd have a nasty surprise coming. No one would be able to see how heartbroken I could be over a silly, fuzzy, adorable kitten.

WHEN I ARRIVED at the Inverness Airport, I walked to the airline that matched the logo on the ticket Gabriel had given me. Our plan—fly to Edinburgh, then connect to Atlanta. I didn't see any of the others yet, so I checked in, turned over my bag, which held all the human-style clothing I owned, and went through security. Between the scanning devices and the quelling of the tears from leaving Sir Raleigh, I had a troll-level headache by the time I found my gate.

Oh, and I'd not flown since returning from medical school in the late 1990s. The difference in the atmosphere shocked me and weighed me down further. Whereas travel had previously been fun, now there was a layer of fear and helpless concern. Excitement on other passengers' faces had been replaced by resignation and boredom in spite of the devices they all carried that would produce any information they wanted.

Without thinking, I pulled out my own device and tapped on the Photos icon. Sir Raleigh's precious little face appeared, looking ferocious although I'd caught him in a yawn. I smiled and tried to block the memory of his yowls from my mind. One more reason to get this assignment over with and return. Surely a magical kitty like that would be welcome in Faerie. My grandmother had a soft spot for fuzzy things, which I'd inherited from her. Neither of us allowed the vulnerability to show lest someone take such attachments as an opportunity for manipulation. That's why noble Fae didn't do "soft."

"Cute cat," a deep voice said, startling me out of reliving the moment of taking the picture.

I turned to see a gentleman had taken the seat beside mine. He looked to be in his fifties, but his green eyes had a certain ageless quality and depth. His hair had started graying at the temples, and he had slight crow's feet at the corners of his eyes, but overall he appeared to be in good shape. The odd thing—whereas I could sense the life force from everyone else in the terminal, this man didn't emanate any sort of energy. If he wasn't a supernatural creature, I'd bet he was a powerful wizard. Either way, he could be dangerous.

"Thanks," I said, simultaneously wanting him to go away and curious about what or who he could be.

"Had him long? I'm guessing it's a him," the man said with a fond smile. "He has a little lad face."

I shook my head. "Just got him."

"Oh?" He raised his eyebrows. "And is he traveling with you? I don't see a carrier."

"He's with a friend."

The man's jaw tightened and his expression hardened into concern. "Are you sure that's wise? He looks very young."

I drew back. What business was that of his? "He's being well cared for."

"And what about you?"

I stood. "That, Sir, is none of your affair." I spotted Selene down the terminal and waved to her. She waved back and started heading toward me.

The man rose, revealing he stood a good head taller than me, and I am not a short Fae. That made him at least six and a half feet tall. "I meant no offense. It can be hard to leave a small creature you care deeply about." The softening around his eyes said he remembered having to do just that, but I didn't care to stick around and find out more. It was quite possible he used a sob story to lure vulnerable young women—all right, young-looking women—into some sort of nefarious trap.

"I will be fine," I said. I'd meant to say, 'I'm fine,' but it didn't come out right.

"I'm sure you will be, although be careful. I don't know why you're traveling, but the world is a dangerous place, especially for young women who get so caught up in cat pictures that they don't notice who's around them. Always pay attention, even when you think you're safe."

He bowed slightly from his waist, then moved on. He carried a jacket but didn't have any luggage, not even a brief-case. I checked to see where Selene had gone, and when I glanced back to make sure the mysterious gentleman wasn't watching where I went, I didn't see him. He'd vanished.

Who was he, and where had he gone? The terminal wasn't that big, there were no restrooms in the direction he'd been heading, and nowhere he could have ducked into. A chill slithered through me. Perhaps he'd been more powerful than I had guessed.

"There you are," Selene said. She pulled a purple carry-on

suitcase behind her. Why had I checked luggage? If she'd been able to pack light enough to not need to, I should have as well.

"Here I am," I agreed, although not with her level of feigned excitement.

She didn't look happy to see me. "Wait long?"

"No, I just got here. Say, did you see the gentleman I was talking to when I waved to you?"

"No," Selene said, "but that side of you was blocked from my view. You look perplexed."

Perplexed didn't begin to cover how I felt.

"Where are Gabriel and Max?" I asked before she could query further. I needed to remember her specialty was the mind.

Selene's pleasantly neutral expression crumpled into disappointment. "Something came up with the Council and the Institute. They said they'd join us later if they can, but they didn't want to hold us up."

"So it's just us, then."

"Yes. Just us," she said too brightly. "Are you hungry? Do you—?"

"Get hungry, yes. But not like you do. If you need to grab something to eat, go ahead. I..." I inhaled, not wanting to reveal too much, but she had to know. She'd have to watch over me. "I have strange reactions to being on airplanes, being separated from the earth. It's better if my stomach is empty."

"Oh. Is there something I need to prepare for?"

I shook my head. "You'll see."

So there we stood, her without her other half and me with... what? A mystery gentleman who gave strange warnings and whom no one else had seen. I'd heard of older Fae hallucinating as their time to sleep in the earth approached, but I shouldn't be even halfway there yet. What could it mean?

I knew one thing—the man was right. I needed to ditch the maudlin pining over a kitten and pay attention. Once we reached our seats on the first plane, I pulled out my phone and deleted the pictures of Sir Raleigh. I couldn't afford the potential consequences of distraction.

Of course, I immediately regretted my actions when the plane took off, and my old friend, airsickness, took over. It's not good for a Fae to be disconnected from the earth or the things she loved. Yes, I loved the silly cat. I regretted deleting the photos, and then we had to run for a connection in Edinburgh, so I didn't have time to recover them before the second flight took off.

It appeared that not only could I not trust my perceptions— my judgment had become questionable as well. What other dangers lay ahead of me, and how could I possibly prepare for them? And how could I do so with an overly concerned psychologist sitting next to me? The Fae didn't do therapy, no matter how much we might have needed it.

SOME PEOPLE COMPLAIN ABOUT NOT BEING able to sleep on planes. I have the opposite problem—I can't stay awake. Thankfully I was seated next to Selene and in first-class, so I didn't have to worry about anyone taking advantage of my semi-comatose state on either flight. When the shoreline disappeared behind us, sleep crashed over me in a foggy wave.

"Is she okay?" someone asked at one point from behind us.

"Yes," Selene said, "she has terrible motion sickness and took something. It's better this way."

Thankful for her coming up with a plausible lie, I drifted back off before I could respond. I fell into dreams in which the roar of the jet's engines provided a constant bass line to my panicked running from...what? What chased me? I couldn't see anything. I ran in the dark, the unnatural scraping noise a disorienting soundtrack to my terror. I only knew that something chased me, and I was without my guardian.

I woke when the wheels touched down, the several feet of synthetic materials separating me from my beloved earth still too much to bear, but I gritted my teeth and forced my eyes to open.

"Good nap?" Selene chirped. How did she look so awake and alert?

I felt like I'd been running for the several hours I'd been out, so I only shook my head.

She patted my hand. "Are you all right?"

"As right as I'm going to be. When can we get off this thing?"

"Soon."

I pulled out my phone and went into the Deleted Photos folder, but it was empty. I refused to cry over it. Perhaps it was a sign I needed this trip to get my head and heart back in alignment with what I truly needed to do—promote the Fae agenda and earn my way back into Faerie.

With Selene's help, I stumbled off the plane and gradually came to more awareness as we walked through a giant terminal, down a long escalator, and onto a strange little train. Then up a long escalator. Did this place have an end?

"Who's meeting us, again?" I asked when we emerged into the arrivals welcome area.

"A couple of representatives from the CPDC," she replied. "But they're not going to be obvious."

I chuckled. "They're not trying to be obvious, but they are, at least to me." I lowered my voice. "There's a large cat shifter and, oh lovely, a gargoyle, waiting for us by the glass case." Their energy stood out among the humans around us. Just my luck, I'd encounter two gargoyle-types in the same week. So much for them being rare.

I led the way since I had seniority in our little group without Gabriel and Max there.

"Doctor, ah, Renee River?" the shifter asked. He looked me over with his golden gaze. As with many shifters, his facial features as a human echoed his creature nature, and he gave me a wide, toothy grin. With his tawny golden-brown hair, he'd be lovely when changed. I was also surprised how young he was, barely over two human decades. When he reached out to shake my hand, his motion and the way his muscles moved under his suit said he kept in shape in both forms.

"That's me," I said and attempted to return his smile, but his companion's glower cast a shadow over my efforts. "And you are...?"

"Corey McLendon," he said. "I'm on the security team for your group. And this is Doctor Lawrence Gordon, one of our scientists."

"Charmed," Doctor Lawrence Gordon, who obviously wasn't, said. His slate gray eyes took in every inch of my appearance under elegantly shaped dark brows. He didn't hold out a hand as his companion had, nor did I proffer mine.

Selene cleared her throat. I supposed I needed to do introductions.

"Right, this is Doctor Selene Rial, the head of their mental health unit." At least I thought that's what she was.

"Close enough," she murmured. She shook hands with the two members of our welcoming committee.

"Corey, Doctor River seems to have had a rough trip," Lawrence said. "Perhaps I should take her for some refreshment in Piedmont Park so she can recover."

The thought of taking off my shoes and digging my toes into some grass, or better yet, the boggy edge of a lake almost made me salivate with desire, but I shook my head.

"I'm fine, but thank you for the offer." I glared at the gargoyle, hoping he'd get the hint I didn't need his help.

"Are you sure?" Corey asked. "We were warned that your

needs may be, um, different." He looked at his companion, and I had a suspicion as to who had played the expert.

The assumption, while correct, made the irritation I'd kept at bay explode in my chest. "I'll let you know what I do and don't need."

"Perhaps it would be better if we were to go to our hotel," Selene, ever the peacemaker, put in. "Freshen up, you know. Are there plans for dinner?"

"Yes, we're housing you at the Crowne Plaza Perimeter," Corey, who looked relieved to address Selene, said. "It has some nice areas for walking, and it's close to a train station should you want to venture into town..."

I noted that the designation of Atlanta as a "town" seemed to fit the understated way the Southerners communicated. Selene chatted with Corey and Doctor Gordon, leaving me the odd Fae out yet again. I supposed I should be accustomed to it, but my little explosion had activated all my nerves, and I wanted to scream until I could reach a green space and hug a tree or something. All right, I didn't know what I wanted, and that meant I didn't know how to ask. Or, I didn't want to throw a Fae-fit and be sent home.

Right, ticket back to Faerie. I took a deep breath, again counting to ten in Fae time, which amounted to four, but it was enough.

I smiled at Corey, but without any extra Fae charm. "Do you know how long it is to get to our hotel?"

"About half an hour, ma'am."

His pronunciation of *ma'am* threw me with its two distinct syllables hung together with a 'y' in the middle. No "mums" here.

"That's pretty much the distance to anywhere in the city outside of rush hour," he added and checked his watch. "But y'all should have enough time to rest up before dinner."

I doubted he knew what my resting up needs would be, but

I nodded. We picked up my bag, went to a waiting car, and drove into the city.

Although I should have felt confident in my sophistication as a Fae, with each passing mile and tall building, my confidence waned. By the time we arrived at the hotel, I didn't know if I could play this game. But what other choice did I have?

I could do one thing—I dropped my bags off in my room and headed downstairs for a walk, hopefully without the not-so-charming Doctor Lawrence Gordon.

7

I spotted Dr. Gordon on the middle level of the three-tiered lobby. He sat at one of the tables and had a glass of red wine and a laptop in front of him. My choices—another elevator ride or walk right past him. Although I hated elevators—being encased in a metal box is one of the Fae's worst nightmares—I tolerated the trip to the ground floor, where doors led outside. The hotel had a lovely courtyard with paths leading into a wooded area, and so I followed the song of the trees, different from home. For one thing, these were younger and less numerous. Also, they wore their early spring buds whereas the ones at home—I mean in Scotland—still worked to get the sap moving and shake off the end of winter. When I walked into the woods, such as they were since I could still hear the road noise beyond, the trees rustled in excitement.

"Welcome, sister," they chorused. *"Welcome to our home."*

I kicked some of the mulch out of the way, removed my shoes, and sighed with bliss when my feet met the cool red clay earth. That was what I needed, not the company of a gargoyle or the too-cheerful Selene, who practically quivered with forced friendliness toward me. I'd be more comfortable if she'd allow her true feelings to show. I suspected she and Gabriel had had some conversations about how to "handle" me, whatever that meant.

A cool breeze, a reminder that it was still early in the season, made the leaves dance with a thousand shades of green, and the scent of early flowers teased my nose. I decided to follow it, and not necessarily on the path, but as it turned out, there wasn't enough space off the path to walk, so I stayed on the mulch. The ground softened under my feet, and with each step, my strength increased. I attempted to bless a sapling that appeared to be struggling, and while her star-shaped leaves perked up slightly, I couldn't reach my full power to heal her completely.

"I am sorry, little one," I told her.

"I appreciate the strength you've given me. I hope it will be enough."

"As do I."

With insecurity and sadness weighing on my soul, I walked downhill toward the sound of running water and found a stream—manmade but still lovely. I crouched at the edge and placed my hand in it, allowing the cool, clear liquid to flow through my fingers. Again, bliss, even if the water was being forced into its path. The brook babbled its welcome, too, and I murmured back to it. Since it had been constructed by people, it lacked a dryad or guardian spirit, and it was happy to have a Fae to converse with. It told me of its path through pipes underground and the stream-bed here, and while it lacked fish, it did have frogs that came to visit and sing on its banks.

I was so intent on listening to the chatter of the water that I didn't notice the intruder until it bumped into me and sent me sprawling into the stream. I leapt up and turned, looking for whoever had dared to attack me, but I saw no one. Dread spread through my gut—was this the same creature who'd invaded my cottage? How had it gotten here?

I reached for the Fae talisman, which I'd kept in my pocket, but the trees rustled a warning—*"Don't bring it out."*

"All right," I said and instead spread my hands in front of me. Water dripped from my sleeves, and the cold dirt on my pants wet my knees, but I drew energy from water and earth. I didn't think I could battle an unseen foe, so I instead cobbled together a shield. It wouldn't withstand much, but I hoped my attacker, if they were even still in the area, wouldn't know that. Their method had shown a lack of knowledge of the Fae. Pushing us into water or toward the earth would strengthen, not hurt, us.

I trudged up the path to the hotel, alert for any change in the feeling of the air or sound. A still gray form made my heart catch in my throat before I realized its color was too light for it to be Sir Raleigh, and he didn't have a bushy tail as this creature did. I knelt by the squirrel, which, as with the waxwing, barely breathed, its energy drained. I placed a hand over it, drew from the earth again, and whispered healing to it. It scampered off, and I staggered to my feet, bracing myself against a tree so I could catch my breath.

No, I didn't have my full strength here, and a sense of vulnerability overwhelmed me before I could gather myself.

I am a Fae princess. I have resources they don't know about.

But would those be enough?

As I made my way back to the hotel, I planned my strategy. I'd feel our hosts out for any threats that had been made or may otherwise exist, and if I had to use my Fae charm, so be it. That was one good thing about Gabriel and Max not being there—they wouldn't be able to scold me for misuse of my powers.

No, the situation at the stream had told me that I needed to use whatever advantage I had.

Before I could change, a knock sounded at my door. I looked through the peephole to see my reluctant travel companion, whose room was next to mine.

"Are you all right?" Selene asked when I opened the door. She took in my bedraggled appearance, her blue eyes wide. "What happened?"

I stuck my hands in my pockets and attempted a casual lean against the doorframe, but the heavy hotel door whacked my bottom and almost knocked me into the hall. Not graceful. With a sigh, I opened the door and beckoned her to enter.

"What are you doing here?" I asked. Could she be connected with the strange being who had taken an interest in me?

She rubbed her eyes. "I sometimes get a sense when something's not right. I hope you, of all creatures, can understand."

"That's pretty vague. And no, things are not *all right*. In fact, something attacked me while I was walking outside."

"What? Where?" If she was lying, she was good at it. I couldn't sense any sort of deception coming from her, and I was typically accurate, although I could be fooled. I didn't necessarily trust my perceptions in my current state.

"By the stream. Something tried to knock me in. Thankfully they didn't realize that whatever they could do, that wasn't going to harm me."

"Because you're a creature of water and earth."

So you think. "Something like that."

"Did you see them?"

"No, it was like the thing at my cottage yesterday. Invisible." And, most disturbingly, it had drawn strength from a living thing.

"That's odd." She looked around the room. "Is everything okay here?"

"As far as I can tell." I wasn't about to let on that I couldn't feel the thing coming, whatever it was, so I went with one of the dumb questions I'd heard the humans ask each other. "How's your room?"

The diamond on her left ring finger sparkled when she crossed her arms. "It's fine. A hotel room. Sort of lonely."

Was she admitting her own sadness to draw me out? If so, it wasn't going to work.

"Don't you have family or friends here?"

She looked at me, her brows drawn in a quizzical manner. "I do, but I haven't reached out to them yet. My life before lycanthropy and after it seems like two separate phases. Two different me's, even. I don't know that they'd understand."

I nodded. I felt the same about my time before and after exile—true Fae versus having to assimilate with humans. Now the uncomfortable thought crept in that maybe I had more in common with people than with my kind.

"Look, I know you're trying to be friendly, but can we get to the important stuff?" I asked. My wet clothes had started to chafe, the water in them now devoid of healing power.

"Yes, of course." She looked disappointed. "What do you need?"

Now that felt more like a human/Fae interaction. Some of the tension left my shoulders. "I think that whatever attacked me today and yesterday is connected to what we're here to do. It has to be. Do you know of something that draws energy from small animals? Is there some sort of local legend here?"

"No, not that I can think of. Small animals?"

I told her about the bird and the squirrel.

"That's horrible!" She scowled, the ferocious expression giving me a hint of the lycanthrope underneath. "And I agree with you—it must be connected. The timing is too coincidental."

"Right, and with that in mind, I don't know who to trust."

She paused and placed one hand under her chin and

propped up that arm with the other one. "Do you trust me, Reine?"

"I just said I don't know who to trust," I snapped. "Why should I trust you? You don't like me. You didn't want me along. And if you're concerned, it's because of Gabriel."

"And you're surprised by this?" She gestured to me. "The first time I saw you, you were kissing Gabriel to get him in trouble. With me. And we weren't even dating yet. Why should I like a troublemaker like you?"

"Why, indeed," I responded, allowing a wry tone to creep into the words. She had a point, although I chose instead to focus on the fact she'd called me a creature a few minutes before.

"But liking doesn't necessarily have anything to do with trusting," she said. "And if you're being attacked by some strange being, you need people around you that you can trust, especially here." She rubbed her arms, although the room temperature hadn't changed. "Something feels off about all this. Can't you detect it?"

"Yes." And I did. I had even before she'd said anything. "But I don't know what."

"Then we need to stick together," she said. "I'm not sure what to expect at dinner tonight, and I need to know you have my back."

Ugh, she wanted to tie my fate to hers. "I agree with you to a point," I said, choosing my words carefully. "Why don't we start with agreeing to watch out for each other, and then we can proceed to mutually agreed-upon sacrifice if necessary?"

She looked at me for a long moment, then nodded. "I can live with that."

"Right," I said, sensing she continued to be disappointed but fine with letting her be. "Can you advise me on what to wear? I've not been to a fancy human dinner in several decades, and Atlanta seems a more casual place."

"Sure, let me know when you've cleaned up, and I'll come back over."

With that, she left. I felt like I'd scored some sort of victory, but over who or what I didn't know. One thing I was certain of —I needed to discover the true story, and fast.

Adorned in the light blue gown Selene had helped me choose —and no, the irony that I wore my mother's favorite color didn't escape me—I descended to the lobby in the metal box. Every time the door opened on the way down, I held my breath, not sure who or what, seen or unseen, would get on with me. So far it was only a couple of tourists and some businesspeople who chatted about what was nearby. I had no idea what a Cheesecake Factory was, only that it apparently manufactured things that weren't cheesecake.

When I walked into the lobby, I looked around, both for my party and for anything that seemed amiss. After the earlier incident by the creek, the strange man's warning in the airport to pay attention played in my mind on repeat. I hadn't been aware enough of my surroundings, but how did a Fae prepare for something they couldn't sense coming?

The energy of Corey the cat shifter and Lawrence Gordon the gargoyle led me to where they waited, near the end of the second level overlooking the restaurant and doors to outside below. I felt exposed rather than comforted by the wall of glass and the trees outside, but neither of them appeared perturbed, so I smoothed my expression into one of polite interest.

"Good evening, gentlemen."

They turned, and their reactions fed my feminine ego. Corey's golden eyes widened, and he looked me up and down without shame. I resisted the urge to twirl for him. I'd put my hair up, so the rainbow fire of my opals sparkled at my ears and throat without any obstruction. I'd carefully arranged curls to fall around my face and hide my pointed ear tips. The silver-colored belt of the dress cinched at my waist, and I carried a white knit shawl for the chilly evening. When I moved, a slit in the blue fabric showed leg up to my mid-thigh, and I wore silver heels.

Yes, this old girl still had it. Lawrence Gordon's reaction was no less admiring, although more subtle, limited to a slight lift of his eyebrows and curl to his lips. I hadn't noticed his mouth before, which was sensual for a gargoyle's. His red silk shirt hugged his physique and set off his swarthy complexion and black hair. Not bad. Plus, he wore black slacks that gave more than a hint of his muscular legs and butt. The mischievous side of me wondered what it would be like to run my hands over his rock-hard—

That was enough of that train of thought. *He's a gargoyle. We don't like gargoyles. One hurt Rhys and caused your exile from Faerie. They can't be trusted.*

"Is your room all right?" Lawrence asked. Again, that dumb human question.

"It's fine. Quite comfortable." Like every other one in this human containment unit, I was sure. Hotels felt like the opposite of home—places of transience, not rootedness.

"Please let me know if you need any live plants brought up for you," he said. Again, trying to help, but annoying nonetheless.

"I'm sure I'll be fine. There are enough trees around the hotel to help me feel comfortable."

"Leave her be, Larry," Corey said with a wink to me. "Don't mind him. He's been quite eager to show off his knowledge of a fellow elemental. Earth, water, and air, right?"

"I see, and something like that." I wanted to correct them—smug males—but I had my directive. And the less they knew about me, the better. Plus I found his directness to be rude. I'd never name another elemental being's aspects in a social situation.

Selene appeared at that moment, looking lovely in a green gown with gold accents. She'd also pulled her hair into an updo, and emeralds glinted green at her throat and ears.

"Doctor Rial," Curtis said and bowed. Lawrence nodded. I didn't miss that whereas they'd greeted me with stunned admiration, they regarded her with respect. My jaw clenched, and I had to tell myself to release the tension. I didn't need a headache distracting me.

"Good evening," Selene said and smiled at each of them in turn. "I hope I didn't keep you waiting."

"Not at all." Corey held out an arm, and she took it. "We're meeting at a restaurant close by. Don't worry, they won't start without us."

She accepted his invitation and placed a hand on the crook of his elbow. That left me and the gargoyle. We regarded each other, and the uncertainty as to what to do on his face mirrored my own. Ah, so he did know protocol to wait for the higher-ranking elemental to make the first move. And the longer I waited to do so, the more annoyance tinged his aura, which I perceived not as colors but characteristics.

I would have enjoyed making him squirm, but the others had almost reached the stairs to the main lobby level. I held out a hand. "Would you care to escort me, Doctor Gordon?"

"It would be my pleasure, Doctor River." He offered his arm, which I took.

I swear I tried not to test whether my perception of his muscles was accurate, but my heel caught on the carpet, and I stumbled, which forced me to grab his biceps. He didn't flinch, only waited while I righted myself. He maintained a neutral expression, but amusement sparked in his black eyes. Once freed from the loose loop of flooring, I lifted my chin and refused to look at him, but I caught his slight grin in my peripheral vision. My cheeks heated in spite of my stern instruction to myself not to blush. Then I heard a snippet of secret conversation I didn't know whether I was meant to.

"You can try not to react, but you're lovely when you blush. More human and less ice queen." Then a snippet of a cartoonish character with light blonde hair in a blue dress and the words, *"Let it go."*

The bastard was comparing me to Elsa from *Frozen*! My cheeks betrayed me by warming even more, and his arm quivered under mine, his amusement leaking through his muscles to my fingertips. I'd never been so glad to get into a car—yet another metal box—in my life.

By the time we arrived at the restaurant, which would have been an easy walk but ended up being a ten-minute drive with all of the other metal boxes on the road, I'd composed myself, and he'd returned to his—ahem—stony silence. Corey and Selene kept up a lively chatter about Atlanta and how it had changed since she'd left. She pointed out places that were familiar and spoke of her childhood. Again, envy poked me in the chest for her "normal" upbringing and shared recollections. The only other being I shared memories with was Rhys, and he and I didn't speak of our past before the banishment. It brought up too much pain and anger, and the one time we'd allowed our conversation to wander in that direction, we'd ended up in mutual blame and recrimination. Never mind that it was the cursed Templar knight and his gargoyle friend who had truly authored our fates. Another reason to not allow Doctor Lawrence Gordon—Larry, as Corey had hilariously called him —to charm me, not even with his secret conversation or his respectable physique. All right, more than respectable. But still.

The car dropped us off at the entrance to the restaurant, and a waiting maitre'd showed us to a private room, where a handful of others waited, including the young woman I'd spoken to through the scrying crystal.

8

When she saw me, Kestrel raised her glass of something pink to me. I tried to signal her with eyebrows and head tilt not to say anything. The woman next to her turned, and I recognized her mother. She looked startled to see me, then whispered something to her daughter that I could easily pick up with my Fae hearing.

"She looks like the woman in the movie you were watching the other night."

"Yes, she does have a strong resemblance to the actress, doesn't she? Or Elsa."

They both giggled, and I resisted the urge to roll my eyes and place a curse on the creators of that stupid movie. Besides, why couldn't I have a resourceful redheaded sibling rather than a deadbeat Fae prince who couldn't stay out of trouble? Kestrel and her mother definitely emanated witch energy, as did the dark-haired man they stood with. He wore an indulgent smile, and the invisible ties between the three of them told me they were a family.

"Doctor River?" A middle-aged man who had the plain energy of a straightforward human approached and held out his hand. His hair had gone gray over a youthful face that sported a matching goatee and mustache, and light blue eyes looked at me inquisitively behind the round-lensed glasses currently in fashion.

"Yes," I said and shook his hand. "Are you Doctor Cimex?"

He chuckled, and his face was so open and friendly I had to smile back. Here was someone who emanated only warmth and welcome, which made me wonder what he could be hiding. Everyone had something.

"You're even more amazing than I'd been led to believe," he said. "Yes, I'm Doctor Cimex, head of the Shadow Project. I see you've already met Larry—I mean Lawrence—Gordon and Corey. I'm hoping we'll all get to be better acquainted. Now, I wanted to make sure, Lawrence said you were a vegetarian."

"Most of the time," I said. "I find I can't eat much of the meat on the market since it's typically been shot through with chemicals, antibiotics, and other things I cannot digest."

Lawrence radiated satisfaction next to me, and I wanted to smack him, but at least he didn't have it completely correct.

"Yes, he said you would only be able to eat organic, locally sourced foods."

"Again, not necessarily, but close enough." I wouldn't give Lawrence the victory even if he had been correct. Then, I recalled my human manners and decided to try to get Cimex to open up. "I appreciate you going to so much trouble to invite and accommodate me."

"Of course!" Cimex threw his hands up like I'd stated the most obvious thing in the world. "There are so few of you walking this side of the veil that I had to. Plus, as I mentioned in my letter, your unique talents will be greatly appreciated for our investigation. Speaking of which..." He walked to the table and tapped a knife against a glass. "Ladies and gentlemen, if you could take your seats. Our dinner is about to begin."

"All right, Kestrel," her mother said. "That's the signal. You said you had homework to do, and the manager said you could hole up in his office for it."

"But I want to stay," Kestrel argued. "I could help." She smiled, but not at her mother. She looked straight at Corey, who grinned back and winked at her.

Uh, oh, if I'd been a fairy godmother-type, I'd have been tempted to help that little situation.

"No, this is government stuff," her father said. "It's better if you don't get too involved. Besides, at least you get a good dinner. You can order anything you want."

"Anything?" Kestrel asked. "Even the lobster?"

"Almost anything," her mother said. She took her daughter by the shoulder and steered her out of the room. "Any dessert you want," she murmured.

With one last glance over her shoulder at Corey, Kestrel left. A waiter shut the door behind her.

"You'll be here," Doctor Cimex told me and placed me between Lawrence Gordon and Kestrel's mother, who introduced herself.

"I'm Beverly Graves, one of the scientists," she told me with a tired smile. "That was my daughter, Kestrel. She's a handful."

"Isn't she old enough to be left at home?" I asked, playing up the insensitive Fae angle.

"Yes, she's in college. Studying criminal justice and hoping to join Corey in the PPP—Paranormal Profiling Program—it's part of the PBI, another shadow organization." She inclined her head to Corey, who lounged against the door. "She'll take any chance to see him," she added in a not-so-quiet whisper.

"Beverly," her husband warned. He sat across from us. "Our guest doesn't want to know all this. At least not yet. How was your trip, Doctor River?"

Arghhh... Why did these humans insist on small talk? And a PPP? Was that why they wanted my talents—because I could identify paranormal creatures by their energy fields?

Then I caught the way Kestrel's father, whom I later found out was named John, looked at me with mixed curiosity and suspicion, then away. What kind of scientist was he?

Worse, what kind of experiment would I be? I snapped into cautious mode—well, more than previously.

Selene, who sat between John, and Cimex, rescued me from having to answer the pointless question.

"I'm sorry if I missed something," she said, "but the itinerary said we'd first meet everyone at headquarters tomorrow. I'm thrilled to be meeting the team already, but are the plans incorrect?"

"Ah, I'm glad you asked, Doctor Rial," Cimex said. "I'll tell you in a moment. Meanwhile, the first course, please," he said to the waiter who hovered by the door. The young man nodded and darted out. Corey closed the door behind him.

Cimex glanced at Corey, who nodded and said, "The room is clear."

Then Cimex spoke, all but a trace of his geniality gone from his face, making his eyes look flat and cold. "The plans are correct, at least as far as the rest of the team is concerned, but I wanted to meet you and your colleagues this evening for a specific reason. You see, we're fairly sure whoever leaked the sample of the CLS vector to an industry contact is one of the team members who isn't here." His eyes glittered, and sorrow over the loss of trust in their close-knit community surrounded him. "This is a chance for us to speak frankly and openly and to give you the true lay of the land. But first, I don't know that we've all been introduced. You met Corey and Lawrence, of course. Our other friends here are John and Beverly Graves. They're talented witches as well as epidemiologists."

And grand poobah and poobah-ess of a powerful local coven, as I recalled. Did their colleagues know?

"What kind of scientist is Doctor Gordon?" I asked.

"I'm a veterinarian," he replied. "There are a few of us at the

CDC and CPDC. Not all of us are creatures ourselves, of course."

"Right." A veterinarian? I guessed it made sense since we were there to look into the Chronic Lycanthropy Syndrome leak, but none of the lycanthropes I knew liked to call themselves "creatures," either. Selene took a drink of water, so I couldn't see how she felt, but her aura indicated she likely found the whole thing amusing.

"Doctor Rial and Doctor River, we're honored for your company," John said. "But we were hoping for Doctor Fortuna and Mister McCord to join us as well."

"What he means," Cimex interrupted, "is that their reputations preceded them, as they were the ones instrumental in developing the cure."

Selene smiled, but she didn't show teeth, and the corners of her eyes remained un-crinkled. "I can understand your feelings, but we all work together as a team. In fact, Doctor River was instrumental in helping us to ward off a plot to interfere with our development, so she is familiar with operations as well."

An awkward speech, but I returned her polite grin and nodded. Fie, now I had to say something nice about her. "And Doctor Rial makes sure everyone stays sane. Plus, her training makes sure she's grounded in both psychological and physical sciences, and if you're looking for a traitor, a psychologist will be most useful."

Selene nodded.

A knock on the door cut off our conversation, and Corey opened it to let in the wait staff, who brought scallops on a bed of sunchoke puree for the others, and the same for me but asparagus rather than scallops. I liked scallops, but the asparagus still sang of the early spring sunshine, so I could tell they'd been picked that morning.

"Are they all right?" Lawrence asked. "They were picked this morning. I made sure to ask."

As if I couldn't tell. "They look delicious."

He smiled as though he'd been the one to pick and prepare them. Gods, couldn't this gargoyle let me eat in peace?

Once our group was alone again, Selene asked, "Do you have any leads or suspicions as to who the leak could be? And what, exactly, are you hoping to accomplish by having us here?"

Cimex nodded and grinned like she'd asked the cleverest of questions. "By having experts like you two here, we're hoping that whoever the leak is will reveal themselves through the questions they ask and the way they behave. Also, Doctor River will hopefully be able to sense any deception in word, deed, or existence. You can tell what kind of paranormal being everyone here is, can you not?"

"Yes," I said, although he'd implied he was something, but I couldn't tell what. Should I reveal the gap in my knowledge? Or ask him later? Or ask Corey, whom I sensed didn't have a single deceptive bone in his body—odd for a security agent. Everyone else had the usual mixture of truth and self-delusion so common to all creatures, human and non-human alike. It wouldn't be so easy to pick out the one liar among so many. The question would be, could I figure out whose secrets had led to the leak?

Our appetizer dishes were cleared, and the main course arrived—Springer Mountain chicken over Logan Turnpike grits for the others, and vegan mushrooms with red wine sauce over grits for me. They were good, but I would have liked to have tried the chicken, which John informed us was the kind many of the high-end restaurants chose. I again responded to Lawrence's overly concerned questions about whether the food was fine.

Once the staff left, I asked, "How, exactly, was the sample stolen?"

"We have a protocol," Beverly said. "Every time someone takes a sample from the fridge, they have to sign it out. We didn't have computer monitoring on it before, but we definitely do now. Someone took a sample after hours, didn't sign it out, and moved the other vials so that we didn't discover one was missing until several days later."

"And there are no security cameras?" Selene asked.

"There are, but they didn't pick up anyone, only the fridge opening and closing that night."

I almost choked on the water I'd been drinking. That sounded like my invisible attacker. Of course everything was related, but how?

"Are you all right, Doctor River?" Cimex asked.

"Yes," I said with a cough. "Went down the wrong way." At least the water was absorbed into my system rather than going into my lungs, which meant I recovered faster than a human would in a similar situation.

"An invisible thief?" Selene asked. "That sounds highly improbable. Had the tapes been tampered with?"

"No," Cimex said. "I reviewed them myself. There may have been something like mist in the shape of a person, but nothing distinct enough to identify exactly who or what it was."

"Could it have been a spirit walker?" I asked, now remembering what had been tickling the back of my mind since the intruder in my cottage.

"A what?" Beverly asked.

"Spirit walker," Selene said. "Someone who can astral project, essentially. But they typically have a form, not an invisible body."

"It's possible," Cimex conceded. "I don't know of anyone on my team who can do that, though, either presently or in the past."

Selene bit her lip, a sign she was thinking. "So there are people who are no longer on your staff but who were at the time of the theft?"

Cimex shrugged. "Only a couple of techs. No one who

would have had the knowledge or connections to have pulled this off. And I'm sure neither of them were spirit walkers. They were human through and through."

Like him, or so I'd thought. It seemed to me that Dr. Cimex had a large blind spot, and that's where we should start.

Selene's gaze met mine, and she nodded.

"If you don't mind," she said, cushioning her request in Southern politeness I could only admire but not emulate, "I'd like to start with those two techs. Could we get their information when you have a chance?"

The lack of directness was going to kill me, but Cimex appeared to appreciate it. "Of course."

Corey let the wait staff back in to clear the dinner dishes and bring in dessert, a lovely strawberry shortcake for everyone else, and...

"I'm sorry, but we didn't get the vegan cake in for the other dessert," the one who seemed to be in charge said. "I can bring another shortcake if you like."

I opened my mouth to say, "Yes, please," but Lawrence beat me to it. "That's fine, just bring some strawberries."

"I'm actually all right without dessert," I said and stood. If I had to stay in there another minute, I would end up taxing myself by attempting to turn him into...well, I didn't know what. But it would be embarrassing. Rather than demonstrating my limits, I decided to leave.

"I'm going to take a walk," I said. "Go back to the hotel. I'm tired, and I need some air."

"Want me to come with you?" Corey asked.

"No," I snapped. "I need some time to myself."

The men stood, and I managed to grind out, "Thank you for a lovely dinner," before walking out. Corey accompanied me to the door.

"Are you sure?" he asked.

"Yes, although if you could do me a favor, I'd appreciate it," I said.

"Anything. What do you need?"

"Could you please hook me up with one of those short-cakes? Bring it to my room later."

He laughed. "Definitely. Don't let Larry get to you. He's a bit stiff—comes with the territory for what he is—but he means well."

I had my doubts. What kind of man came between a woman and dessert?

"Thank you." I made a quick stop at the ladies' room and then walked into the cool night air, remembering to pay attention to my surroundings. But a Fae could still be surprised no matter how careful she was, and I knew within three steps that I was being followed.

9

W hoever it was stayed about ten feet behind me as I walked alongside the busy road back to the hotel. Thankfully there were sidewalks, although still not wide enough to give me a comfortable distance from traffic.

How did I know I was being followed? The echoed emotions of the person behind me that they needed to catch me, their intent so single-minded I couldn't help but feel it.

My previous attacker had been silent and swift, unde-tectable even to my finely tuned Fae-dar. No, this evening's pursuer lacked that kind of subtlety. Could the earlier one have been a spirit walker? Possible, although the ones I'd met in that form had more identity and substance. But they'd also been trying to get my attention in a good way.

The hotel driveway was coming up, and I'd have to walk behind a small copse of trees in order to follow the sidewalk to the front door of the hotel. I'd be vulnerable there, but then, so would my follower. Once I stepped into the shadows of the wood, made starker by a nearby street lamp, I ducked behind a large tree with Fae speed and waited. My tracker's breathing came quick and desperate, and I pounced them when they walked by, putting them in a choke-hold with one elbow and pulling their left arm behind them. The scents of strawberry shampoo and fear wafted up to me, and something in a plastic bag bounced against my leg.

It was the young witch Kestrel. Not sure who was more surprised. I let her go, and she backed away but didn't drop the bag.

"What was that for?" she asked.

"Why were you following me?" I gave her my best pissed off Fae look, although I struggled not to let her see my amusement...and relief.

"Why were you walking so fast?" she asked. "I tried to catch up with you, but..." She took a deep breath. "Corey sent me with this." She held out the black plastic bag, in which a clear clamshell container held a piece of strawberry shortcake, a couple of thick paper napkins, and a fork—also plastic. Hadn't anyone here heard of compostable restaurant materials?

"Thank you." I took the bag from her. "I appreciate you delivering this to me. And if I was walking fast, I was annoyed. Not at you," I added quickly. I didn't want to hurt her feelings. It wasn't her fault that her parents hung out with an annoying gargoyle, and the scrying stone had indicated she could be a valuable ally. "Did you get to try it?"

"No." She pouted. "Corey sent me after you before I could."

"Let's go inside and split it," I suggested. It didn't seem fair that she'd given up her dessert to bring mine. While Fae didn't typically care about what was and wasn't fair to humans, I did hate to deprive someone of the opportunity to have a good dessert. Plus, the girl could be useful.

"Can you eat that? Doctor Lawrence says—"

"Doctor Lawrence doesn't know a mushrooming thing about me," I snapped.

"Obviously," she said with a wry smile. "Otherwise he would have made sure you got dessert."

"Precisely. Come on." I didn't like how the shadows moved as the wind stirred the early spring foliage around us. There were too many places for my invisible assailant to attack me from. It was bad enough it had invaded my home—would it deprive me of comfort in my natural surroundings, too?

Kestrel and I walked into the hotel lobby, and she went to the bar to grab a couple of plates for us. I spooned out the chocolate cake, whipped cream, and strawberries and attempted to divide them equally. Again, not my usual game, but I needed this gesture of goodwill to go a long way.

"This is good," she said after her first bite. "I've never had chocolate strawberry shortcake before."

"I may have once. I don't remember. Desserts tend to blend together after a while unless they're extraordinary."

She paused before putting her next bite in her mouth. Each of her forkfuls held equal amounts of chocolate cake and whipped cream as well as two strawberry pieces. "How old are you, anyway?"

"That's not a polite question." I took a bite—bliss. And another stab of anger that the gargoyle had cake-blocked me and almost deprived me of this pleasure. "How old are *you*?"

"You didn't answer me. That's not fair."

"There's no fair in Fae," I told her. "Older than your country, how about that?"

She had the grace to look surprised. "Really? You don't look a year over two hundred." Her grin held mischief.

For the first time in years, I laughed freely. "Thanks, I think."

"I'm twenty," she said with a sigh. "Almost twenty-one."

Aha, an in. I could guess where that sigh came from. "And how old is the handsome Agent Corey?"

She grinned, and the light hit her cheeks at the perfect angle to show her pale freckles. She was already pretty, but she'd be a true beauty given a few years. Whoever made her face light up like that would be a lucky gentleman.

"Twenty-five. He's already through the Academy."

"What Academy is that?"

She rolled her eyes, reminding me how young she was. "The PBI—Paranormal Bureau of Investigation—Academy."

"Right, they mentioned that at dinner."

"You probably don't have it where you are," she said. "It's an American thing." She took the last bite of her shortcake. I finished mine as well.

"Thanks for bringing dessert," I said.

"No worries." She stood and gathered up the plates and utensils. "I should get back. My parents will be wondering where I went. By the way, please do me a favor and don't mention their coven connection to anyone."

Ooh, another secret. "Why not?"

"Their scientist friends won't like it." Her phone buzzed, and when she looked at it, her face fell. "And there they are." She hit a button on the screen, then said, "At hotel with Doctor River."

"Don't your parents' colleagues know they're witches?" I asked.

"Yes, but not that they're so involved with something outside the lab. That's one of the things about the CPDC—they don't look favorably on outside entanglements." Her frustration came through in her tone, and I could guess why. They wouldn't like Corey the security shifter being involved with Kestrel. Or perhaps they watched him so closely since he was at the PBI.

Only the first night, and already so many threads to unravel and secrets to use. I could barely contain my glee.

A strange hum filled the air, almost like the thrumming of a bass string that had been plucked and allowed to vibrate indefinitely. "Do you hear that?" I asked.

"Hear what?" Another tone, discordant to the first that almost drowned out her words. "All right, they're going to pick me up."

"That weird hum. Or drone. You don't hear it?"

She gave me her inquisitive look. "No... Do your kind not react well to chocolate? Or non-organic ingredients?"

"Insolent chit," I said, but grinned to take the sting out of my words. "I handle chocolate just fine, and a little of the other stuff. No, something odd is happening."

"Right... Well, anyway, you have my cell number. Call me if you need anything. More dessert, maybe. I'm always up for a chocolate run. Oh! And you have to try Insomnia Cookies. Hey, where are you going?"

I ran to the elevator, and once in it, I knew I had to get to my room. The noise hadn't just been an oddity—it had been a summons.

When I threw open the door, the moonlight coming through the window illuminated a small gray form on the bed. His one white paw practically glowed.

A tracking spell pinged off the back of my head, but I didn't pay attention. I walked to the bed and put a hand on Sir Raleigh. He wasn't breathing.

10

Kestrel appeared at the door, her parents behind her. They must have been the source of the tracking spell. "What is that... Oh! A cat?"

I gathered Sir Raleigh to me. He was colder than I'd ever felt him, and I wondered just how far he'd come through whatever medium he traveled through to find me. What had happened to his collar?

My phone buzzed—Veronica. *"Have lost cat. He chewed through his collar. Have you seen him?"*

"He's here," I texted back.

"Is he okay?"

His little chest rose and fell once, and I cuddled him to me harder, pulling from the trees outside to give him whatever energy I could. He struggled, his life force trying to recover, but I didn't know if it would be enough.

"You need a vet," John said. "I'm calling Lawrence."

"No... Wait, all right." The last being I wanted to see was the gargoyle, but I didn't want Sir Raleigh to die. He'd fought so hard to come find me. If he didn't make it, it would be my fault.

I shouldn't have left him. But I'd had to. Where had he come from?

I continued to breathe energy into Sir Raleigh until Lawrence arrived carrying an old-fashioned doctor bag. Kestrel and her family bowed out and left to give him room to work. Lawrence gently took the kitten from me, laid him on a hotel towel, and listened to him with a stethoscope, his movements precise and gentler than I expected for a gargoyle.

"I need to bring him to the office. I have an incubator where I can warm him up and give him sub-cu fluids if necessary." I almost didn't recognize his professional tone

"Do what you have to do," I said. "I can pay whatever it costs."

He looked up at me, his dark brows almost meeting over his nose. "I'm not sure I want to bargain with a Fae."

That might be what he didn't want, but I knew what I desired to do—grab him by the collar and shake him until he helped my cat.

"I won't trick you," I said. "Please, just help him."

He wrapped Sir Raleigh in a towel and handed him to me. "He's attached to you, obviously. Take him to the front. I'll pick you up."

I didn't know what kind of car I expected him to drive, but the practical—and dare I say boring?—Honda Civic wasn't it. At least it was the expected dark gray. Gargoyles couldn't help it —they were drawn to stone-colored things.

I cuddled Sir Raleigh and got in. Lawrence arched an eyebrow at my expression.

"What?" he asked.

The cat seemed to be breathing more regularly, so I felt okay with teasing him. "It's just typical. The color of the car, I mean."

His lips twitched—an almost smile? "Well, my bright red convertible is in the shop."

"Figures."

He drove us through the night to a campus guarded by brick gates, then through those to a building, where we took an elevator to a subterranean floor. Even through the metal box and its concrete cage I could feel the red earth of the Georgia hills welcoming me and lending me their strength, which I funneled to the cat. He alternated periods of breathing regularly and then going frighteningly still.

Once we were downstairs in a veterinary clinic that didn't have any animals, Lawrence took Sir Raleigh from me, stuck a needle into him—I had to look away for that part—and started a fluid drip. He rubbed something on Sir Raleigh's gums and then placed him in a metal device. He didn't close the lid, though.

"That should keep him warm enough," he said. He positioned a tiny cuff over Sir Raleigh's leg with the white paw. "To monitor blood pressure and heart rate," he told me. "What happened to him? How did you sneak him over here from Scotland? There's a quarantine for a reason."

I stroked the kitten's head and willed for him to be all right. "I didn't sneak him over here. He came on his own."

"He what?" Lawrence crossed his arms and gave me a classic Fae-style stern look. "How?"

I mentally went through the pros and cons of being open with him.

Pro—perhaps he could help me figure out how to keep the kitten from teleporting, to use the modern term. It had been annoying before. Now it had gotten dangerous.

Con—I didn't trust him. Nor, I realized, did I trust Doctor Cimex or any of the other team members. Not yet, anyway. There was still too much left unsaid and unrevealed.

Pro—he was a vet, so he had an oath to keep, didn't he? I had taken the Hippocratic one in medical school, but I didn't know if vets had something similar. Even if not, he surely had an ethics code. He'd been nothing but gentle and professional with Sir Raleigh to this point.

Con—he was a gargoyle, which meant he'd betray me at some point. They always did that to my people, being concerned with the survival of their species over all others.

Pro—he hadn't yet given me a reason not to trust him. Annoyance didn't count. And he did seem to know a lot about mythical creatures, even if the knowledge wasn't entirely correct in my case. But then, we didn't allow full knowledge of who we were or what we could do out into the scientific world, so he could be excused for some inaccuracies.

And I really did need to know what was going on with my cat. The cat, rather. All right, it seemed the decision had been taken away from me—Sir Raleigh had decided he was my cat. I'd simply have to figure out how to take him with me into Faerie once I was allowed back in. My grandmother liked curiosities, so she might let him stay. I didn't doubt he'd follow me, anyway.

"He's not a normal cat," I said and checked to see Lawrence's reaction.

To my surprise, he smiled without any mockery although his tone teased. "No cat owner thinks their cat is normal, but I suspect you mean something else."

I told him about Veronica rescuing the mother cat and her kittens, and how this one had a tendency to disappear and reappear, mostly on my shoulder. I also informed him of Sir Raleigh's fast growth rate and seeming intelligence. All right, I may have embellished that last part, but I didn't doubt he was a very smart kitty.

"Have you ever heard of or read about anything like it?" I asked.

"No," he said and scratched Sir Raleigh under the chin. The kitten purred once. "But he's responding very well to what we're doing, so he has at least somewhat of a normal physiology. I want to keep him overnight to observe him." Then he yawned. "I'll need to get some coffee."

"Why don't you go home to bed, and I'll watch him?" I asked. "I can see things you can't and I'll call if something seems wrong."

His own pro/con process showed on his face, but he finally rubbed his eyes.

"Right. Cimex had us all in early, so it's been a long day. Don't hesitate. If anything is even a hair off, or you have a flicker of suspicion, call me." He gave me his number.

"Will do," I promised. "I won't let anything happen to him."

"I know you won't. Well, then, good night."

"Good night." I listened for him to exit the clinic, and then I turned to see Sir Raleigh looking at me. I sat beside the incubator and rubbed his ears. "Well, you gave me a fright, wee lad. How are you feeling?"

He didn't move, but the life force that had been waxing and waning steadied. I continued to pet him for about half an hour until he glowed brightly to my Fae-senses. Then he disappeared from his monitors, incubator, and towel and reappeared on my shoulder. With a happy chirp, he chewed on my hair.

"All right, then." So he obviously felt better, and now we were stuck. An inconvenience or gift from the universe? "Shall we see what we can find in Doctor Gordon's files? Maybe we'll figure out what they're hiding from us."

LAWRENCE HADN'T LEFT any lights on in the rest of the office, but I didn't mind. I could see well enough in the dark, an ability my fellow Fae envied. My mother always said it was because I'd been born the night of a new moon, but I didn't know whether to believe her. She wasn't exactly forthcoming about my history.

Rhys, on the other hand... I knew the circumstances of his birth and early life better than my own, him being the favored child.

Of course my wayward brother came to mind. He loved snooping and gathering information to use against people. I whispered the unlocking spell he'd taught me and opened the first file cabinet in the office that had "Lawrence Gordon, DVM" on the door. I flipped through the top drawer, and, not finding anything beyond boring personnel stuff, moved on to the next one. Sir Raleigh had resumed his perch on my left shoulder, and I kept awareness of his purring and breathing, my own heart skipping a beat each time he paused. His life force continued to thrum happily, so I guessed he was all right, but I had a newfound sense of how fragile he was—how fragile all life could be, really, even for one as almost-immortal as a Fae.

The front of the second drawer held more human resources things—apparently Lawrence helped out in more than a veterinary capacity—but the back of the drawer seemed too close to the front. Indeed, when I compared this drawer with the ones above and below, it was obvious that there was some sort of compartment.

"Nothing too secure to stop a curious Fae," I murmured. Sir Raleigh agreed with a squeak. Or maybe it was a yawn. I scratched his head before I continued.

The edges of the not-so-false back lined up so flush I almost broke a nail trying to find and pry them apart. There had to be a lock somewhere, but where?

Finally, I found a tiny hole in the side, and with the help of a paperclip and another unlock spell, I got the front to pop off. A small compartment held handwritten notes and messages to Lawrence. The first didn't seem that bad...

LAWRENCE,

The deadline is getting closer, and I haven't seen the files. How is your end of the project going?

— G

WHAT IN THE world made that a secret document? And who was G? I kept reading.

LAWRENCE, I've told you that the protocol you're suggesting will never fly with C. Stop insisting, or he'll discover what you and I have been planning.

ALL RIGHT, but what protocol? Where were his notes?

Then, something more sinister.

LAWRENCE, I've become aware of the missing item and attempted to report it as per protocol, but the system was down. Do you know anything about it? I thought we weren't supposed to deliver until a week from Thursday. Please clarify.

COULD the missing item be the CLS viral vector sample? And could G be John Graves? The handwriting looked masculine. Were Lawrence and John the ones who had stolen the vector and delivered it to Cabal Laboratories? Why would Lawrence have kept the notes, though? Was he intending on double-crossing John?

That would make sense for a gargoyle. But to what end? He'd be implicated, too. Or was he planning to cut a deal?

I took pictures of the messages, replaced them and the door, and then closed the drawer and locked it back up. He'd never know we were there.

My stomach rumbled, but I knew I didn't need to eat. Sir Raleigh had gotten restless and hungry, so we returned to the laboratory part of the office, where I found some kitten kibble for him. He ate daintily in spite of his gnawing hunger pangs. Again, what sort of creature was he? What type of cat could disappear and reappear? A troublesome one, to be sure, but I felt like I missed something big and obvious.

Thinking of the mystery surrounding Sir Raleigh brought my thoughts back to Lawrence and John. What had they been conspiring to do? And were they working against Cimex? Disappointment made a surprising and heavy weight in my chest. I should be thrilled to find out Lawrence would end up being yet another traitorous gargoyle, but I found myself less happy than I expected. And what about John, with his sweet wife and daughter? He must be putting his family at risk.

After Sir Raleigh finished his kibble and drank some water, I decided to go back to the hotel. No cell signals got through to the clinic, so we took the elevator to the top floor and walked through the glass doors into the night. To my dismay, I found a familiar vehicle parked in front of the building.

Lawrence leaned against his car, arms crossed, and an unhappy expression on his face.

"And just what do you think you're doing?"

11

"N-nothing," I lied and gave him what I hoped was a winning smile.

"Then perhaps you'd like to explain how the cat is on your shoulder and not in the incubator or hooked up to the monitor." He held up his phone. "I had just gotten home when all the alarms went off." He looked every inch the grumpy gargoyle.

So he wasn't upset over me snooping... Phew. Not that I felt badly about my actions. I'd never had a guilty conscience and didn't plan to start now.

And...maybe I could work this to my advantage. I couldn't confront him with what I'd found without revealing my guilt, but perhaps I could earn his trust and charm it out of him. That would, of course, mean having to put aside my aversion to gargoyles, but I could deal if it meant I'd get answers.

"Do you have anything to say?" he asked. "I told you to call me if something changed."

"No," I said and drew out the vowel as seductively as I could. "You told me to call if something went wrong. There's a difference. Sir Raleigh made a miraculous recovery thanks to your quick thinking and care."

He gave me a look full of suspicion and no charm, but he didn't argue. "Then you wouldn't mind me taking a look at him."

"You'll have to ask him. By the way, he teleported from the incubator, I didn't unhook him."

Sir Raleigh peeked out from underneath my hair and gave one of his kitty chirps. He sounded quite proud of himself.

We followed Lawrence back into the clinic, and he looked Sir Raleigh over, then pronounced him to be fit.

"No sign of any trauma," he said. "I suppose he's good to go with you." Then the ghost of a smile. "Not that I could stop him."

"Right." I didn't have to fake my smile or my pride in Sir Raleigh's ability, which had started to grow on me. I had to respect a creature determined to make his own destiny.

"All right, then, I'll give you a ride back to the hotel," Lawrence said.

"Thank you."

"But he'll have to ride in a carrier. I'm not going to risk him."

So Lawrence was a rule follower. Noted, although that didn't make sense with him conspiring with John Graves to double-cross their lab. At least he spotted me a litter box, bowls, and enough food and litter for a few days. I'd have to not allow housekeeping in, but I was fine with that.

Sir Raleigh deigned to be put in a carrier, and I attempted to engage Lawrence in conversation on the way back to the hotel, but he kept putting me off. I declined to be upset—I could tell how tired he was. When he dropped me off, he didn't say much, only that he'd pick me and Selene up at nine. I used a slight glamour—all I could manage so far away from home— to keep the front desk people from noticing the cat and supplies and made it to my room with no trouble.

Huh, so I'd have to figure out how to get past that stony exterior. Luckily no gargoyle could ever resist a Fae.

I CAUGHT a few hours of sleep with a warm cat nestled in the crook of my neck. While I didn't know what I'd do with him during the day, I relished the comfort he gave me. The whispers of the trees outside the room sounded unfamiliar, and the noise of the nearby interstate hummed constantly like the buzzing of angry insects. Finally, with Sir Raleigh's purr in my ears, I fell asleep.

Of course I rose with the sun, and I listened for Selene in the next room. The outer door opened and closed, and then the shower ran. What had she been doing? Had she gone out to meet someone without telling me? What would Gabriel think?

The sleep fog cleared in an instant. As soon as I heard the shower stop, I moved to the door between our rooms to knock on it and see if she had time for a chat or wanted breakfast. Not that I needed her approval, but I wanted to tell her about my investigations from the night before and the results. The bathroom door opened and closed, and I heard her talking to someone. It took me a second to realize she was on the phone.

"I just got back from the gym," she was saying. "Jet lag is a bitch." Then a laugh. "Yeah, she's been a handful. Max didn't tell me about her airsickness thing." Another pause. "Right, Fae get airsick. Who knew? It looks like narcolepsy."

At that point, any honorable human or Fae would have stopped listening, but I wanted to know what she was saying about me. And I had *not* been a handful.

"No, she stalked out of dinner in a huff. Over dessert." A soft chuckle, although it didn't sound friendly or comforting since it was aimed at me. "No, I don't know what she's going to do. Are you sure it's safe for me to be here alone with her?'

Not safe? I hadn't put her at risk. I'd only had enough of the insufferable Lawrence Gordon. Who I was now going to have to pretend to like to get information from him.

I'd intended to share what I'd found and plan with Selene, but there was no way now. Not if she thought me to be a useless drama queen, as the humans liked to say. And if she thought I wasn't safe, it meant she didn't trust me.

"When are you guys going to be able to come?" she was asking. I wanted to know the same. Let them see that I'd been doing the useful work and she'd not accomplished anything. Then we'd see who was a handful.

I wouldn't be able to hear the answer, so I moved away from the door before I gave myself away, either with a noise or a Fae energy spike. I understood she had some sensitivity. Instead, I sat cross-legged on the bed and tried to calm myself. Sir Raleigh crawled into my lap, and I pet him instead of focusing on my breath, which worked just as well. Why did everything have to be so complicated?

WHEN SELENE KNOCKED on my door about twenty minutes later, I'd regained my composure and my unruffled Fae demeanor. I hoped. She didn't seem to act any differently or notice anything amiss when I opened the door. Instead, her eyes widened, and she put her hands over her mouth before exclaiming, "Oh! Is that the kitten?"

Sir Raleigh, the little traitor, trotted right up to her and sniffed her hand. Soon, he purred under her caresses, and she, in turn, cooed over him, telling him what a handsome kitty he was and oh, how soft, and...

And it took every bit of willpower for me to not roll my eyes. Sure, she could be sweet to the cat, and to my face, but I know what I'd heard. Well, if she thought I was a handful before, just wait.

I ordered Sir Raleigh to stay in the room while I went to eat. I almost referred to myself as his Mommy but stopped. While I wanted to bring him with me into Faerie, it wasn't guaranteed he'd be welcomed, and I didn't know how his strange talents would manifest there. If anything, the overheard conversation reminded me not to allow anyone to get too close.

The ache in my heart at the thought of leaving him permanently steeled into annoyance at what I'd heard on the phone. How should I act? I vacillated between deliberately trying to not be overly dramatic and deciding, Fae it, I should be myself, and she could deal with it. At breakfast, I sent back my order for them to remake it because the waffles weren't crispy enough, and I sulkily settled for coffee because they didn't have my favorite tea. Selene didn't say anything, and she maintained a politely neutral expression, which further annoyed me. Right, she was a psychologist—they were trained to do that. The only sign of tension was the slight dimpling of the corners of her mouth, and her inability to look me straight in the face said she definitely was cataloging my actions for a report to Gabriel later. Speaking of which...

"Have you talked to Gabriel?" I asked. I had to remember not to show I knew she had.

"Yes, he called this morning after I messaged him that I was up." She stirred cream into her coffee, and her gaze flicked to the bar to our right. I pretended to find something in my hair on that side and took the opportunity to see where she'd looked. Right at a large bottle of Bailey's. Excellent—both the taste in alcohol with coffee and her desire, whether conscious or unconscious—to self-medicate when dealing with me.

"Did he say when he and Max are joining us?"

"No, he said they're still dealing with a thorny issue at the

Institute. He didn't want to say over the phone what it is." She sighed. "It's tough..."

"What is?" I added another half-packet of raw sugar to my coffee, regretting my snobbishness. It wasn't bad, but the tea had been better.

"Him not being here. I'm not the investigator. I'm not sure what to do."

I studied her from under my lashes, which had thankfully remained dark through my entire life and had not faded when my hair went from blonde to ice. Selene wore makeup, but I could tell she hadn't slept well from the matching bags under her eyes, a complete set of two. Regret for giving her a hard time flickered in my core, but I sternly reminded it that she'd been mocking me to Gabriel over the telephone. If she wanted my sympathy, she'd have to be nice to my face *and* behind my back.

"Well," I said brightly, "we'll just have to do the best we can. Maybe we'll discover something today." Like how Lawrence and John were behind all of it. Perhaps there would be some clue to confirm what I'd read and how to bring it into the open without revealing I'd snooped. I did recall from a medical forensics class that going into someone's personal things could bias a jury against you or even cause the evidence to not be allowed at the trial. And I wanted the case to be open and shut so there would be no reason to keep me here, no ambiguity to cloud my case for re-entering Faerie.

After a delicious breakfast, we reconvened in the lobby, this time with Sir Raleigh hidden in my hair.

"What do you think of Lawrence Gordon?" I asked.

Selene shrugged. "I don't blame you for walking out last night. It's infuriating when someone thinks they know you better than they do." She slid me a glance.

"Thanks for acknowledging that." *But not for playing up the drama with your fiancé.* "I guess we'll have to deal with him.

Maybe he was feeling insecure. What do you think, Doctor Rial?"

"Well, Doctor River, I guess we'll just have to see."

When Lawrence picked us up, he pointed to the carrier in the back seat, and I coaxed a reluctant Sir Raleigh into it. Selene took the front, and I sat behind her with Sir Raleigh in his carrier belted beside me.

"How did you sleep?" Lawrence asked. In spite of his short night, he looked completely rested and cheerful. Selene and I gave polite affirmative answers, and off we went.

As soon as the car started to move, Sir Raleigh began a pitiful chorus. He and I locked, eyes, and then he disappeared, reappearing a half second later on my shoulder with a satisfied purr.

"All right," I told him in my secret conversation voice, but quietly in case by some weird chance Lawrence could hear me. *"You can stay there, but pop back into the carrier when we arrive okay?"*

A meow in my head told me he'd heard and agreed. Indeed, what sort of cat could hear and understand secret conversation?

On the way to the CPDC, Lawrence informed Selene of Sir Raleigh's surprise appearance and how he'd saved him. I refrained from rolling my eyes and instead gratefully acknowledged his help. Then Selene looked back at me in the rearview mirror with an arched eyebrow. Oh, well, let her wonder.

In the light of day, I could see the abundance of trees, all wearing their early spring gowns of peridot and light emerald. Now awake, they whispered hello to me, and I to them. But the more joy that filled me with my communicating with them, the more Lawrence scowled.

"Do you have to do that?" he asked.

"What?" I looked at him, all innocence.

"Talk to the trees." He shook his head. "Sorry, their whispers remind me of nightmares I had as a child."

"What sort of nightmares?" Selene asked.

This could be interesting. I sat back and let her do her therapist thing.

"Of being lost in the forest, and the trees would try to help me, but then I'd get more lost, and eventually, I'd fall down a deep, black hole I couldn't escape from."

"That sounds terrible," Selene agreed. I pulled myself back from the delightful thought of him being stuck in a pit and returned my attention to the conversation.

"It was."

Now I stifled a snicker at her frustration that he wouldn't open up more.

"How old were you when you were having them?"

His lips moved, perhaps a sign of him doing the math internally. It occurred to me that I didn't know how old he was. Elementals aged slowly, especially when around their pet elements, and Atlanta certainly had enough granite, iron, other minerals, and water to keep a gargoyle happy. I'd heard they thrived in cities, where stone tended to be as much aboveground as below with the buildings, but sometimes the water pollution got to them.

"I suppose it was from ages five to fifteen," he said. "Can't think of why, though. Sorry, Doctor Rial. Doctor River, do you ever have nightmares?"

I bristled internally at such a direct personal question, but I forced my expression into a thoughtful one. "No, not that I can recall. I don't sleep much, so maybe I don't have the chance."

"That's what I thought," Lawrence said, practically crowing with satisfaction. I wanted to hit him, but I didn't want to injure myself, the cat, or Selene in a car crash. "We've just started a paranormal sleep lab, and we're attempting to see how our sleep differs from the humans. Doctors, if you wouldn't mind, you'd likely be a great matched sample set with your similarities in intellect and perceived age."

Perceived age? What in Hades was that supposed to mean? Selene looked out the window to her right, but her shoulder shook, and I knew she was chuckling.

"I couldn't stand having the electrodes stuck to me," I said with a shudder at the thought. "Nor could I sleep with someone watching me."

"Ah, right, I'd forgotten—Fae and some metals," Lawrence replied. "I'll have to check into materials. It's possible we have ones you could tolerate."

"No, thank you. I am still not interested." Hopefully I wouldn't have to be around that long.

"Ah, well, here we are."

I swore that if he said one more "ah," I'd give him something to "ow" about.

Be charming, be charming, be charming...

He turned into the campus and slowed the car, and Sir Raleigh disappeared from my shoulder and reappeared in the carrier, where he curled up and pretended to sleep.

No, if Lawrence was indeed guilty of industrial espionage, the last thing I wanted was for him to experiment on me.

12

Instead of going to the elevators, we stayed on the main level of the humble brick building and went through two keycard-guarded doors to the main CPDC lab. Of course Dr. Cimex had everyone lined up like we were visiting nobility to Downton Abbey. The scientists and techs didn't look too happy about it. Americans never liked it when Brits came over and tried to tell them what to do, but as soon as Selene opened her mouth and turned up her "bless your heart" accent, they relaxed.

I didn't pay that much attention to introductions. Why should I? I knew that Lawrence and John were guilty. But I might need an ally on the inside, so I told myself to tune in.

"...and this is Leah," Cimex was telling Selene. "She's our newest tech, and she's already showing great promise. John couldn't get along without her."

Oh, really? Leah, a petite brunette with big green eyes and a pixie-like face, blushed and sent a side glance to John Graves. He smiled indulgently, and, more interestingly, Bev stiffened, her smile draining from her eyes.

Hmmm... Scandal in the laboratory? That could be interesting...and advantageous.

"How long have you worked here?" Selene asked.

"Three months," Leah chirped. "Doctor Graves knew me from the hospital and told me to apply when the job opened."

"When did that happen?" I asked Cimex, who beamed at his people. It was interesting that Leah hadn't been invited to dinner. Because she was a suspect? Or irrelevant? And who had she replaced?

His smile didn't falter as he looked up. "Now let me see. Right, we did fire someone right after the incident." By which, I presumed he meant the loss of the vector. "Not that we had any concrete proof. No, wait, he, ah, left. Said he had a family situation he had to take care of."

"Do you know what happened to him?" Selene asked.

"No, but I could give you his information."

"Did you think it at all suspicious that he quit right after the, ah, incident?" I tried to make my question as friendly as possible, but I'm not sure I managed to keep the implied, "you idiot" out of my tone.

"We did consider it," Cimex said. "But he didn't have access to that part of the laboratory. Only a few do. I'll give you a list."

"That would be helpful," Selene told him.

After a few more scientists and techs trotted up for their turn in the dog and pony show, we adjourned to Cimex's office, where Lawrence joined us along with Corey. Although the office had looked big before we entered, the presence of so many people turned it claustrophobic. Plus, whoever had decorated it had come from the school of industrial scientific chic. The painted cinder block walls, diplomas, and metal and surplus storage-vibe of the furniture made it feel shabby, not like the office of a department head.

"Here's the list of the people whose key cards will let them in to the room where the top-secret samples are kept." Cimex handed Selene a list. I held out my hand for a copy, but he shook his head. "Sorry, I only have one. Can y'all share?"

Selene and I, who sat across his desk from him, leaned in and looked at the list together. It included Cimex, Lawrence Gordon, the Graves couple, a behavioral epidemiologist I recalled meeting because of how beautiful she was—all dark hair, eyes, and skin—and a couple of techs, who assisted the scientists on the list.

"Had anyone seemed unhappy, or did they act differently before the incident?" Selene asked.

"Now that you mention it, Mickey—that's the tech who left —had gotten a poor performance review, his first while working for us, and he'd been here a while. He said it was because of his family situation. He couldn't keep his mind on his work, or so he claimed."

So far I wasn't impressed with Cimex's sleuthing or management abilities, and Selene's expression said she felt the same.

"Anyone else?" she asked. "I know it's been a while, but any direction you can give us will be helpful."

Cimex, Gordon, and Corey all glanced at each other. "We'll discuss it," Cimex said. "Now, why don't y'all look around, talk to people? See what you can get a feeling for. Doctor Rial, I understand you have some empathic abilities."

"They're minor," Selene said. "Nothing magical, just good observational powers."

I kept myself from snorting. She hadn't figured me out yet.

Sir Raleigh, who'd been napping on my shoulder since we arrived, stirred and woke. He yawned, and the sound finished with a squeak in my ear. He kneaded my shirt with sharp claws, and the pinpricks of pain on my right shoulder nearly made me miss Selene's final question.

"Thanks, and please let me know if you do think of anything. By the way, did you call campus security when you noticed the sample missing?" Selene tucked the list in her purse.

"We have our own security." Cimex gestured to Corey. "Agent McLendon's superiors can let you know what they found. Basically—and embarrassingly—it was a minor breach of protocol that led to a big problem."

"Right." Selene stood, and I did likewise, but I had one more question—something it seemed no one had thought to ask.

"What about the industry contacts?" I asked. "Has no one managed to get in touch with them? They should be happy to sell out their supplier now that they've made a mess of things with CLS."

"That's another issue," Cimex said with a sigh. "The head of the project at Cabal Pharmaceuticals has disappeared. Believe me, a lot of time and resources were wasted trying to track him down."

I nodded. "Guess we'll get started, then."

We walked out of the office and paused by the door. Sir Raleigh less-than-gracefully let himself down by half-climbing, half-crawling down my shirt and pants. While I was glad he was using his limbs and not blinking in and out, I didn't appreciate the resulting small holes in my clothing.

"Will he remain unharnessed?" Lawrence asked.

"I suppose so," I said. "I trust he'll stick close by." I gave the cat a stern look, not that I knew how much good that would do.

"I need some air after that close office," Selene murmured. "Reine, care to join me?"

"Definitely."

"I'll accompany you," Lawrence said.

"No, no, that's not necessary," Selene told him with a gentle hand on his arm. "We're going to be fine, and I'm sure you have important work to do."

"Well, I do have some reports to catch up on," he grumbled

good-naturedly. "Doctor River has my cell phone number if you need me. And Corey won't be far away."

Indeed, the golden-eyed cat shifter hovered nearby. Lawrence left, and Selene and I walked out with not just one, but two feline shadows, since Sir Raleigh seemed inclined to follow us, as did Corey. At least he hung back unobtrusively, but I guessed he'd have cat-sensitive hearing.

"Do you mind?" I asked and put as much Fae persuasion behind my words. "Doctor Rial and I would like some privacy to discuss things."

"Of course, ma'am. I'll be nearby, though, so holler if you need anything."

"Will do."

Once he moved far enough away, or so I thought, Selene asked, "Can you do anything to mask...?" She gestured between the two of us.

"Not too much. My powers are greatly attenuated here." I sighed and leaned against the brick. We were on the east side of the building, so while the air was chilly, the wall had absorbed some heat. The mineral and fire baked my back and rear end and soothed some of my anxiety, but not all of it.

"What do you think?" she asked, still softly.

"That they're each hiding something," I replied. "But I don't know what's relevant and what's not."

"Did you know they're calling us consultants since Max and Gabriel couldn't come?" She snorted. "That's the problem of not being able to publish our work in the mainstream literature— no one here will recognize my name."

"If we're consultants, they need to pay us," I grumbled. She laughed.

"So what's our next step, do you think?" she pulled out her phone. "It looks like we're in charge, after all."

"I'm curious about that tech."

"Me, too."

I pushed off the wall and focused on my cat, which I'd kept in my peripheral vision to make sure he didn't wander off too far. Sir Raleigh chased something on the nearby lawn, then looked up at something we couldn't see, arched his back, and growled. Something stirred the blades of grass a few feet away.

"Do you...see that?" Selene asked.

"Yes." I grabbed the kitten. "Corey!"

13

W e almost smashed into Corey as he rounded the corner of the building.

"What is it?" he asked.

"Something..." I trailed off. It occurred to me that if we were dealing with an invisible foe, that talent fell under either astral projection or shapeshifting, and we still didn't know who to trust.

"Something spooked her." Selene took over smoothly and shrugged. "Fae. What are you going to do?"

Corey's golden gaze lingered on her sweaty face and too-wide eyes. "Right."

"Psychologists, what are you going to do?" I said with a mocking shrug. "We need transportation somewhere."

"I'll take you," he said with a grin he mostly aimed at Selene. Sucker. "That's my job. Cimex has assigned me to watch over y'all."

"Oh, I'm sure we'll be fine," I said, but the hairs along my back and neck hadn't stood down after our brief encounter with... Well, whatever it was. I guess I didn't sound convincing because he pulled his keys from his pocket and motioned for us to follow him.

"Car's this way, ladies. Where are we going?"

Selene followed him, but a tug on my jacket nearly made me jump out of my skin and drop the cat. Instead, I clutched him tighter and turned. He squeaked indignantly, so I loosened my hold.

"Yes?" I asked Leah the tech. She held up a cat carrier.

"Doctor Lawrence said to give you this in case you decided to go somewhere." She smiled, and her entire face lit up. I could see how John Graves would get suckered in.

"Thanks." I ignored the hard side-eye Sir Raleigh gave the object. Leah didn't immediately turn to go back inside, although she shivered in her lab coat. "Is there something else?" I asked.

"Yes," she said. All traces of mirth left her face, leaving her looking serious and older. "Doctor Cimex lied to you about the secure room where the fridges and freezers with samples are. They should be locked, but the keypad developed a short and sometimes wouldn't open, so someone—I don't know who, probably Doctor Graves—rigged it so all you have to do is press the same number four times, and it will open. It saves us a lot of time."

"That sounds...illegal," I said.

"Yes, it probably is," she agreed. "But it's how it is here, and how it was when I got here." She paused to make sure I got her hint—that the lock had been broken before the previous tech left. I nodded. She continued, "The rest of the organization doesn't take what we do seriously, so we're not watched as closely, and we get away with more. And they're only human, after all."

"And you're not?" I asked.

"Not entirely." And with that cryptic comment, she whirled around and went inside, leaving me speechless, a rare condition for me.

"Well, Sir Raleigh," I said and scratched his head with my free hand. "This gets more and more interesting."

Corey opened the back door for me when I reached the car. Selene already sat in front and had her phone out. "It says that Mickey lives in Tucker. Is that far? I admit I'm turned around." She gave him a helpless look, and he blushed. I guess I wasn't the only one who'd decided to try to charm information out of someone. Her strategy seemed to be working better than mine.

"It's a little out of town, but not too far," he replied. "Doctor River, would you like to secure the cat?"

Although it had been phrased politely as a question, I heard the command in his tone. I pointed to the open carrier, and Sir Raleigh gave me a "really, this again?" look but slunk inside. He turned around, laid his head on his paws, and fixed me with a baleful stare through the bars of the door.

"It's not for long," I promised. I wished he could speak so I could ask what he'd seen outside, what had made him growl. Although he couldn't weigh more than a pound, he'd made a truly hair-raising sound that resembled something I'd heard before. I couldn't put my mental fingers on it, though.

Corey and Selene chatted about the city and how it had changed. It seemed to be a never-ending topic of conversation, so I once again stared out the window and tried to commune with the trees. As usual, they whispered their greetings, but this morning they added signs of caution, that I needed to be careful and watch. Their admonitions sounded so much like what the man in the airport had said to me I suspected there must be a connection. But what could it be? And how could he have passed his message on to the trees?

Unless he was a Fae like me. My Fae-dar hadn't gone off, though I'd been upset enough that I could have missed a slight signal, especially if he was from a different region. We responded most to those who'd spent a lot of time close to us.

Not that I'd spent much time with any other Fae except for Rhys in the last few centuries.

A familiar word brought my attention to the front of the car —Culloden.

"Did you ever go to the Highland Games there?" Selene asked. "Since your dad was on the athlete circuit, I thought you may have. They stopped a while ago."

"In Scotland?" I asked. "And they're still going."

"No," Corey responded with a chuckle. "In South Georgia. Tiny town, but they played up the name connection. You're familiar with the original?"

"Quite." The battle had drawn me and Rhys out of Faerie. Tasked to spy, we'd split up...

I blinked away the memories.

"What is it like?" Corey asked.

Thankfully Selene answered him. I didn't want to think about it. Instead I focused on the mental image of the nearby standing stones, a place of balm and healing for me, even if they didn't open for me to allow me to pass into Faerie again.

Corey pulled up to a small ranch-style house in a quiet neighborhood. The yard showed that someone cared for it, and tulips and other colorful bulb flowers nodded in the morning breeze along the walk and in the front bed. The sight lifted my spirits. Perhaps if Mickey was a gardener, I could connect with him.

Corey turned off the ignition, got out, and opened my door, and then Selene's.

"Perhaps it would be best if you didn't come," Selene suggested gently. "He may be more likely to open up to us."

Gutsy move on her part. It seemed that opening up was exactly what Cimex and his crew didn't want the guy to do, but Corey shrugged.

"Suit yourself," he said. "I'll be here if you need me. Just shout. I'm sure I'll hear you."

My cheeks heated with shame at how I'd panicked. But I didn't think my reaction unjustified, if unexplainable. Sir Raleigh stayed in the cat carrier. I supposed he was angry with me and didn't want to come out, so I didn't think anything of it. Besides, some people didn't like cats.

Selene and I walked to the front door, and she rang the doorbell. It chimed throughout the house in the descending major and minor third chords of Beethoven's Fifth Symphony.

"Ah, so he's got some culture," I said.

Selene laughed. "Let's hope he's home."

The door opened to reveal a man wearing flannel pajama bottoms, a stained white T-shirt, and a flannel robe, which he tied as he looked us over. His gray and black hair stuck out at awkward angles from his head, and his eyes were bloodshot and bagged. Whatever he'd taken to sleep, it was still with him.

"C'help you?" he mumbled. The fog of dreams still surrounded his aura, which I only saw for a second before it blinked out of sight. That's how my third eye worked far from home—in spurts rather than consistently. I'd be a disappointment to any investigative team unless I could channel more energy to it, but I was still adjusting.

"Hi, I'm Se—Serena Rogers," Selene said. "This is my associate Farrah Pendragon. We're private investigators and were wondering if you could answer some questions for us."

He ran a hand over his face, and his fingers whispered against his gray-mottled black stubble. "'Bout what?"

"About the lab you used to work for," Selene said. "The secret one, you know. We've been hired by the government to look into it."

Her excuse sounded flimsy to me, so I gave him a little glamour push, nothing hard—he still had plenty of room to make his choice—but he nodded and stepped back.

"'Bout wanting to talk about that place. No one will listen to me."

We followed him into a house that seemed too light and airy to house its occupant. Light wood, wide arches, and white walls made it look bigger than it was. I'd used the same techniques in my cottage when I'd had it built, oh, a few hundred years prior.

"Please have a seat. Coffee?" he asked.

"No, thank you," Selene and I chorused as we sat on the tan leather couch he'd indicated.

"Fine. I want some." He went into the kitchen and called, "Ask your questions, ladies! I'm listening."

Selene and I looked at each other. We really should have planned that out better.

"What can you tell us about working in Doctor Cimex's lab?" Selene finally shouted back.

After a long pause, his voice floated back to us. "Nothing. I signed an NDA." He came back, again tying his robe. He appeared more alert, the red gone from his eyes. Had he made coffee or done some sort of speed in the kitchen?

"But you said you wanted to talk, and no one would listen," I said.

"Right." He ran his hand over his hair. "I'm sorry, I'd just woken up from a bad dream." He shrugged, hands out. "I'm afraid I can't tell you anything. Doctors Lawrence, Graves, and Cimex were a joy to work for. Too bad I had to leave."

"And why was that?" Selene asked.

"Oh, you know..." He looked up like the answer was on the ceiling. "Family stuff?"

Selene and I traded another glance. Something was definitely wrong.

"You are Mickey Michaels, right?" I asked.

"Yep, that's me, Mickey." He stabbed at his chest with this thumb.

Then it hit me... He'd gone to make coffee, but by now we

should have heard and smelled it brewing. But there was nothing.

"Well, we're sorry to have bothered you," Selene said. We stood and moved toward the front door. "Please let us know if you can think of something."

"How? You haven't given me a card or anything." He held out his hand. "I'll take one, if you please."

This had gotten even stranger, and I had a wide reference range for *strange*. Selene and I hurried toward the door, but he moved quickly and blocked us. "Come on, now, ladies," he said. "You don't want to leave so soon. We've just started to have fun." He reached into his robe pocket, and—

A yowling mass of gray fur appeared out of nowhere and attacked his head. He stumbled away, trying to fight off the cat, and the revolver he'd been about to pull on us clattered to the floor. Selene kicked it away. I couldn't have touched it—too much of the metal I couldn't tolerate—but she could have at least used it to cover us.

Selene pulled open the door, and I followed her. "Raleigh!" I shouted. The sudden weight on my shoulder told me he'd joined me, and this time I didn't mind the sensation of his claws digging into my shoulder.

Corey moved toward us, his weapon drawn, and Selene and I ran to the car. He went into the house and was gone for a few minutes that felt like many more before he came out.

"Doctors," he said. "What were you running from? There's a naked, unconscious man in the kitchen."

"Wait," I said. I put my hands on Corey's cheeks and forced him to look into my eyes. His energy flowed through my palms, and I could tell it was him, although I couldn't explain how.

"What?" he asked.

"We're dealing with something very dangerous," I explained. "Something your gun won't help you to defend yourself against." I opened my mouth to say more, but something invisible slammed into me, knocking me to the ground and jolted my breath out of me. Raleigh jumped at it again, and it fled. Still, my brave little cat walked in a circle around me, growling and hissing until, satisfied, he sat beside my head. Corey helped me to a sitting position as my breath returned, and I gathered the purring cat to me.

"What is it?" Selene asked.

"A soul-eater," I said. "At least I think so. Let's go inside and take a look."

We followed Corey into the kitchen, where we found the comatose body of Mickey Michaels, coffee filter in hand, but without his clothing, which lay in a heap by the front door.

"Poor guy," I said and rubbed my eyes. "I wish I'd figured it out earlier. I should've known when I saw the drained animals."

"Drained animals?" Corey asked. "I don't follow."

"It's how it was following me. Taking the form of animals so I couldn't sense it. Soul-stealers can take the form of humans and animals, and they need to steal their energy in order to do so." First a bird, then a squirrel, and now...

"Where did it come from?" Corey asked. He looked concerned.

"It's a type of dark Fae, and most cultures have a different name for it. You know how they say fairies steal children? This is the truth of the legend," I told him. "And the fact that this one is getting closer and taking on larger forms says it's growing stronger."

Selene pulled out her phone, then frowned at it. "What do I do? Call the police?"

"No, we have a different way of handling things like this," he said. "I'll call our organization. They have a special medical unit for such things. Mister Michaels will be safe there."

"Who is it?" Selene asked.

"Branch of the TS," he replied. "Sorry, that's all I can tell you. Would you mind waiting outside? Do you feel safe?"

I nodded. "Our friend is likely going to need to take time to recover from his or her most recent sojourn." But did I trust his organization with Mickey?

"And I need some air. Truly," Selene said. I followed her outside, all the while cooing to Sir Raleigh and telling him what a good kitty he was. He purred, and he allowed Selene to hold him, too, until she stopped shaking.

"Thank you," she said and put him on the ground, where he set about sniffing the lawn and beds.

"For what?" I asked.

"For letting me hold the cat. I know how attached you are to him."

"I..." I couldn't argue with her. "You're welcome. Have you not seen anything like that? There was no blood."

"That doesn't help much. The poor man. What if our being here led to his attack? And what if he doesn't wake up? He felt...empty."

I refrained from telling her that our presence likely had led to Mickey Michaels' death, if not now, then soon. He was a weak human, after all. The Fae Court called it collateral damage when two parties at war took out possible allies and...spies.

"Ohhh..." I said, the realization hitting me so hard it hurt. "He didn't just know about the lab. He knew about the bigger picture. Hades on a stick!"

"Wha...?" Selene was giving me that wide-eyed *I'm not keeping up with you* expression a lot that day.

"And somehow the cat knew. That's why he didn't come in. I think."

"I'm not following you," Selene said.

I wasn't following me. The thoughts flew through my brain

so fast I couldn't catch them. "Give me time to sort it out. It'll make sense. By the way, Leah told me that the lock on the secure storage room door has been broken for a while, even longer than she's been there."

"So Mickey Michaels could have been the culprit," she said.

"Likely not if he was attacked to keep us from getting information," I replied. "It's definitely a sign we're on the right track, though."

She looked back toward the house, from which Corey emerged.

"And that we need to work more quickly before more innocent people get hurt, Reine. I know you're a Fae and don't hold our lives in high regard, but please tell me you have at least a little humanity."

And with that little speech, she got in the car, shut the door, and wouldn't make eye contact the entire ride back. She and Corey ignored me, as per usual, but instead of pondering revenge as I previously would have, another thought occupied my mind.

Now that a dark Fae had come into the picture, I needed to find some way to call my mother.

14

How was I going to call my mother? That was the big question. I had my talisman, but I still needed a place to use it. As far as I knew, the United States didn't have standing stones. While I had no doubt there would be spaces sacred to the indigenous peoples, I didn't know how to start looking for them. Well, I did. Fae knew how to use the Internet, but I also didn't know if such places would be similar enough in energy to draw my mother out, especially since she would have to use strength to push through, and while she was more powerful than me, she would also be weakened by being so far away from home.

A scrying stone wouldn't work, assuming I could find one. It couldn't call into Faerie, at least not with the amount of power I had, and I'd likely be incapacitated for days afterward. Not a good condition for dealing with a soul-eater.

My own skin crawled at the thought of such a being—a hybrid between the dark Fae and a powerful dark witch. They were rare and only emerged when called forth by a powerful shaman, witch, or other Fae, which was why I needed to talk to

Mother. If anyone in the Light Seelie Court had summoned it, she would know or could find out.

Sir Raleigh lay curled in my lap, no doubt exhausted from his encounters with the creature. How had he known? And, as I sorted through the memories of the encounters, I recalled something else. I had seen the shadows of wings around Sir Raleigh.

Could he be a grimalkin, another Fae creature? I'd only heard of them since they were of the gray Fae, or the result of a rare cooperation between the Light and Dark courts. I petted him and felt along his shoulder blades, and he purred, but I couldn't feel any wing knobs or anything else that would indicate he either was going to grow or manifest them. But he traveled between dimensions, so what if he had them in whatever space he moved through?

Every encounter with the kitten gave me more questions about him.

Corey dropped us off at the lab and parked the car, and we all walked into the building.

"Are we safe here?" Selene asked. "I didn't think about it earlier, but now I'm worried. Especially since we're dealing with something invisible."

"We should be," Corey told her. "The exterior walls as well as the ceiling and floor are lined with silver-coated lead, and our most powerful spell-casters have put wards up. No critter should be able to get in or out without invitation."

That explained the hush I felt when I entered, like my senses for the outside world had been cut off. I'd been too preoccupied to notice it that morning.

We followed Corey back to the inner office. Cimex looked up, his expression startled. "Back so soon?" he asked. "I thought y'all were going to lunch."

"We encountered a problem."

"What sort of problem?" Cimex put his pen down, lining it

up exactly along the top line of the document he'd been reading. Indeed, his entire office spoke of preciseness and lacked the clutter I'd been accustomed to seeing in other scientists' spaces. If a cluttered space was the sign of a clear mind, what did a neat space mean?

"A soul-eater."

Cimex's eyes appeared to grow in size to fill out the space behind his round lenses. "Are you sure?"

"Yes," I said. "It attacked Mickey Michaels before he could tell us anything." I refrained from saying that the man certainly seemed eager to reveal something to us. Selene and I would have to put our heads together to see whether we could talk to him on a different plane. Maybe Kestrel Graves could put us in touch with some local witches.

"I called the TS," Corey said.

It then occurred to me what he was referring to. "The Truth Seekers? That band of vigilante witches?"

Cimex held up a hand. "It's all right, Doctor River. We've been trying to make peace with them, and they've proven useful liaisons with the local law enforcement."

"What are they?" Selene asked.

I couldn't stifle the urge to roll my eyes, so I lifted my gaze to the heavens—all right, ceiling—with a heavy sigh.

"Merlin started them. They think they're our law enforcement, but there's no central supernatural government, so they don't really represent anything, and they don't have any power."

"And the Fae have never acknowledged their authority," Cimex added. Unnecessarily, I thought. Maybe he missed my eyeroll.

"So where were they when CLS became a problem?" Selene asked. Right, she'd been changed involuntarily, so she had some feelings about the matter.

"Their argument is that they monitor supernatural interference of humans, not vice versa," Corey explained.

"They missed the Order of the Silver Arrow, then," I muttered. "Was Wolfsheim not important enough to watch?"

"I don't know," Cimex replied, but his pleasant expression didn't waver. "Perhaps they knew that the Lycanthropy Council's Investigator had it under control."

"Riiiight," I said. "So, they'll clean up the mess. Good. What about the soul-eater?"

Now Cimex's face molded itself into a serious cast. Watching him fascinated me. He had a lot of expression for a human male. How had he become the leader of a scientific organization? Didn't human politics require more deception?

Or was he that good of an actor?

"I don't like the thought of you two being in danger," he said, now the picture of concern. "I'm afraid I have to insist that you not go anywhere unaccompanied. I'll also have our spell-casters come put wards on your hotel rooms."

"Maybe just Bev," I blurted. If John was tied somehow with the CLS issue, he might be in league with the soul-eater. Then my cheeks flushed as I recalled Kestrel's admonishment to keep her parents' roles a secret.

"Why?" Cimex asked. He didn't seem surprised. Maybe their secret was their coven involvement.

A deep voice answered before I could, and the condescending tones of Doctor Lawrence Effing Gargoyle Gordon filled the room. "Because female Fae have strict rules about who can do magic in their spaces. They only allow women to cast near them. Men's magic is too strong."

I opened my mouth to argue, but my mother's caution to not let them know too much truth about us came back to me. But too strong?

"Something like that," I replied through clenched teeth, not willing to give Lawrence more satisfaction than absolutely necessary. When had he snuck in?

"Very well," Cimex said. "Thank you, Lawrence. Why don't

you accompany Doctor River since you seem knowledgeable about what she needs? And Corey, you watch Doctor Rial. I'll arrange for you gentlemen to have hotel rooms near theirs."

"You can do that?" Selene asked.

"We have ties to lots of the hotels," Corey said. "They'll contact us for the occasional exorcism, even though it's not exactly what we do. But they're grateful, and we have a lot of favors to call in."

Huh. Not only did they study paranormal diseases, they were also mediums. "Do you have a medium on staff?" I asked.

"No. We've sometimes used Kestrel Graves," Corey said, and I caught the pride in his tone. "She's young, but she's shown some talent in that direction."

"She hasn't settled into her powers yet?" I asked.

"No, she's a slow bloomer," Corey responded. Then he bit his lip and looked away.

Ah, so the feelings between the two were mutual. What kept them apart? Did Mama and Papa Graves not approve of the potential mating? Thanks to my Scottish colleagues, the rules against witch-shifter pairings had been rescinded as it had become apparent that forbidding them hadn't worked, and the Lycanthropy Council and Wizard Tribunal were, for the first time in centuries, trying to change with the times and create an alliance for this brave and strange new world.

"That's all right," Selene said and did her hand-on-the-arm thing. "It's sweet."

I suspected there would be some conversations while Corey guarded her, and jealousy again lanced through me. Not that I wanted to play fairy godmother on any level, but I didn't want to be left out, either. I couldn't resist a spark of love that brought light and joy in a difficult situation, even if I knew it would never be mine.

～

Lawrence brought me and Sir Raleigh back to the hotel. This time I got to sit in the front seat, but Sir Raleigh still had to be in the back in the carrier. I could feel his resentment.

What was happening with the kitten? It felt like he connected spiritually to me more every day, never mind how he liked to literally attach to me. I would have to get thicker shirts or maybe something with shoulder pads. The thought of wearing shoulder pads made me smile.

"What are you thinking?" Lawrence asked. He glanced over, and his lips curled in a slight grin.

That made my humor flee. "Nothing." No way would I tell him I was pondering sartorial suicide to accommodate a cat.

Sir Raleigh chirped from the backseat.

"The cat disagrees. I've been thinking about his unusual talents. Have you ever heard of a grimalkin?"

I didn't want to say yes, but I also didn't want to lie outright —those got you into trouble eventually—so I said, "Maybe."

He went into lecture mode. I folded my hands so I wouldn't strangle him.

"It's a type of dark Fae creature. They're often in the form of animals, and they display normal behaviors for their avatars, but they have strange abilities. There are no two alike."

"He came from a litter," I said, not bothering to correct him or educate him about the gray Fae. Mostly because I didn't know much about them. Hades, half the light and dark Fae didn't believe in the gray, but something told me they were real.

"How did the mother cat feel about him?" Lawrence gave me a side glance. "Often they'll masquerade as a young animal, but sometimes they're rejected."

"Veronica—the woman who had him—said the mother cat was perturbed by his disappearing and reappearing and didn't want to nurse him."

"Aha." His condescending tone made me wish I'd lied after

all and said she hadn't had a problem with him. "So it's possible he was planted. The question is, by whom?"

"Indeed." I glanced back to see Sir Raleigh watching me with his gold-rimmed green eyes. He licked his nose. Cheeky little thing.

"Too bad he can't talk," I said. "That would solve many of our puzzles."

"He may eventually. Then you might not be able to shut him up." Lawrence shook his head. "That's been my experience, anyway."

"Wait..." I turned to look at him more fully just as he angled the car down a side street and the sun highlighted the—pun intended—chiseled planes of his face. When he wasn't being an ass, he could be good-looking.

Too bad he liked to spend so much time being an ass. But he had information I needed.

"So what you're telling me is that you've encountered these grimalkin creatures before?"

"Sure. Like you, I'm older than I look."

I sat back and folded my arms, more embarrassed than anything that while I'd been fending off his trying to know me more, I'd missed his lack of self-disclosure. "How old are you?" I asked.

"Old enough to not give a straight answer to a Fae," he replied. His words came across as teasing, but I caught the thread of caution that wound through them. So he was also old enough to know about the traditional enmity between our peoples, even before Rhys' fateful encounter.

"Right." I looked out of the window. "Because you'd rather be the expert on me but not have anyone know you that well. C'mon, Lawrence." I looked at him and caught him looking back. We both turned our gazes forward, at least from what I could see out of the corner of my eye. My cheeks heated for some strange reason.

"C'mon what?" he asked.

"Tell me something about you. Something beyond the professional vet and scientist persona." Something that would make spending excessive amounts of time with him bearable. Even beyond my mission for the Fae, to keep our true identities and abilities hidden, I hated being the subject of observation and study, and that's what he had been doing. And now I'd be stuck with him. I couldn't leave—that would be seen as abandoning what I'd been sent to do, which would close the gates of Faerie to me for good.

"I love animals," he said.

I shook my head. "Not good enough. I already knew that. It's one of your few redeeming qualities."

"Oh, so you admit I have others?"

"Don't push your luck, Gordon." And bless the Fates, I smiled. Actually smiled because I was enjoying our banter. "Tell me something that's not obvious."

He drummed his fingers on the steering wheel. "I'm from Scotland, too," he murmured.

"What?" I turned to look at him fully. "How long have you been here? You've got a boring American accent."

His soft grin hardened into a line, and the muscles moved beneath his jaw. Heat spread from my cheeks to my scalp.

"I mean," I said, "it's very neutral."

"My buddies in school teased it out of me." His grin returned, but only half of it. "Listening to you brings back memories." His smile faded again.

"Not good ones, apparently." I wanted to keep him talking. This crack in his tough guy scientist exterior fascinated me.

But the tension returned to his jaw, and he shook his head. "They don't matter. Now tell me, have you thought any more about that sleep study?"

～

LAWRENCE WALKED me up to my room, then left to get some things from his house since he'd be moving into the room next to mine. Selene would be transferred to the one on the other side of him with Corey beside her.

Once alone, I pulled out my laptop. I hated the thing, as I did most modern "conveniences" and appliances, but I did appreciate the access it gave me to necessary research when I was in a hurry. My preference, of course, would be to go to a library and spend time among trees that had been, but in this case, plastic and electric waves would have to do.

The scrying stone had shown me Kestrel Graves, and so I typed her number into my communications program. Luckily, she picked up.

"Oh, it's you," she said. She didn't sound happy. "Calling for more dessert?"

"Don't tempt me. They forgot to feed me lunch."

"Oh!" She looked around and picked up her phone. "Do I need to order something for you? You can probably get delivery from just about anywhere."

"Thank you, but I'm not helpless." I'd already called room service, who were happy to accommodate my dietary preferences for natural, organic ingredients.

"Right. So what can I do for you?"

"I was told that the CPDC used you occasionally for your mediumship skills, and I need to reach a spirit who may be hovering on the edge of moving to a different plane."

Rather than looking proud, she cast her gaze downward.

"What?" I asked. "It's nothing to be ashamed of. Some of the greatest witches in the history of the world could talk to the dead."

"It's not that..." She sighed. "I sometimes can do it, but then it goes away. That's what's happens to all of my magic. It comes, and then it goes away. I'm useless." Her eyes turned shiny, and she wiped her cheeks. "I'm sorry, I shouldn't cry."

"No, you should. That's terrible."

She coughed what sounded like a sob. Right. I didn't know how to do this human feeling better thing.

"I mean, that's got to be so frustrating." I imitated what I'd seen Selene do when we thought we were talking to Mickey Michaels.

"It really is," she said. "I think I'm going to be the greatest... whatever...and then I can't do it anymore after a few days."

"But Corey highly recommended you."

"Really?" That dazzling smile appeared, but then her expression clouded. "He's sweet, but he doesn't understand. Hell, even my parents don't."

"But they're witches."

She lowered her voice even though she presumably was at home by herself. "And they're the leaders of the most powerful coven in Atlanta, and I can't take over from them if I have wonky powers."

"Right." I hadn't put it together before, but John Graves being a coven leader with a succession to defend made his and Lawrence Gordon's collusion more interesting. "And what about Doctor Gordon?"

She shot me a coy look. "What about him?"

I rubbed my eyes. "He's annoying, and he kept me from having cake the other night. What do you think?"

She laughed, a welcome change from her melancholy of a few minutes before. "He's a little stiff, sure, but handsome, don't you think?"

I raised my eyebrows. "No, I do *not* think."

"You're just saying that because he cake-blocked you."

I laughed at her using my expression. It did sound slightly dirty. "Right, but if I'm going to be stuck with him, I need to know more about him. Like, where does he come from? How did he get involved in the CPDC? Why does he think he's an expert on all things Fae?"

She tilted her head. "Why are you stuck with him?"

Oh, right. She didn't know about the soul-eater. I doubted her parents would tell her even if they found out, and I did hope that Cimex would inform his staff.

"Because I was attacked by an evil creature today, so Doctor Rial and I are under a twenty-four-hour-watch."

The words must have clicked in her head because she sat up straighter. "Who's watching her?"

Clever girl. "Agent McLendon."

"Dammit!" She balled a fist and hit her knee. "Why isn't he watching you?"

"Why, don't you think I'm a threat?" I asked, secretly laughing at her jealousy. "Aren't I young and pretty enough to catch Corey's eye?"

"Pretty, yes. Young, probably not."

Well, then. I should have made her squirm harder for that, but something inside me softened at the memory of her distress at her magical issues. It never felt comfortable to fall short, especially when it was beyond one's control.

"All right, I should punish you..."

A panic-stricken look crossed her face. Good. At the very least she needed to be reminded of what she was dealing with.

"...but I won't. Don't worry about Doctor Rial. She's engaged."

"But she doesn't have a ring."

"She doesn't often wear it. She doesn't want to lose it when..." I almost said, 'she shifts,' but I didn't have the right to reveal Selene's secret. "...when she travels." Another little lie. How many would I rack up before the day ended?

"I can understand that." Now she looked dreamy. "When I get engaged, though, I'm going to wear that sucker everywhere, even to bed."

"Are you and Corey that serious?"

"No." She sighed again. "He's too caught up in his work, and it's frowned upon for people in the program to fraternize. They say it could be distracting in the field."

"Right." Humans and their rules. Someone knocked on my door. I called, "Just a minute!" Then, to Kestrel, "Well, my food is here. If you think about something useful regarding Doctor Gordon—or someone who can help me talk to a spirit in a different plane—let me know."

"Will do! And give me a few. I do know a good medium who can help me out if I can't manage. I'll get in touch with them and get back to you."

"Thanks."

Kestrel's pleasant expression hardened into something else —warning? "Don't thank me yet. No one in my parents' coven does anything for free."

The screen went dark, so I answered the door. A young man stood there with a tray. He smiled and asked, "Can I come in?"

I didn't want him to see the cat, and I also didn't want to invite anyone into my room—basic magical creature security protocol, that—so I shook my head.

"I'll take the tray, thanks. Just tell me where to sign." I did as he instructed, took the tray, and backed into my room as quickly as I could.

Sir Raleigh climbed into my lap when I sat, and I shared a little piece of cheese from my sandwich with him. Even if Kestrel could help me find a medium, I still had the quandary of no spot with enough natural energy to call my mother.

Sir Raleigh mewed and kneaded on my thigh.

"But first, we need to clip those claws." I suspected that would be the biggest challenge of the day, or at least I hoped it would.

I finished lunch and had just found the clippers Lawrence had loaned to me when my phone chimed with a text—*Backup medium found. Séance in an hour?*

15

I called Selene to let her know about the plan. Lawrence hadn't returned yet, and I figured if I was with Corey and Selene, I'd be safe, so he wouldn't mind us going without him.

I was wrong.

I opened the door to find a glowering gargoyle on the other side.

"Going somewhere?" he asked, his arms crossed like a geeky paranormal club bouncer.

"Yes, with Corey and Selene."

"In case you forgot, *I'm* supposed to be watching over you. We're playing man-to-man, not zone defense here."

"Is that a sportsing thing?" All right, I knew what he was talking about, but I couldn't resist the impulse to annoy him.

"Yes, and you've been around long enough to know what that means. Where are you going?"

There would be no getting around him, so I decided to come clean and figure out what to do with him as we went along.

"To a séance. Kestrel and one of her friends are going to help us catch Mickey Michaels' spirit before he either goes back into his body or leaves permanently. After the attack he sustained, either is possible."

He bloody still didn't move. "How do you know he hasn't already?"

"We don't. So, if you'll kindly get out of the way, we have a better chance of catching him." I tried to push past him, but of course he didn't budge. Finally, he stepped aside. "Rock head," I muttered.

We met Corey and Selene in the lobby, and we all piled into Corey's SUV. I listened to the trees' murmurs to calm my racing heart. Could we finally be getting the break we needed? Would this information lead to my homecoming to Faerie? With a path home now open to me, strewn with rocks though it may be, the urge to return had grown into a visceral pull. I clasped my hands so I wouldn't allow my impatience to dance through my fingers.

We arrived at a mixed-use development and parked in front of one of the stores. Kestrel met us out front.

"Excuse us for a moment," Corey said. We walked into the store, and when the heels of my boots met the wooden floors, the crystals on the shelves greeted me in a familiar chorus.

"What is it?" Lawrence asked.

"What?"

"You're smiling. Truly smiling, not the polite grimace you've been giving us."

Well, that wiped the happiness from my face. "Nothing."

He pulled out his phone, and I imagined him making a note —*Earth elemental energy strong in this Fae. Smiles at crystals.* Or some such nonsense.

Meanwhile, I'd kept an ear on Corey's and Kestrel's conversation.

"You don't have to do this," he said. "You said you were having trouble."

"Well, *you* decided to make me look good and recommend me, so what was I supposed to do?"

"Say no? You're allowed, you know." His tone told me this wasn't the first time they'd had such a conversation.

"Yeah, but my parents heard about it, so..."

"So, you're allowed to say no to them, too. I was trying to help."

"Well, don't." Kestrel huffed and came into the shop. She waved to the clerk, a teenager who barely looked up from his phone, and we followed her into a back room. Six chairs sat around a round table covered in a black velvet cloth. Jewel-toned cloths hung from the ceilings and walls, and I looked around for the crystal ball that must be in there somewhere. The center of the table held a shiny silver candelabra with four places. A slight, dark-skinned woman with platinum blonde hair and gray eyes smiled at us.

"This is my friend Aria," Kestrel told us. "She's the medium I told you about."

"I'm pleased to meet all y'all," Aria said. Her accent held a trace of Southern, but in general she sounded like Selene and many of the other Atlantans we'd talked to—neutral. She glanced around to everyone, and then her eyes widened when she saw me. "And I am honored you are here, Princess."

I cringed. "Please, call me Renee."

"Princess?" Lawrence asked.

"Long story," I said. "Let's get to it, shall we?"

Aria had us sit around the table, and she took the position opposite Kestrel. "I understand we're summoning a spirit in transition?" Aria asked.

"Yes," Selene said, but didn't offer any more explanation.

"Very well. Kestrel warned me that you couldn't say much

about your mission here, but I do sense you're in danger, especially you, um, Renee."

A medium had just warned me of danger. I wanted to dismiss her claim as part of her act—weren't they always supposed to do that? But her words echoed through the crystals in the room.

"Yours isn't the first warning I've received," I said.

"Then I hope whatever is at the end of your path is worth the risk." Aria placed four new white candles in the pewter sconce in the middle of the table and lit them in clockwise order starting with the one aligned to the north. "Now everyone join hands, and I'll summon my spirit contacts to see if they can find your lost soul. What is his name?"

"Michael Michaels," Selene told her, giving her the tech's legal name.

Aria sat beside me and held my left hand. Lawrence had my right one. Everyone closed their eyes but me—I wanted to see the tricks. What would happen? Table knocking? A shadowy white figure made of gauze and sticks? Or perhaps table levitation?

Then I caught sight of Kestrel's face, her forehead scrunched with earnestness. Hades, I could be a coldhearted bitch. Here she was trying to help us, and I couldn't buy in because it was all too stereo—

My chair shook. I leaned back to search for some sign that it was being manipulated, but I didn't see anything.

"Kestrel, do you feel that?" Aria asked.

"Yes," Kestrel said. "Something is here."

I looked around and didn't see anything, but another tremor rumbled under the floor. If Aria had hydraulic effects installed, I'd give her props for using modern methods to invoke a Victorian experience. Then the temperature plummeted, and every hair on my body rose. The logical half of my brain chalked it up to Southeastern US-grade air conditioning, but the other half started to be impressed and buy in—at least a little—to the possibility of spirits. The doubt that had sprung up when we walked into the faux-Victorian parlor began to ebb.

"Spirits, we thank you for your help," Aria intoned. "Please help us to reach the soul of Michael Michaels, who liked to be called Mickey and who may be journeying between planes. Ophelia, are you here?"

Her spirit channel was named Ophelia. Perhaps she'd be a drowned waif-like spirit who'd—

"What's up, witches?" Then a cackle. "I've always wanted to pop in and say that." Aria's voice, which had been slightly breathy, came out deep and with a resonance she shouldn't have been able to physically manage. More disturbing—her hand, which had been warm, had turned into ice.

Hades, this might be real. Excitement warred with anxiety. If things got out of control, would I have enough power to intervene? Whoever spoke through Aria had a strong and potentially malicious presence. But this could be important.

"Who are you?" Kestrel asked. "Spirit, I command you to identify yourself."

"Oh, do you, now?" The spirit mocked her. "Look, witches, I only have a few minutes here, and I need to talk to the Princess, here. You know, the one who's too important to close her eyes for a silly little séance put on by goofy little spell-casters who want to play medium."

Aria opened her eyes, and her irises had darkened to black. Her lips spread to reveal teeth with slight points to them, and I knew what I was dealing with.

"Speak, dark Fae," I said with as much royal command as I could muster. Sir Raleigh hissed, and I stroked his head. He quivered, but not with purrs. Who knew kittens could feel such rage?

"This thing goes beyond some stupid investigation into who

told what to whom. No, you're dealing with something much bigger, much—aaaaugh!" Aria arched back and clutched at her throat. "All right, all right, I won't say too much." She returned to an upright posture, and after a couple of gasps, said in a less flippant tone. "Listen, Princess. Align yourself with the fangs. They'll know what's what. And they may help with what you're here to do."

"Thank you," I said. "And what do you ask in return for this?"

"No free in Fae, eh? You know the rules. But I didn't make the bargain beforehand. Just remember your old friend Troubadour when you get home."

I didn't have a friend named Troubadour, but he wouldn't give me his real name, especially not in mixed company. "I will remember this."

"And keep an eye on that one." She/he nodded to Sir Raleigh. "You're right that no gift is freely given in Faerie." Then Aria appeared to deflate, and Corey, who sat on her other side, caught her before she slumped to the floor. The candles blew out, but rather than the typical sweet candle-smoke smell, they gave off a peaty odor. It wouldn't mean anything to anyone but me, but I got the hint—an old bog god had come to visit.

Aria opened her eyes—back to their normal color—and asked, "Did we find him?"

"No," Kestrel said. "Something else came through."

"Damn." Aria closed her eyes again, and I checked her pulse. Strong, but her energy said she'd been depleted.

"Damn yourself," I told her. "You must be one hell of a strong medium if you could hold that being for as long as you did. No more spells or summonings for you for the rest of the week."

"But the Equinox is tonight."

"But nothing." I put a hand to her cheek so she'd look at me. "I'm serious. Trust me. I'm a Fae princess and a doctor."

"And you're in trouble," Lawrence said.

Right. I'd managed to forget he was there.

"That's not an unusual situation for me," I told him. What could Troubadour have meant, *Align yourself with the fangs?* Did he mean vampires? They didn't exist outside of the Collective Unconscious, did they?

But then, there weren't that many Fae outside of Faerie.

We made sure Aria was all right. She promised to rest for the remainder of the day, and I suspected she wouldn't, but I couldn't force her. When we emerged from the séance room, the store had turned gloomy, and we found the sky had clouded up.

"Doctor River, I do have one thing to ask," Kestrel said.

"Right, I should check you, too. You were channeling along with her, weren't you?"

She batted my hand away. "I tried, but I was blocked." She looked down and shrugged Corey's hand from her shoulder. "No, I have a favor to ask you in exchange for bringing you here."

Right, no free in Fae. "What would you like?" I asked.

"My parents would like you to come along to our coven's Equinox ritual and celebration tomorrow morning. You don't have to do anything. It's more to show you off."

Oh, goody, another human social event. But I'd agreed, so... "Thanks for the invite. And the honesty. Guess I'll be coming along, then."

"Okay. I'll be in touch." She turned and walked to her car, a red Ford Mustang convertible. Someone loved their little girl— or wanted to make something up to her.

"Well, then," I said to Lawrence, Selene, and Corey, who gazed after Kestrel. "Looks like we need to find some fangs."

"I'll make a call," Lawrence said. "But it can only be the two of us."

"That's all right," Selene told him. "Corey's pulled some

records for me, so it looks like we've got a long evening ahead searching security logs for abnormalities."

WHEN WE REACHED our adjoining rooms, Lawrence had suggested we keep the door open. I still felt the residual energy of my conversation with Troubadour, so I consented, if only to have a protective, if annoying, presence nearby. Well, besides the cat, who'd crashed out. Being ferociously cute must be exhausting.

Lawrence pulled out his cell phone, then held it to his ear.

My curiosity got the better of me. "Who are you calling?"

"Someone who may know of a club with fangs." He gave me a sly grin. "I have famous friends."

"No, wait, I don't believe you. You're not that much fun. Why would famous people like you?"

He arched an eyebrow at me. Right, I should be nicer considering he stood on the cusp of doing me a favor.

"I mean, how did you meet them?"

He rolled his shoulders back. Could I be annoying him as much as he did me?

"I went to school with the Steel brothers."

"Which... Oh, the billionaire and—what does the other one do?"

"He's a news anchor. And he has a favorite club."

"Interesting." That could dull the monotony. And he was friends with a journalist. That added a new layer to my suspicion—had he been selling information?

"That sounds fine. What time do we go?"

He punched a couple of things on his screen. "Hey, Ted, it's Lawrence. So, I have a wager for you..." He walked into his room and closed the door. I thought about listening, but I didn't want to expend any unnecessary energy. Finally, he came back through, but only briefly.

"I'll meet you here in an hour. Try not to get in trouble before then."

"I'll do my best." But I wasn't making any promises. At the very least, I needed to come up with a strategy to turn up the charm and extract the information I needed from him.

16

When Lawrence picked me up, I made sure he had plenty to distract him from any probing questions I might ask. I wore an ice blue minidress with a faux fur wrap and my favorite blue diamond earrings, which had been given to me by an ice witch. They matched the necklace that her sister and rival had given me. I never told the other sister they'd managed to give me their mother's bridal jewelry. Instead, I hoarded the jewels and the drama for my own enjoyment...and other purposes. The earrings would draw attention to my eyes and the necklace to my décolletage, which honestly didn't need much help, at least from what I could tell.

But when I saw Lawrence, I almost forgot my distract-and-extract campaign.

He'd dressed in an electric blue shirt and a tailored set of pants that must have been cut and sewn to highlight his narrow hips and round ass. I knew men didn't want to describe their butts as perky, but I struggled to find a better word when he turned away from me to summon the elevator. He'd allowed his hair to dry in waves rather than the tight gelled helmet he typically wore it in, and his stubble had grown in. An elemental effect? Sometimes the men could change their beard style like women did with their hair. And his eyes, rather than being black chips, looked dark gray, and they widened when he saw me.

"Are you ready?" he asked.

"Definitely."

He peered around me into the room. "What about the cat?"

I patted my purse, which looked like a clutch, but which had the magical property of being able to hold whatever I put in it. "In here. He crawled right in. It'll be fine."

I'd been surprised, but Sir Raleigh had hopped right in when I'd told him that was the only way he'd be able to come with me. Not that I could have stopped him. I hoped inviting him along would encourage him to behave. I didn't dare wear him on my shoulder, as usual, but after that afternoon, I didn't want to be without him, either. At least one of us could sense the soul-eater. As it grew stronger, it would be able to mimic other creatures' energy, making it difficult to detect.

To my surprise, Lawrence didn't argue. Huh. Perhaps he knew about magical Fae purses? My curiosity about him grew. And, grudgingly, my respect. He seemed capable of playing the same level of game I did.

"I've asked the valet to bring the car around," he said. "It should be downstairs at any moment. Shall we?"

"Sure." I walked past him and felt his gaze linger over the curve of my waist and my own unapologetically perky ass. Or maybe I wished for him to check me out. By the time we reached the elevators, a slight flush had come to his cheeks and lips, and I smiled. Bingo.

Another surprise waited for me when we walked out to the car. Rather than his sensible black vehicle, a sleek dark gray convertible sat sparkling under the lights. I didn't know many car names or kinds, but I recognized its low-slung body and curves as belonging to the expensive category. And, I'm not going to be ashamed to say, it was sexy as hell. But I wasn't going to let on I thought so.

"Oh." I pouted. "I thought you said it was red."

"No reason to give the cops too many excuses to pull me over," he told me and opened the door on the passenger side. I got in, but carefully, both to make sure my dress hiked up just the right amount and to give him ample opportunity to check out my long legs, which I knew looked particularly good in the silver pumps. I watched him from under my lashes and couldn't complain about where his gaze lingered.

The hook was set. I hoped. He hadn't pulled his phone out to make notes about me, although I didn't know what he'd say —*Fae princess looks like sexy Elsa.*

He got in and asked, "Do you want me to close the top? It's chilly this evening."

"No, it won't bother me."

In spite of the pollution that always fouled the air around cities, I found the atmosphere to be bracing. I imagined squaring off against him, preparing for a battle of wits with the prize being information. I only wished I knew what to ask without giving away that I'd snooped. Vague words in notes didn't help much, but he must be involved.

He drove us through a wooded area, which became residential, and soon we turned on to a large road that took us into town. The buildings grew just as the trees must have beforehand, and the whispers of the large oak, hickory, and pines turned into the whimpers of small decorative trees and the sullen silence of glass, steel, and concrete. I avoided cities as a rule. They felt loud both in the noises of their engines and machinery and in the absence of the familiar murmurs of nature, no matter how many trees they had. And to give it credit, Atlanta had its share of trees, which did greet me, although not with the full chorus of forests.

"Where are we going?" There, start with an easy one.

"To an eighties club. Ted and I like to hang out there and remember our misspent youth." He smiled, and I barely caught the words, "Well, his at least."

Again, I wondered how old Lawrence Gordon was. With elementals, unless they were very old or very young, it was impossible to tell. Could he and I have more in common than I thought? I'd lived for several centuries both before and after my exile, and yet I looked like a young human woman, probably in her thirties, although my white hair made me look older to some.

"Which eighties?" I asked. "Eighteen-eighties? I imagine the music may be a bit bombastic. Seventeen-eighties? I do love me some Beethoven. Or sixteen-eighties? Baby Bach?"

He laughed. "Right. Did you know all those composers?"

"Not all of them. Chopin was surprisingly shy, in spite of his reputation." And I think he might have been dead by then. I could never keep my composer dates straight. "What about you? What's been your favorite period in history?"

He shrugged. "Each has its own merits. I try not to get stuck in the past."

Ouch. I was not stuck in the past. I appreciated it. I learned from it. I knew from my experiences that I shouldn't do certain things, like trust gargoyles.

"Sometimes the past can be useful," I said, attempting to lighten the heaviness our conversation had taken on. "Besides, I like the perspective it gives me. Kingdoms come and go, but certain things like music live on. It gives me hope for humanity and the world." Where in Hades had that come from?

Lawrence laughed, and the sound made me want to join in. Could Doctor Uptightpants be loosening up?

"So, you're an optimist? I figured all Fae were pragmatists."

"I'm most definitely an optimist." Well, maybe opportunist would be a better term, but I wouldn't admit to it. "By the way, how did you become such an expert on us?" I again tried to keep my tone teasing, but either he didn't want to answer, or my timing sucked because he turned into a Valet line. Two young men rushed up to the car once it stopped. One of them opened my door and didn't try to hide the fact he checked out my legs. The other one opened the door for Lawrence and took the keys.

"Please be careful with it," Lawrence admonished, all business again. I attempted not to roll my eyes.

"Of course, Sir. It will be my pleasure."

He held out his arm, and I took it. "Ready?" he asked.

For what, I didn't know, but I nodded. "Ready."

LAWRENCE GUIDED me with a hand on the small of my back through a hallway and into a spacious club. Mirrored light fixtures hung from the ceiling, and the walls were painted an iridescent blue. The black lights made the off-white and black furniture glow in dizzying patterns. I felt not so much that I entered a space as that it absorbed me and transformed me into another element.

As for Lawrence almost touching me, his hand radiated warmth, an anchor in the cold environment. Cool lights. Cool colors. Cool backlit bar with a bartender dressed all in white with white-framed mirrored sunglasses. The color—or lack thereof—of his attire seemed a strange choice—what if he spilled something? But his deft movements showed me a mess would be highly unlikely. It's possible he got paid more than some day job professionals.

"Would you like a drink?" Lawrence asked.

I nodded. "Wh— Red wine, please. Whatever hasn't been open for too long."

"You drink red wine?" His raised eyebrows gave him a comically surprised expression.

"Sometimes." When I needed to drink something I didn't like too much so enjoyment of the beverage wouldn't distract me. Something about the place felt off. Subtle magic ebbed and flowed with the music. A powerful wizard had been here, and, I suspected, hung around somewhere. I shouldn't care, but I disliked not knowing who I was dealing with.

Or what I was dealing with. When I turned my head to watch Lawrence walk to the bar, I caught a whiff of something dead. Or undead, as the case may be. The sun had just set, so it would be time for the dark creatures to come out and play. Surely "allying with the fangs" wouldn't be so easy.

"Is everything all right, Miss?" A tall man had materialized to my right. He was dressed the same as the bartender, except his glasses had clear lenses. His all-white suit hugged his frame tightly. Where did the supernaturals in this town get their clothing tailored? Probably by someone with their own preternatural talent.

"Everything is fine, thanks." I waved my hand. "This place is...unusual. Or is it?"

The man barely moved his lips when he spoke, but I understood every word.

"We attend to every detail. It confuses the humans and inferior beings such that they don't notice there is royalty among them." He inclined his head toward me.

"Royalty?" I asked and looked around.

"You don't have to pretend here, Princess," he said. "My boss is honored for your presence and would like to request a word with you and your date. He said he will meet you in the VIP area at your earliest convenience."

He bowed and melted away, or at least seemed to before I could correct him about Lawrence being my date.

My gargoyle non-date returned with my glass of wine and an amber-colored cocktail for himself. An old-fashioned? That would be funny.

"Got a text from Ted," he said. "He's running late. Are you all right hanging out for a bit?"

I accepted the wine and took a sip. Nothing like the vintages we drank in Faerie, but it would do, and the bitterness of the tannins would keep me grounded.

"That's fine," I said. "We've been invited to the VIP area. Maybe we can see what's there."

Lawrence's eyebrows again slid up his forehead, two dark curves of surprise. "How? No one gets into VIP here—not even Ted, and his brother is a partner."

"Ted's brother has interesting taste in friends. Shall we go?"

"May as well." But he didn't smile.

He pulled me to my feet and placed a hand on my elbow. Unnecessarily, I might add. I didn't have any trouble keeping my balance in my heels. We walked toward a blue velvet curtain, which parted just wide enough for us to walk through. Back there, the *thump-thump-thump* of the club muted into a heartbeat rather than an ear assault, and candles in sconces lit the way up a black marble staircase. I didn't see who had lifted the curtain, probably a machine or something. Humans did like their effects.

I preceded Lawrence up the stairs, which were steep enough that his face was at eye-level to my ass most of the way. Another likely intentional touch for rich men to have the opportunity to ogle their dates. By the time we reached the top, neither of us were out of breath, but I had developed a dislike for whoever we were to meet. I imagined him to be large, thick, and intimidating-looking with rings on his graceless hands.

Instead, a woman awaited us in a space lined with black and red velvet couches and maroon damask wallpaper. The entire room had a Victorian vampire vibe, but she did not. She wore a blue and white striped dress that clung in all the right spots between the floor-skimming hem and the halter neckline. Her hair, the same color as mine, hung straight, and her large blue eyes were so light as to be almost white. She smiled with red lips.

"Ah, Princess Reine," she said. "I thought it might be you. Who's your handsome friend?"

"I'm sorry," I said and tilted my head. "Do I know you?"

She laughed. "I'm sorry," she said in a tone that almost mocked me. "Of course you don't. I'm Ashlee Wyatt, the club's owner. Well, one of them."

Her energy stayed fairly contained, which made her difficult to categorize, but she had that same close-lipped smile as the man downstairs.

"I didn't think vampires existed outside of the Collective Unconscious," Lawrence said, almost making me jump. I'd all but forgotten he was there as I attempted to piece together what vampires were doing in Atlanta and if we were in any danger. I would have kept my sunlight power at hand if I knew I could access it. The thought popped into my brain that perhaps allying with fangs could put us in more danger.

Sir Raleigh appeared on my shoulder, and I had to catch him so he wouldn't slip off and take my wrap with him.

"Bad timing, Little One," I told him, although he looked so cute in my wrap I couldn't be mad he'd potentially ruined my intimidation factor.

"Is that...a cat?" Ashlee asked. She drew back, her left upper lip curled in disgust, which revealed one of her fangs.

"Of a sort," I said. I got Sir Raleigh situated on my shoulder. Thankfully the wrap's thickness protected my skin from his needle claws. He vibrated, although not with an audible sound, so I couldn't tell if he purred or growled. Or both.

"Animals are not allowed in my club," she said sharply, then took a breath. "I mean, for anyone except for you, Princess."

"Thank you," I said and scratched Sir Raleigh under the chin. "You wouldn't be able to keep him out if you tried."

"No, I see how he's not an ordinary cat. Nor are you an ordinary Fae." She crossed her arms, then uncrossed them and folded her hands in front of her. "May I ask why you're here in my territory, I mean, club?"

That hadn't been a slip. I almost scoffed at the thought that she would be threatened by me. Not because I couldn't take her down, but because I had no interest in vampire politics. In fact, by revealing herself and her colleague, she'd put herself in more danger. The TS, as Corey called them, didn't like nightmare creatures to establish themselves in the waking world.

"I'm here for drinks with friends," I said and raised my glass. "Good choice, by the way. Cheap and drinkable. That's a tough combination to achieve well."

She inclined her head at my left-handed compliment.

"Thank you, Princess. Can I count on your discretion? You will find you can count on mine as well. There are many who would be interested in knowing you're on this side of the Atlantic."

"I promise I won't tell."

"Gargoyle?" she asked.

"I won't say anything," he promised. "In fact, if I could ask you a few—"

I elbowed him. Seriously, had he really been asking if he could study her? I couldn't take him anywhere.

"Right," he said with a cough.

"By the way," I said, "do you know of any dark Fae creatures that have come through here lately?"

Fear flickered across her face so quickly that anyone with normal human vision would have missed the slight widening of her eyes, twitch of her eyebrows, and tensing of her lips.

"Why, are you missing some?"

Her question threw me off. "Why would I be missing any? I'm not a dark Fae."

"Oh, right," she said. "You don't—I mean, you're absolutely right. And no, I don't know of any."

What in the world did she think she knew about me that I didn't?

"Are you sure?" I asked.

"Oh, absolutely." She smiled, showing her fangs, and I knew she lied through all her teeth, pointy or not.

"Please let me know if you do find out about any."

"How do I reach you?" she asked.

That was a good question. I didn't want to give her my phone number. Lawrence gave her his, and I appreciated his cooperation in playing secretary. I assumed I could trust him with at least that.

I wished I had thought to ask more follow-up questions to Troubadour's advice. I didn't want to give away our mission, but I couldn't figure out how she could help us. Then Sir Raleigh disappeared from my shoulder and reappeared by one of the couches, which he promptly disappeared under.

"Dammit," I said. "Raleigh, get back here."

As undignified as it was, I went to the couch, knelt beside it, and shone a light underneath it. Raleigh had disappeared, but a cream-colored rectangle caught my attention way in the back. I reached for it and pulled out a business card.

"What is it?" Lawrence asked.

"A business card, from one of your patrons, I presume, Miss Wyatt?"

I blew the dust off of it—how long had it been under there? —and the embossed lettering came clear. It read, *Robert Cannon, PhD, MPH, Program Director, Cabal Pharmaceuticals.*

"That's the industry contact who's missing," Lawrence murmured in my ear. His warm breath stirred my hair and made me shiver in a good way.

"Do you know who this is?" I asked Ashley.

She took the card between her left thumb and forefinger. "Oh, yes, he was a regular until about six months ago. Why?"

"I can't say," I told her. "Do you know where he is now?"

"No."

"Can you tell us anything about where he may be?" Lawrence persisted.

"No, and please don't ask again."

She knew something but wasn't telling. I wished I could truth-spell her, but I lacked that ability. "How much is the information worth?" A vampire couldn't resist a good deal.

"More than my life, Princess. Well, enjoy the club. Your party's drinks are on us." She forced a rictus-like smile. "Our bartender Adam makes a great Old-Fashioned, as you've already found."

"Thank you for letting me know," I said. "And please do let me or Doctor Gordon know if you think of anything." We said our goodbyes, and I again preceded Lawrence down the stairs. When we reached the landing, a gentleman stepped aside. He looked familiar, like...

Like the main in the airport! I turned to ask him, but he put his finger to his lips and shook his head, then darted up the stairs.

"What was that all about?" Lawrence asked.

"We can talk later," I told him. "Those like her have good ears, even if they're not pointed."

"Right, I understand that the point somehow enhances your hearing. Would you be willing to do some tests so I can test that hypothesis?"

I gave him my best pissed-off-Fae look and said, "No."

He didn't seem offended. He merely shrugged, said, "Ah, well," and then, "Look, there's Ted!"

17

I n my days living among the humans, I'd learned that while it helped to grow with the times, some things never changed—those with power, prowess at physical acts, great beauty, and money drew the attention of others. I'll admit to some confusion at the new brand of celebrity, of those who were famous without doing much, but those had always been around, too. They tended to fade from awareness and memory more quickly than the others.

Theodore Steele resembled his more-famous brother Jared. Not surprising since they were twins. Indeed, he received his share of double-takes and murmurs as he walked in, and he pushed his hand though his dark hair, his eyes bright and smile brighter. The male vampire in all white bowed to him and brought him to our table, which had miraculously remained empty in spite of the club having filled.

A server brought drinks before we asked for them—red wine for me again, another mixed drink for Lawrence, and something fruity looking and smelling for Ted. He and Lawrence greeted each other like old friends with the half-hug back-pat gesture of men. Then Lawrence directed Ted to me, and Ted's smile grew brighter.

His energy was...interesting. If his brother was a rarity—a weather wizard, so I'd heard—Theodore was an oddity. Not rare, but strange in that he must be some sort of wizard, but I couldn't tell what kind. Whatever it was, it came with a good measure of charm, and his handshake warmed my skin.

"Ted, this is Reine, a friend," Lawrence told him. "Reine, Ted."

"Oh, a friend, huh?" Ted winked at me. "Don't let Rocky here fool you. He'll commit eventually. And then get his heart broken. Happens every time."

"That's a lot of assumptions, Sir," I replied, allowing ice into my tone. Dammit, now I was Elsa-ing myself.

His grin didn't dim. "I call them like I see them, Ma'am. There's no reason to deny what will happen eventually."

His words echoed through my brain, and I caught it—he was a fortune-teller. An interesting occupation for a newsman. But then, prognostication came with its fair share of error.

"I'd stick with talking about what's already happened rather than trying to say what will," I warned. "The future is too unstable for complete accuracy, even for a future-telling witch."

He laughed. "She figured it out in less than five minutes, Lawrence. You owe me twenty."

"Hey, that's not fair!" Lawrence smacked him on the arm. "You gave her a hint as wide as a barn."

"Wait," I looked between the two of them. "You had a bet going?" Oh, right, Lawrence had mentioned a wager.

"Yes," Ted said. "To see how fast it would take you to figure out what kind of wizard I am. I bet less than five minutes within meeting me. Lawrence said at least seven since my 'energy'"— he made air quotes—"is so murky."

I didn't know whether to be angry or amused. Lawrence made a note in his phone, so I went with angry.

"How dare you?" I asked, pitching my voice so I didn't yell, but the words cut through the noise just the same. "I'm not an experiment, you putrid pile of rock."

"Putrid pile of rock," Ted said. "I'll have to remember that. She's clever, Lawrence."

"Don't try to charm me, Madame Fortune," I told him. "You aided and abetted that experiment." I stood. "I need some air."

They protested, but I pushed through the crowd, which closed behind me.

"Let the lady have some space," I heard a voice—the vampire?—say behind me. The door man opened the glass door for me, and I walked into the chilly night.

Sir Raleigh purred against my neck, around which he wrapped his tail, and he nudged my cheek with his head. I laid my right hand against the side of the building. The composite material covered in paint didn't give me any solace, so I walked along the sidewalk until I found a tree that seemed big enough for me to lean against without danger of breaking it. I'd somehow found a quiet side street, and I didn't sense anyone near me.

No, someone was coming. I stiffened, not sure if I should prepare for an argument, a physical fight, or an apology. I went for the second one since the energy coming from the intruder on my private moment didn't feel like gargoyle or wizard. It was wilder, darker... Sir Raleigh quieted, allowing me to listen with all my senses, physical and mystical. The creature approaching wasn't the soul-eater, and as far as I could tell, didn't *intend* harm. But I knew strong and powerful beings could easily maim without meaning to. Running would be foolish. Fighting... I could possibly win, but only after great harm to myself. So, I took the wisest course. I quieted all I could—mind, breathing, even heartbeat as much as possible—and went still. Many beings wouldn't notice me even though visually I stood out from the dark surroundings like a white and light blue beacon.

The intruder stepped into the fullness of the streetlight, revealing it wore a long coat and fedora-style hat. I could barely see his face, but what I could make out resolved into familiar lines. He smiled, his eyes the only warm part of him—a shade of blue that looked familiar but which I couldn't place even at this, our third meeting.

The strangest part wasn't him. It was Sir Raleigh. The cat emanated...excitement and eagerness?

"Having fun with your tree hugging?" the man from the airport asked.

"I needed some air." And alone time. But now, faced with his amusement, I heated with shame. My excuse sounded flimsy, especially considering the soul-eater that could be lurking about.

"Is the air out here so different from the air in there?" Now his tone held slight mockery.

"Yes, as a matter of fact, it is." I stepped away from the tree and held the cat close to me. He'd been leaning so far forward I didn't want him to fall.

"Ah, so you have your cat again. Good. That way you won't be distracted by pining away for him. May I?" He held out his hands.

I didn't want to let go of Sir Raleigh—what if the man took off with him, and worse, what if Sir Raleigh went willingly— but I reluctantly handed him over. The strange man had an air of authority I'd only encountered in my mother, grandmother, and grandmother's consort.

He gently took the cat from me and held him in one large hand while he stroked him and turned him, seemingly examining him.

"Tsk, where did that white paw come from, Grimalkin?" he

asked. Sir Raleigh chirped and purred at his touch. Little traitor.

"What did you call him?" I asked.

"Nothing." He handed Sir Raleigh back to me. "He's a lovely little cat. Do keep him close."

"I plan to. Sir, who are you?" I asked, the desire to know tugging the question from the middle of my chest. He had a certain magnetism. Not sexual—surprising, since that's how I tended to approach men—but caring, oddly, although he'd not done anything to indicate he would or did beyond his vague advice.

"I'm no one, Reine," he said, and sadness edged his voice. Then anger. "No one you should know, anyway."

"But I want to," I said, again surprising myself. "Please, Sir, are you Fae?"

He barked a laugh. "Not that any you know would claim as part of their court." He lifted a hand, his fingers slightly bent, and I imagined someone's face being cradled in his palm. He dropped his arm. "Forget you saw me," he said. "I shouldn't be speaking to you, interfering..." He shook his head. "Remember what I told you—stay alert. Stay aware. And no matter how badly you think you want something, very few things are worth your future."

I noticed he didn't say life, but future. All right, he must be Fae. Those were classic vague Fae instructions. Before I could ask anything further, he stepped into the shadows and disappeared. The air moved around me as it filled in the space he left, and I shivered. Not only was he Fae, he likely belonged to the dark Fae. That would explain why he had business with vampires.

"What is he, Raleigh?" I asked and placed the cat back on my shoulder. "And more importantly, what is he to me?"

I wasn't used to the emotions the stranger brought up, of caring and tenderness. And worry for my well-being. But why would a dark Fae care what happened to a princess in the court of his mortal enemy?

It appeared I had my own mystery.

A WHIFF of decay alerted me to the presence of the soul-eater just before the cat dug his claws into my wrap, bowed up, and hissed. His vocalization turned into a low growl.

That got me moving. I ran as quickly as I could in my heels to the club, and I darted inside. I caught the arm of the white vampire and said, "Quick, get a message to your mistress that a very dangerous dark creature is about."

He shook himself free from my grip, demonstrating how strong he was. "She's aware of him."

"No, not that one. Not the one who came to meet her. Another one." I leaned close to him. "A soul-eater."

White eyebrows rose and disappeared under his ridiculous bangs. "Are you certain?"

"Yes."

He nodded and vanished into the crowd. I found Lawrence and Ted at our table. Again, I didn't know what to feel—didn't they worry? But they had respected my need for time alone. And they both rose when I approached.

"I owe you an apology," Lawrence said.

"Yes, you do, but it will have to wait. The soul-eater is around. It's outside."

"Are you all right?" He ran his hands over my arms, leaving warm tingles in their wake. I must have gotten colder than I realized for that reaction to happen.

"Yes, I'm fine. I've told the manager." I looked around. The young, beautiful people around me lounged, drank, and danced without any idea of the danger in their midst. What should we do? Evacuate the club? Try to draw the creature away? What did it want?

"Whatever it is, Ashlee will take care of it," Ted said. "She doesn't allow other dark creatures to interfere with her business."

"Maybe it didn't follow me in, then." I tried to open my senses to sniff for it, but the sights, sounds, and smells of the club assaulted me, and I had to slam everything shut to human levels.

The vampire manager appeared—could he teleport? I'd heard some vampires could—and said, "Mistress would like a word."

In a few minutes, Lawrence, Ted, and I stood in Ashlee's office. The large windows behind her showed the scene below, a blue, white, black, and multicolored spotted tapestry.

"What evil have you brought?" she asked me, her arms folded and her light eyes glowing faintly. Hades, she must have been pissed.

"I didn't bring anything," I said. "It's been following me."

"Why? And who unleashed it?"

"That's what I'd like to find out," I told her, an idea forming in my mind. "I suspect it's connected to our earlier questions."

She snorted. "About Robert Cannon? What could he possibly have to do with a soul-eater?"

"Perhaps if you were to help me ask him, we'd find out."

She tapped her bottom lip with one claw-like nail.

"I admit I am intrigued. Very well, I will help you find him. But you must promise me that you'll share any information you find out from him about this...thing."

"Definitely. I'm as interested in binding it as you appear to be."

"That would be an interesting experiment, Princess. How do you trap an invisible creature? But I would like a new pet since your grimalkin isn't up for grabs."

Sir Raleigh hissed, but softly.

"Never," I said. "What can you tell me?"

She grabbed Robert's card from a nearby table and wrote a telephone number on the back of it. "This is his private number. Tell him Ashlee sent you. I cannot promise he will cooperate, but it's the best I can do."

I nodded. "Fair enough. Can you keep us safe in order to get out of here?"

"Yes." She snapped her fingers and the manager appeared again, this time from the top of the staircase. I was pretty sure he didn't materialize from thin air—he just had a flair for sneaky entrances. She gave him rapid-fire instructions in a language I didn't understand—interesting, since I had a good ear for most tongues.

"Rae will take care of everything," she said. "Stay here for an hour, and then you will be safe to go."

I wanted to trust her, but I kept my senses open for signs she deceived me. The fact a vampire club existed told me that the old rules didn't apply anymore, so I needed to be extra careful.

After the allotted hour had passed, we walked out of the club into the cool night and a scene from a horror movie. A dead bouncer lay sprawled on the sidewalk. Behind him, something had scrawled three words on the wall with his blood—"I'll get you."

18

My two companions drew their phones out faster than gunslingers in western movies. Lawrence had his to his ear faster, and Ted snapped pictures.

"What are you doing?" I asked.

"Collecting evidence."

I arched an eyebrow, wrapping myself in haughty Fae attitude so I wouldn't scream, cry, throw up, or otherwise show any sign of weakness. How had I managed to keep a low profile for almost three hundred years and now be the target of a dark Fae predator?

"All right," Ted admitted. "Getting pictures for a story."

Rae walked out, and his reaction surprised me. He looked at the dead bouncer with wide eyes behind his lightly tinted lenses, and his mouth made enough of an *o* that I saw his fangs for the first time.

"You have an interesting way of taking care of things," I said.

Rae shook his head and knelt by the man, who when standing must have been almost seven feet tall. "He was supposed to take care of it." Rae felt for a pulse. He shook his head. "This creature you've attracted... It's very bad."

Strange words coming from a vampire, but I declined to comment.

"What does it want with you?" Rae asked. He stood, his white clothes miraculously unstained, and wiped his hands on a white—of course—handkerchief.

"I wish I knew." Then, when his eyebrows rose above his glasses, and he tilted his chin forward, I added. "Truly, I don't know. To 'get me,' whatever that means."

Rae shrugged.

"Better you than me. But be careful." And, before I could thank him for his concern, he added, "If that thing comes anywhere near her, I'll come find and kill you, princess or no." Then he turned around and stalked inside.

I wanted to curl in on myself like a boiled shrimp, have a good cry, and not deal with anyone for at least a week. I thought I'd left with a new ally, but as it turned out, I'd made an enemy, or at least potentially made one.

Red and blue flashing lights alerted me to the fact that we were about to be caught at a crime scene. Lawrence, Ted, and I left. Before we did, I sent a little zap to the surveillance camera so it would seem to have shorted out when we walked outside and therefore would have no record of us. I had no desire to deal with the human authorities. I suspected the supernatural ones would be bothering us soon enough.

The valets had either cleared out when the soul-eater energy appeared, or maybe Rae had sent them home. I couldn't picture him doing something so caring, but I also hadn't expected him to threaten me, so obviously I'd underestimated the vamp. Perhaps by design—who would take a vampire dressed like a washed-out version of the angel in *Good Omens* seriously?

We found our cars, which had the keys inside them, and

Ted wished us a good night. Rather than getting into his car, he unlocked the back seat and pulled out a makeup case. "Got a cameraman on the way," he explained. "We'll report from the scene."

"Don't tell anyone we were there, okay?" Lawrence asked.

"No worries," Ted replied. "Your secret is safe with me. Just... be safe, okay? I don't know what that thing is, but it's nasty, from the looks of it."

We bade him farewell, and Lawrence shook his head when he slid into the driver's seat and pushed the button for the roof to close. "He's either the dumbest or bravest guy I know."

Sir Raleigh had crawled into my lap and had started to purr. I stroked him, grateful for the comfort.

"He should be fine. I don't sense the soul-eater anywhere around, although sometimes I don't know it's there until it's too late. This one, though," Raleigh blinked at me and yawned.

"Has he done anything else interesting?" Lawrence asked. I told him about Raleigh attacking the soul-eater earlier, and he nodded.

"Sometimes dark Fae creatures can see others of that ilk where the rest of us can't. It's sounding more and more like he was sent to be a guardian to you."

I shook my head. "By who? My mother doesn't have command over the dark Fae creatures, and I don't have any family or friends among them."

"No one in the Unseelie Court?" Lawrence asked, his tone teasing. "Not even a former lover or flame?"

"No one," I repeated, "and I have yet to have a lover who would do anything so kind for me." I refrained from mentioning I only took lovers when I wanted a good shag. Otherwise emotions got messy, and they'd just turn on me, anyway. It was the price of royalty—use others before they could use you.

"Sounds like a lonely existence," he said.

I turned toward the window. "I don't know that you're one to judge. I haven't seen any evidence of significant others in your life."

"I'm close to the Graveses," he argued. "In fact, I'm Kestrel's godfather. But those of us in the lab don't socialize much outside of it. We've got too many secrets to be comfortable."

"But you have Ted," I observed. "A journalist. How do you keep your secrets around him?" Seriously, now we were having this conversation?

Lawrence shrugged. "He's different. We've known each other for so long we don't need to talk enough for me to worry about secrets slipping out. Plus, he has his own. We trust each other."

Or you trade secrets, I wanted to say. I tried to remember who had first broken open the case about Chronic Lycanthropy Syndrome. I'd read about it on a medical news site, but it had been a few years. Something tickled my mind—had it been in Atlanta? And could the thing John Graves had been referring to be news of the new disorder, not the viral vector sample? Had they been trying to alert the public?

That didn't quite fit into my theories, but as a scientist, I knew I had to consider all the possibilities. At this point, I was still in the land of speculation.

Raleigh dug his claws into my legs, and Lawrence swerved hard, making me bump my elbow against the door. I directed my attention to the road in front of us but didn't see anything.

"Did you see that?" he asked.

"No, I was looking out the side. Did I see what?"

"A car crossed the median and was coming right at us. But then they corrected and went on their way." He checked the rearview mirror. "At least I think they did."

"Probably some idiot on their phone." I soothed Sir Raleigh, who turned in circles, his nose in the air. "At least I hope." Then, of all the inconvenient things, my stomach growled.

"So... When's dinner?" The clock on the dash said it was almost ten o'clock.

"I don't know of anything around here that will still be serving." Lawrence frowned. "Wait, there's a Vietnamese place, but they switch to takeout only after nine. Does that sound okay? They use mostly organic ingredients and have some vegan dishes to cater to the neighborhood."

"That sounds great." My stomach agreed.

He gave me the name of the place, and I pulled up the menu on my phone. Soon enough, we had bags of delicious-smelling pho and banh mi, and I had to keep Sir Raleigh from crawling into them to investigate.

When we got back to the hotel, I was ready to wish Lawrence a good night, but he reminded me of Cimex's command.

"We'll eat in your room," he said. "Then I'll stand guard while you sleep."

Great. At least I'd managed to score a chocolate dessert so the night wouldn't be a total loss. Could I even sleep with a gargoyle nearby?

AFTER DINNER, Lawrence left me alone for a few minutes so we could get into nightclothes. I wished for a moment that Selene still had his room. In spite of our differences, I wouldn't have minded talking to her. The desire surprised me, as did the hope that Kestrel wouldn't hate Selene too much for occupying Corey's attention. The two of them could be good for each other—Selene with her womanly wiles and secrets, and Kestrel with her innocence and cleverness. Yet another human dyad that would make me feel left out, but that's all right, I was used to it. Let them screw each other up.

I typically slept in a gauzy nightgown, but that wouldn't do with Lawrence nearby, so I put on a T-shirt and a pair of shorts I'd gotten from the hotel gift shop. It amused me to have "Peach" emblazoned across my rear end. When Lawrence came into the room wearing a pair of black satin pajamas and a dark red robe that he'd tied but which left the planes of his pecs showing, I had to pretend really hard I wasn't impressed by his physique. He'd showered, and his hair curled with the damp. The look he gave me said he wasn't immune to my charms, and the thought flickered through my brain that I wondered if he'd be into a one-night stand. But no, that would make things too awkward. More awkward than our current gawking at each other, to be sure.

"You can hang out in your room with the door open," I finally managed to say. "You don't have to stay in here. I'm a kicker, so you don't want to be in bed with me." No matter how much I wondered what it would be like to be in bed with him.

"No, I promised I wouldn't leave you alone." He sat in the chair by the desk.

Sir Raleigh hopped down from the bed and onto his lap.

"And now I have company."

"Traitor," I murmured, but the sound of Sir Raleigh's purring vibrated through the air between us and soothed me. I turned off the light, rolled over, and went to sleep. And straight into a dream.

I was walking through an unfamiliar place. It was the time of night when everything looked gray, and there's just barely enough light to make stuff out, even for a Fae. Humans would be blind, but I could at least see shapes, if not textures or variations in colors. Still, I felt disoriented, and I moved slowly, carefully placing my feet since I couldn't see the ground, which sloped upward.

A need drove me to keep moving. I had to warn someone of something, but I didn't know of what, or to whom I carried the warning. I only knew I needed to continue, to push through the fog and fear.

Stone met my hand, and the familiar energy of the standing stones flowed through me. I placed both my palms and my forehead on the rock, tears of relief running down my face and making warm splashes on my fingers. I knew where I was. And I could feel a sliver of opening in the metaphysical wall between here and Faerie.

Physicists talked about parallel dimensions, but experiments couldn't show them a full one. I was from one, and I couldn't explain how to reach it, only that something we did in certain places where the barriers thinned or at certain times of the year when the veil fluttered. Now a doorway opened, but the energy shoved me backward. I stumbled and landed on my knees. A bright light made me look up to see my grandmother.

Shakespeare had called her Tatiana. Others referred to her as Maeve. I knew her as Grandmother, which was as much an honorific term as a description of relation. She looked down at me, her ageless face stern.

"What do you think you're doing?" she asked.

I looked around. Her glow illuminated the stones in my familiar clearing. "Kneeling."

She shook her head, apparently not finding my answer suitable.

"No, child. What are you doing in that world, in that far-away land?"

"I've been fulfilling my mission. I'm ensuring that they don't find out the truth about us." Not that it had come up all that much, but at least I was trying.

"And how are you doing so?"

"Mostly by changing the subject. And I'm trying to find out how the so-called expert knows so much about us." There, that should help.

"I have a new task for you."

Great. I didn't allow my dismay to show, but she must have felt it because she then said, "I know the desire of your heart is to return home. And I have heard your pleas, even if your mother thinks she hides them from me."

Interesting—"your mother" rather than "my daughter." And why would she hide my pleas from my grandmother?

"What do you need me to do, Grandmother?"

"There is a plot against me..."

I snorted. It came out before I could catch it. "There's always someone plotting against you."

"I am aware of this." The corners of her eyes crinkled, the closest she'd get to a smile without Faerie wine. "But this plot involves those close to the throne. I need you to determine who or what is involved."

"How can I do that if I'm not in Faerie? Or..." Hope exploded in my chest and I scrambled to my feet. "Am I being let back in?"

"No, I'm afraid not. You must complete your current mission first. But keep your ears open. What happens in my realm has echoes in the one you're living in." She started to fade, and I fell to my knees again, grabbing for her dress. My hands passed through her, and I cried out.

...and woke myself up to find a large winged creature standing in my room.

19

"What in the ever-living Fae?" I asked and scrambled backward. I turned on the light, not believing my eyes. Lawrence stood there, but it wasn't him. But it was. My mind ping-ponged between the two —*was-wasn't, was-wasn't.*

I'd seen shifters, plenty of them, but this was my first gargoyle in ages. He still wore his silk pajama bottoms, but rather than being loose, they stretched and strained over his bulging thighs and—oh, my. I hastily slide my glance upward to his stone-colored abs and pecs, all clear of hair. He looked like a statue of some sort of demon, complete with horns and tusks.

"Are you all right?" he asked. His voice had become deeper, more resonant.

Sir Raleigh slithered out from between the bed and night-stand and walked over to him, sniffing his feet, which had also grown and sported mean-looking claws, as did his now giant hands.

"Uh, yeah, I'm fine. What made you—?" I waved at him.

"You cried out and sounded so terrified and sad, this happened."

"Wait—I did that?"

He nodded. "Did you not know that my people used to be the guards for yours?"

Okay, score one for him. Did he always have to be the damn expert? Still...

"No, I did not. That's interesting." And made the betrayal that had maimed Rhys that much worse.

"So, there are certain things..." He shrugged, and he grimaced. "One moment, please." He folded his large, black leathery wings and walked into his room. He had to duck to get through the door. A groan split the air, and I clutched a pillow so it wouldn't resonate so much in my chest. I didn't follow to see if he was okay—shifters liked their privacy, whatever kind they were.

"Mrowr?" Sir Raleigh asked. He leaped on to the bed beside me, and I noticed he'd had another growth spurt.

"You keep that up, you're going to be too big to fit on my shoulder," I told him, but I appreciated the distraction. Then the noise stopped, and the silence that rushed to fill it pressed on my ears.

"Lawrence, are you okay?"

No answer.

"Son of a Fae," I murmured and hopped out of bed. I found Lawrence sprawled out on the floor of his hotel room, his arms spread out like wings, and his satin pajama pants clinging and pooling in all the right places. Although he no longer had the large chest and stone abs of a gargoyle, I couldn't help but notice he must have spent some quality time in the gym. Concern made me frown. In spite of his apparent physical strength, something had laid him low. What could have done that? And what would help him?

"Hades. You're annoying, but I don't want you to die!" An unfamiliar emotion—doubt—crept into my chest as the unsettling realization hit me that he knew more about me than I did about him, about gargoyles in general. I knew my human and Fae anatomy, and I'd treated most paranormal creatures in my day—plenty of other shifters, definitely, since they tended to get in trouble. But no gargoyles. Since he'd shifted into a humanoid form, would his needs be different?

I had to act quickly, or soon it wouldn't matter. I was the physician, and he needed my help. I felt for a pulse, which I found, although faint. A quick examination didn't reveal anything obvious was amiss. Did he have some sort of disorder? Again, I wished I knew more about gargoyles and what happened after they shifted. Perhaps this was normal. But wouldn't he have told me so I would know he'd need recovery time?

I made a quick call to Selene's room and woke her.

"What is it?" she asked. "And where did you go tonight?"

"To a club. Met a couple of vampires. Got chased by the soul-eater again." I shuddered. "But that's not important. Get Corey. Something is wrong with Lawrence."

She quickly arrived with Corey in tow, his golden eyes full of concern.

"What happened?" he asked.

My face heated, and I hoped they didn't think my blush indicated something too exciting had been going on.

"I had a nightmare, and he shifted into his gargoyle form," I said. "Then he shifted back. I heard a long groan, then nothing, and found him like this."

Corey also did a quick exam. Lawrence didn't move.

"Is this normal?" I asked. "Do gargoyles pass out and need recovery after shifting?"

"Not usually," Corey told me. "I've only seen him shift a couple of times, and it's impressive. He doesn't ever seem the worse for wear. You're the doctor—medical doctor—can't you make sure he's all right? Do some sort of exam?"

"I can try, but this far away from home, I'm very limited."

Home, wherever that was. In truth, I didn't want to get too close to Lawrence through an energy exam. I may find confirmation of what I suspected, but I hated the invasion of privacy it could entail. But I had to do something. His breath had become shallow, and his skin clammy.

I cupped his face and resisted the impulse to smooth my thumbs over his jaw bones. They were nice when he wasn't talking. I closed my eyes and opened myself to what his body wanted to tell me.

Of course, the first thing was his physical attraction to me. That hadn't been hidden when he was in gargoyle form. Not one bit.

Then, the next layer—anxiety. Not guilt, though. If he'd had any part in the vector being stolen, he didn't regret it at all. Interesting.

I continued to dig and tried not to pay attention to the stray thoughts and memories that floated around in the energy fields of most people, either paranormals or mundanes. Then I got to the source of the issue—something in his stomach.

What was it, though? Some sort of toxin. It had a sickly greenish energy, and I recalled the mixed drinks he'd had. I'd have some questions for Ashlee and Rae once I saw them again. While he'd digested the drinks, the energy residue of whatever had been in them had gotten caught between his pelvic and solar plexus energy centers. I nudged it along, and it exited his body with a long, loud fart.

Everyone recoiled. Whatever it had been, it was powerful enough with a stench of rotten eggs and...something I couldn't quite place. Hmmm... How had it gotten into him? The vampire club? They had seemed odd, but not murderous. Well, beyond the typical vampire issues. In the food at dinner? I guessed it was possible.

His skin had returned to its normal temperature, his

breathing to steady, and his pulse to strong. Finally, after I'd lost count of my breaths, his eyelids fluttered, and he stirred.

"Take it easy," I said. "Don't try to get up too quickly."

He didn't pay attention to me and struggled to raise himself to his elbows. He finally focused on me, then looked at Corey and Selene. "What happened?" he asked, his voice thick.

"You were poisoned," I said. "What do you remember?"

He managed to sit, and we helped maneuver him to the bed, where he sat with his back against the wall and propped up with pillows. "I remember being at the club. Then dinner. Some sort of discussion. Then you cried out in your sleep, and..." He trembled. "I had to shift. Something made me. Something in your voice."

"What in my voice?" I asked.

"You sounded so frightened and sad." He rubbed his eyes. "It activated the protective side of my personality, and my inner gargoyle came out."

"How romantic," Selene mouthed. I almost kicked her.

"Right," I said. "You mentioned that your people used to protect mine. But I don't remember any of that in Fae lore."

"It was a long time ago. I don't know what happened to make the arrangement stop."

"This is all lovely," Corey broke in. "But we need to know who tried to kill you, Mate. And with what."

"Something that wouldn't take effect until he shifted," I said, finally putting it together. "When was the last time you did, Lawrence?"

"At the last new moon," he said. "I go flying when the sky is darkest."

"So that was, what, two weeks ago?" I asked. "Crap. It could have been at any time. Did you have meals with anyone? Go out with anyone besides Ted?"

He nodded. "I ate at the lab several nights as we were

preparing for your visit. We got takeout. Anyone could have put something in the food."

"Wait a second," Corey said. "How? The only people there were you, me, Cimex, and the Graveses and none of us would hurt you."

"Except it seems that someone tried to," I pointed out. "Do you remember anything about trying to change, Lawrence? Anything that could help us figure out what they gave to you?"

"I felt like I was trying to shift against a tide, like it wanted me to stay trapped in my gargoyle body forever." He looked down at his very human hands, which in this form, had lovely long, tapered fingers. "I had to fight to come out of it. Like when I was a fledgling."

"Is that a young gargoyle?" Selene asked.

"Yes, after my first shift. It happens to all of us—the temptation to stay that way. But when we do, we end up turning into the thing we hate being compared to the most—stone animals doomed to live in caves or on top of roofs."

"And what about this time?" I asked.

"It seems like a very gentle way to ensure I don't get too involved with whatever's going on," he said. I had to agree. My suspicion about his activities with John Graves seemed unfounded. Perhaps I'd misinterpreted the notes. It had been known to happen before, especially when my mind was on something else.

"Do you have any enemies outside the lab?" Selene asked. "Or even any disgruntled employees?"

"No." Lawrence shook his head. "I mostly spent time with the animals."

"Any incensed pet parents?" Corey asked.

"No, not that I know of." He shrugged. "Sorry I'm not being much help."

"That's all right," I said. "Let me ponder for a few minutes and see what I can come up with." Not that it was my responsibility to figure out his enemies. But he must have at least one, and evidence pointed more and more at one of his colleagues, someone he trusted. Was now the time to confess I'd snooped and ask about John Graves?

Corey shooed me and Selene out so he could help Lawrence dress. Sir Raleigh stayed in the room with the two men, and he served as an unexpectedly good spy. I heard every word through his little cat ears.

"What happened?" Corey asked.

"Not sure," Lawrence replied. "Hit me like a dose of swamp gas. When I shifted back to human, I felt like my guts were being twirled around by a giant, burning fork."

"Is it one of the secret protocols?" Corey then asked.

I raised my eyebrows. His voice grew louder, and the rumble of a purr started in the background. Clever kitty—he was asking for pets so he could get closer and I could hear everything.

"I don't think so. I'll have to ask Bev about it. She's the one who's been working on shift disruptors. But how could someone have gotten it?"

Corey's reply came through, clear and grim. "The same way someone got the vector. It's got to be the same culprit. Who have you been with or near that could have sneaked something into your food or drink?"

"That's the weird part," Lawrence said. "I've been very careful to only eat or drink around our core group in case something like this would happen."

"Do you think it's the Fae, then? She's definitely hiding something."

I bristled. Weren't we all?

"No." Lawrence sounded all too confident. "I'd be able to tell if she meant me harm. I should be able to tell if anyone did, but humans are murky. They've got so many layers of thought energy, it's hard to sort through all of them."

"So, what about Kestrel? Have you been able to read her yet?"

I smiled. So, I wasn't the only one willing to use another's powers to snoop on someone's feelings.

"Not yet. She's been too close to Reine the last couple of times. The Fae's energy masks everything around her."

"Interesting. Could our culprit be using that?"

"Maybe."

"Speaking of Fae, better shoo the cat back into her room. She'll be pissed if he's gone."

Sir Raleigh reappeared, looking very pleased with himself and I rewarded him with a nice ear rub. In the end, I decided I needed more evidence, which I could perhaps get at the Equinox gathering.

20

A s it turned out, rather than Lawrence sleeping in the chair in my room, I slept on the other side of the bed in his. Otherwise there was no way Corey would leave.

Six-thirty came way too early.

"Where are we going?" I asked Lawrence as we pulled out of the hotel drive. I clutched my tea, but it hadn't hit my brain yet.

"To the Equinox gathering." Apparently, the sarcasm was strong in this one no matter what happened.

I refrained from rolling my eyes—barely. "Yes, I'm aware. I mean, where is it going to be?"

"Stone Mountain. Some of the members have an in there."

I remembered the picture that had flashed up on my computer screen, and I clutched my crystal talisman in my pocket. Could I draw enough power there to contact my mother to ask her about the soul-eater? It would be worth a try. But then how would I stick close to Lawrence and John and see what they were up to? I'd have to find a way to do both.

"What are you planning?" he asked. He glanced sideways at me.

"Nothing. Keep your eyes on the road." It depended on what kind of ceremony the witches performed and how savvy they were. Surely they wouldn't mind me syphoning off some of their power? It was for a noble cause, after all.

"I don't know if I believe that," he teased, a slight curl to the corner of his mouth I could see.

"Well, you know us Fae. Always up to something."

His expression hardened, and he muttered, "Don't I know it?"

"What's that supposed to mean?"

"Nothing. Hang on. I need to figure out this traffic."

His phone's screen alerted him to an alternate route. So, not much for him to figure out, but I got the hint—he didn't want to talk about it. It seemed that he, too, had negative gargoyle/Fae history. Something to do with a guardian gone wrong? Or—and it should have occurred to me earlier since I knew my own people—a Fae betrayal? I leaned my head back and closed my eyes. Normally a few hours' sleep sufficed, but so far away from home and my source of strength, I found my energy waning. Until...

As we approached Stone Mountain, a granite knob that rose from the rolling hills around it, I tasted mineral at the back of the roof of my mouth. We parked, and I took a deep breath. Although we hadn't come that far from the city, the air felt clearer, the atmosphere greener. The trees whispered their welcome, and Lawrence scowled. Right, he disliked tree noises, something about nightmares. Well, he could deal. With each step, I felt stronger and younger, more like myself.

Sir Raleigh mewed, and I placed him on the ground and rolled my shoulders. I swear, he'd grown another half inch and half pound, and now he could hop along after us and keep up without any trouble. I scooped him up again when we got to the cable cars and walked inside. I looked out of the window once we were seated and let out a little groan.

Someone had defaced the granite mound with giant carvings of men on horseback. "Who are they?" I asked.

Lawrence looked at me, his eyebrows raised. "Confederate generals. Right, I forgot you wouldn't know."

"Why would I?" I whispered an apology to the hill. A slight tremor shook the gondola, and Lawrence grabbed my forearm.

"What was that?" he asked.

"I apologized to her. She said she appreciated it."

"She?"

"The spirit of the hill, a daughter of Gaia. There are still a few around."

"And you can talk to her?"

"Only in basic sentiments. Their language is even older than ours."

He pulled out his phone and made a note. I huffed, and this morning my mission seemed almost impossible. How could I be myself without giving the scientists any information about us?

When we arrived at the top, we walked through the little terminal and outside. Light streaked the sky, and warm gold limned the horizon. Although a chilly breeze ruffled my hair, I smiled. I might not need the Equinox ceremony to draw the power needed for my long-distance Fae call. Before I could make up an excuse and sneak off, Beverly and John found us. Kestrel followed, wearing a long white dress, denim jacket, and a sulky expression.

"We're so honored you could make it, Doctor River," Beverly gushed.

"Yes," John said. "It is a true blessing to have you here."

I refrained from asking, "Really?" Fatigue marked circles under his eyes—guilty conscience or fear of being found out, perhaps? But he didn't look surprised to see Lawrence. Not that he would have expected him to shift yet.

"I couldn't say no," I told them with what I hoped was a

charming smile, then added before they could get too offended, "I'm glad to be able to celebrate the Equinox." There. Let them think they wasted a favor, that I might have come anyway with a simple invitation.

"We'll be over here." Beverly led us to an area behind the gondola terminal and down the hill a little ways.

There, a clearing in the trees held about a dozen people, all in long, white robes or dresses with jackets or sweaters over them. John donned his robe over his turtleneck and corduroy pants. Lawrence and I remained in our street clothes, and I felt like we stood out, but intentionally. Indeed, the curious glances of the coven members made my skin prickle. Lawrence's face had settled into its typical stony neutral expression, and I looked away before I could trace the line of his jaw with my gaze. I might or might not have done that while he'd slept that morning.

"We're not allowed to have a bonfire," Beverly told me. "It's been too dry this spring."

"That's too bad. I'm sure you've got a backup plan."

"We do. Lots of candles." Her face lit with mischief, and I laughed.

"Letter of the law rather than the spirit?" I asked.

"Exactly. Oh, there they come."

Two other people, a man and a woman, entered the clearing and carried a box, from which they brought forth and assembled a large candelabra. Their sure movements said they'd done it several times, and soon they had lit the twelve candles in the outer ring and five in the center ring.

The sun approached the horizon with the sensation of a rising wave, and I felt its nearness like a whispered good morning.

Could they feel the balance of light and dark tipping toward the light? My talisman vibrated with a subtle thrum—a summons coming through. Now, how to get away...

"We'll form the circle now," John said, his voice carrying clear and true. The timbre surprised me, and when I looked at him, I saw not a slightly disheveled and exhausted scientist, but a high priest, confident and assured in his power. Beverly joined him, looking every inch as regal. Kestrel stood beside her father, and he nodded at her reassuringly. She swallowed and dipped her chin.

What were they up to?

I stood beside Beverly, and Lawrence placed himself to my left.

John held up his hands and intoned, "Let us welcome the sun on this sacred day of Ostara. The world woke at Yule, then dozed as she nurtured the seeds and roots of life. Now she stretches, fully awake, and new life bursts forth from the tip of every branch. Let us sing of life and balance and healing for our planet and ourselves."

Something about his opening speech must have been off since the coven members exchanged looks. But no one said anything, and John began the chant in a language I knew and that made homesickness well in my chest—Gaelic.

Beverly grabbed my hand, and I squeezed hers.

"They weren't expecting him to ask for healing for ourselves," she said in secret conversation.

I almost dropped her hand but decided not to. *"Who needs healing?"*

"Kestrel. She cannot hold on to any of the powers that try to manifest in her. She could be a powerful witch, but they keep slipping away."

"Sometimes it takes time," I reassured her.

She didn't break her chant, and I caught her slight head shake in my peripheral vision. *"Not this long. Never this long in either my or John's family. Can you help her?"*

Ah, that's what this was about. *"You do know it's dangerous to ask one of my kind for help."*

She dipped her chin, and her lips tightened. *"I am aware, but we are desperate, Princess. I am throwing myself on your mercy."*

Her candor made my heart ache. When had my mother ever done anything so bold for either my brother or me? *"Since you are being forthright, I will be as well. I don't know if I can help your daughter. I'm not in possession of my full power here."*

Beverly's frustration flooded through her hand with surprising power, and I let go. My talisman continued to vibrate, and when the coven members closed their eyes and lifted their arms for a series of incantations, I slipped away.

SIR RALEIGH and I crept out of the clearing and to a place where the granite was exposed. The sounds of the coven faded when I stepped on to the rock, and the atmosphere around me shimmered with rainbow light. The sharp chill of morning warmed to a softness scented with wildflowers that had never grown on Earth. For the second time that morning, I caught my breath with homesickness. I had found a doorway, although I couldn't feel any way to open it.

The air in front of me clouded, and my mother appeared. Or, rather, a transparent version of her.

"Greetings, Daughter, and blessed be."

"Greetings, Mother, and blessed be." Before she could launch into whatever she wanted from me, I added, "I have questions for you. I'm in danger."

She displayed nary a change in facial expression, just her same, haughty look. "You knew this mission wouldn't be easy, Daughter."

"I didn't know what to expect. You didn't give me any guidance." In fact, she'd never given me any, now that I thought of it. "I need your help, Mother."

"What do you expect me to do?"

"Can't you even ask about what the danger is? I don't know —act interested instead of like you're waiting for me to be done with a tantrum so you can say your piece?"

Sir Raleigh twined around my ankles, and his rumbling purr brought me out of the frustration and panic seeping through my chest. I picked him up and held him to me.

Her lip curled. Finally, a change to Miss Stoneface Fae, even if she expressed disgust. "I am concerned, Reine," she said. "But I know you can handle whatever is thrown at you. You always have."

"I don't know about this one. There's a soul-eater about. Do you know of anyone powerful enough to have summoned it? And anyone in Faerie who doesn't want me to succeed on my mission?"

She thought for about half a second, then shook her head. "No one. But you know that our court doesn't have contact with the dark Fae."

"What about the gray Fae?" I asked. There had always been rumors of a third court, one not as organized, comprised of Fae who refused to choose sides. While I chose to believe those rumors, others did not.

"They don't exist," she snapped.

Hmmm, that had been more emotion than I expected.

"But is it possible they could? That they could be interfering to make mischief for both sides, to cause another war?"

"They don't, Daughter. At least not in the way you think they do." She pressed her lips closed. Aha, so they *did* exist, and she'd said too much.

"So, what do I do about this thing? It's getting stronger and has already killed a human. And threatened to 'get' me."

"You'll figure something out."

I placed Sir Raleigh on the ground and stood to my full height to face my mother. "I don't want to figure something out. I'm asking for your help, Mother." I never thought I'd ask another Fae to not have confidence in me, but I found myself frightened. And not just for myself, but for my colleagues here. Dear Fae, could I call them friends?

No, Fae didn't have friends. And they certainly didn't have gargoyle lovers in spite of growing mutual attraction. I imagined Lawrence pulling out his phone to make a note—*"Does not play well with others."*

I knew when to give up. "What did you want of me, Mother?"

"I wanted an update. It's difficult to see what's happening at such a distance. It's fortunate you came to the Ostara ceremony, but our time together grows short. They'll soon notice you're missing."

"Progress is slow. Whoever leaked the vector covered their tracks well." In truth, I didn't know what to tell her. I needed to check with Selene to see how her interviews of the staff were going, to see if any information taken together pointed to someone. My money—human and Fae—was still on John Graves. He was definitely covering up something.

"You need to try harder, Daughter." That was the fourth time she'd called me Daughter rather than by my name. It brought to mind the dream I'd had about my grandmother and how she hadn't used the term.

Could my vision have been more than a dream? And could my mother have been lying to me all along?

Then she added, as though I could ever forget, "You know what's at stake."

"Right, my future." As the strange Fae gentleman had said. She faded, and the bite returned to the air. I walked back to the ceremony with more questions than answers, and one burned in my mind brightest of all—at this point, did I have more in common with human or Fae?

I slipped into the circle at the end of the chant, and Lawrence opened his eyes. He smiled when he saw me, but the

dark curve of his eyebrows held a query. Had he seen me leave?
I wouldn't be the only one with questions.

And the warmth his smile gave me made me doubt that I
would cast myself as unequivocally Fae.

AFTER THE CEREMONY, Beverly thanked me with true Southern
politeness, but she'd gone cold. I didn't blame her. She'd asked
for help, and I couldn't give it to her. I respected her pragmatic
streak and wondered if she'd been behind Kestrel inviting me
to the ceremony. My mother would have cast aside a useless
Fae as well, but at least Beverly loved her kid. I couldn't
imagine her telling Kestrel to "figure it out" if faced with potentially lethal danger.

John thanked me more warmly, and he practically vibrated
with exhaustion. Guilty conscience leading to poor sleep, or
had the ritual drained him? Or had my foray and the power my
mother and I drew for our contact done it?

Lawrence and I opted to take the path that wound down the
side of the hill rather than the cable cars. Our little hike gave
me more time to soak up earth energy. If I had a Fae battery, it
would have been at a solid sixty percent by the time we reached
the bottom and walked along the sidewalk to where he'd
parked the car, sixty-five when we drove off. I promised the hill
I'd be back. Although it wouldn't charge me to a hundred
percent, I'd take what I could.

Once we got into Lawrence's car, he asked, "Where did
you go?"

I snapped into innocent Fae mode. "When?"

"During the chant, when we all raised our arms. I felt you
leave."

Oh, Hades. I'd healed him, and in spite of my weakened

state, I must have accidentally made some sort of connection with him. That would make it difficult to lie.

"I went to talk to my mother. She summoned me."

He didn't look at me, but he nodded. "Your Faerie mother?"

"I don't have another one, unfortunately."

My bitterness must have come through because he asked, "Didn't go well?"

"Not at all. I was hoping she could tell us more about who may have summoned the soul-eater, but she didn't have any answers." I sighed. "She never does."

"And what did she want with you?"

Rather than his typical probing tone, he posed the questions gently.

"She wanted an update on the mission, on finding out who leaked the vector." I chose not to tell him about my true mission of keeping proprietary Fae information secret.

"Why does she care?"

"That is a good question." In truth, my being there made the possibility of the scientists gleaning information about us Fae more, not less, likely. Especially when it came to a certain curious gargoyle who already had some knowledge that he could test and tweak.

He didn't ask anything else as we drove to the CPDC, and I didn't volunteer any information. Why did my mother want me there, in truth? And why hadn't I questioned her more? Because she knew exactly what to dangle in front of me to make me comply. So, did that mean I wouldn't be allowed back in Faerie? No, she'd made a Fae bargain. If I fulfilled my part, she'd have to let me back in, unless she'd found some loophole.

That made me feel worse. If there were such thing, my mother—indeed most Fae—could be described as an expert on loopholes.

21

At nine o'clock, the core team convened for a donut and coffee breakfast meeting in Cimex's office. Lawrence didn't take one, citing a new low-carb diet, but I knew the true motive for his abstaining. I was hungry, so I took a filled donut with bright pink icing from the box.

"You eat donuts?" Lawrence asked.

"Yes, and don't you dare make a note in your phone about it," I teased.

He laughed. "Noted."

I ate the sticky sweet pastry while Selene and Corey gave their report of what they'd found in the files they'd been reviewing—essentially nothing.

"And how are the staff interviews going?" Cimex asked.

"I'm still working on them," Selene told him. "Although nothing has popped out as particularly incriminating for anyone. You're sure you've told us about all of the projects here?"

Cimex nodded, his face open and guileless. If I could pick a runner-up suspect, it would be him. No one was that nice, especially no one who worked for any government.

"Yes, I have given you all of the information I have," he said. "I suppose that something could be going on behind my back, but it would be difficult to hide."

"So, no one was working on mapping out the DNA of paranormal creatures," Selene said. "Just to confirm?"

"Not exactly. The CLS vector was originally designed to be a treatment for pups who were having difficulty expressing their lycanthropy when they came of age."

I looked at John and Beverly, who both studied their hands. Their pup wasn't expressing her talents well, although I couldn't think of what use the vector would be for a witch. They had a long history of not getting along with lycanthropes.

The meeting adjourned as most committee meetings did, with not much being revealed or decided. Selene and I walked into an empty conference room, where she and Corey had brought the piles of folders.

"How did the ceremony go?" Selene asked.

"It was fine." I filled her in on the Ostara ritual and the parts of the conversation with my mother that Selene would need to know, namely that we were on our own with the soul-eater. "How about your end?"

She sighed and put her hair back in a ponytail with the elastic she kept around her wrist. "I feel like we're missing something obvious, but it's so in our faces that it's out of focus and we can't see it."

"Or it's being hidden from us."

She looked up, her blue eyes wide. "What do you mean?"

I pulled out my phone and showed her the notes I'd found. Then I surprised myself by saying, "But I don't know if Lawrence was involved in the vector leak. These must refer to something else."

"Oh?" She looked at me with a grin. "I think someone is developing feelings for a certain gargoyle. These look pretty suspicious to me. Have you asked him about them?"

"What? And no to all of the above." I couldn't admit my feelings to myself, so definitely not to her.

"Seriously, what's going on with you two?" she asked, her blue eyes wide with curiosity. Humans. They thought they could sniff out scandal from a mile away, and once they found one, they couldn't let it go.

"Nothing," I said. "What about you and the handsome Agent McLendon?"

"Nothing." She crossed her arms and lifted her chin, so I knew she'd felt more challenged than I had. "He's very attached to the Graves girl, and as you well know, I'm engaged to Gabriel."

"Still, one shifter's as good as another, eh?" I asked with a wink. Gods, why couldn't I have a normal conversation with the woman? Something about her made me want to challenge her, make her squirm.

"No, and why are you such a bitch?" she snapped.

Oh, so the stress *was* getting to her. I took a deep breath. There was no need to make an enemy of her, even if all my instincts told me she was competition. While we might need human cooperation, it didn't mean we liked working with them.

"I'm sorry," I grated out. I hated those words. I filled her in on the vampire encounters and the soul-eater's stalking of me and threat.

"So, on one hand, you suspect Lawrence is involved," she said. "On the other, he's been nothing but protective of you."

Huh, I hadn't realized that had come through. Maybe she was a decent therapist, after all.

"Yes, I've been trying to watch him to see if I can find evidence of some sort of misconduct, but so far, he's been a bit of an ass, but nothing else."

"Are you sure that's all?" she asked.

I narrowed my eyes. "You doubt me?"

"Well, he's been poisoned, and it may have something to do with him guarding you. Did that occur to you?"

Actually, it hadn't. What if he had become a target because he'd been assigned to watch over me? Or, if what he'd told me was true, maybe it had occurred because someone guessed he would be guarding me.

So, what did that mean for me?

"Right, but that would make him innocent, right? At least of the breach, of giving the CLS vector sample to the industry rep."

"Maybe, maybe not." She tapped her lips with a long index finger. "Perhaps he later had regrets, changed his mind. It happens."

I refrained from snorting. She didn't know gargoyles very well. Admittedly, neither did I, but I did know one thing. "Gargoyles are notoriously stubborn. Once they set their mind on a course, they'll see it through no matter what." Which made me wonder if the one who'd assisted in Rhys' maiming had been working on a bigger mission. That sent a shiver down my spine.

"Then at the very least, he bears watching," she said. "I can't do all this by myself, Reine."

I drew back. "What do you mean, do all this by yourself? I'm helping."

"By doing what?"

The force of her irritation drove me back another step, and Sir Raleigh ducked under the table. "What do you mean?"

She'd just gotten warmed up and continued, "Interfering with séances, going to vampire clubs—yes, Corey knew where you were—playing with your cat, and attending Equinox rituals? You've gotten ceremonial duties, and I've been doing all the work."

"Hey, what happened during the séance wasn't my fault. And all this is tied into what's going on in Faerie somehow."

"It's never your fault, is it?"

What the...? "Oh, I know what this is about," I said. "You're still pissed about me kissing Gabriel. And you still don't trust me."

Before she could answer, a soft knock echoed through the room. A soft voice called through the door, "Doctor River? Doctor Rial? May I have a word?"

I took a deep breath and gestured for Selene to answer.

"Yes," she said. "Of course."

The door opened, and the behavioral epidemiologist walked in. She looked between the two of us with her dark features drawn into an expression of trepidation. How much had she heard of our argument?

"I'm Latonya Francis," she said. " I've been looking for the opportunity to talk to you outside of the hearing of the investigative committee. You see, I have information about John Graves."

Aha! I knew it. "What sort of information?" I gestured for her to take a seat, and Selene and I did likewise.

"I am not sure how to explain it. I was in the lab late one night and saw him here as well." She looked between the two of us.

"In the lab?" Selene prompted.

"Yes, but in the hallway between Cimex's office and the file storage room. He looked around, and I ducked back around the corner. And then he disappeared."

"Disappeared?" I asked. "What do you mean?"

"When I looked back, he'd vanished, and I heard a click. He didn't come back toward me, and he also didn't go the other way. I would have run into him."

"So, you're saying there's a secret room." Selene sat back. "That would make sense. Especially considering how we keep running into dead ends. They're not telling us everything, and I bet the key to the mystery is in there. Can you show me where later?"

"Yes, this evening. The lab typically clears out around seven. Shall we say nine?"

"That works for me," Selene said. "How about you, Doctor River?"

I caught the edge in her tone. I had better be there, or I'd forever be branded the slacker Fae. "I'll be there. But what to do about our shadows?" I explained to Latonya about how we'd been assigned Lawrence and Corey as our guards.

"Corey isn't an issue," she said. "I've long suspected he's here as a spy for the PBI. But I haven't been able to get close enough to tell him my concerns. As for Lawrence..." She smiled. "Honestly, I don't know. He's always been gentle and kind, especially with his animals. I'll leave that up to your discretion."

Sir Raleigh took that moment to make an appearance, and he hopped on to my lap.

"Oh!" Latonya's grin widened. "Is that your cat?"

Cat, not kitten. At this point, Sir Raleigh had lost his kitten roundness and turned into a dark gray mini-panther with one white paw.

"Yes, he's my emotional support animal."

Selene coughed, likely to cover a laugh.

"He's darling. May I?"

She held out a hand, and Sir Raleigh sniffed her fingers. He pressed his head under her palm, and she scratched him behind the ears. I can't explain how, but he intimated to me that I could trust her. All right, then. He jumped down to the floor.

"Thanks so much," I said and stood. The others also got to their feet. "So, tonight at nine? Here?"

"Yes. See you then." She walked out.

"All right, partner," I said to Selene, who appeared to have settled. "What's our task for today?"

Again, before she could answer, someone knocked. "Reine? Selene?" It was Lawrence.

"Yes, come in," I said.

He walked in, and he held the card Ashlee had given us. "I called and got Robert Cannon. His assistant agreed he'll meet with us in an hour."

"All right, then," I said. "I should do that interview in case he needs a little Fae-style push to give us the info we need."

Selene's eyes narrowed, and she inclined her head toward Lawrence, but all she said was, "Oh, okay. I'll continue interviewing people here."

"Reconvene around lunchtime?" Lawrence suggested. "I'll pick something up for the four of us."

Smart man, keeping in control of his food. "Sounds great," I said. "Would you excuse us for a moment?"

"Fine, meet you outside."

Once the door had closed again, and I locked it, I turned to Selene. "Let me make sure I read your hint right. I'll keep a mental eye and ear on the interview for any signs Robert Cannon and Lawrence have had previous contact."

"Smart move."

"Also, one thing to consider—remember, someone poisoned Lawrence, so he may be less involved than we think. I'll have to explain later."

She astonished me by smiling. "You're just full of surprises, aren't you? Yes, tell me later. That explains why you're suddenly more into him." Then she shocked me further by putting a hand on my arm. "Don't screw it up by doing what you normally do—pushing people away."

My jaw dropped, and she walked out. How dare she say that to me?

And, worse, how dare she be right?

22

"Where are we going this time?" I asked Lawrence. This was getting to be a habit.

"Not sure. He gave me GPS coordinates, and it looks like it's in the middle of nowhere."

"Is there a lot of 'nowhere' in Georgia?"

"You have no idea."

Indeed, in twenty minutes we were outside of the city heading north. Occasionally we would pass exits with stuff on them, the usual assortment of fast food restaurants and gas stations, but even those got sparse after we turned on to a secondary highway.

I leaned back and closed my eyes, more fatigued from the events of the previous day and night than I wanted to admit. The charge I'd gotten from the mountain that morning still held me at about sixty percent, but the underlying exhaustion from being so far away from my home territory lingered. Fae didn't get sick like humans, but I imagined this must be what it felt like to fight a virus on the cusp of going into a full-blown flu.

Sir Raleigh curled up on my lap, and his soft purr

comforted me.

I must have dozed because the next thing I knew, Lawrence pulled into what looked like an abandoned rest area and turned off the engine. He checked his phone.

"This is the place," he said. "Did you have a good nap?"

"Yes, thanks."

"I didn't realize that Fae snored." He typed something on to his phone, and I grabbed it from him.

"I do not!" I said and looked at the screen. He'd typed, *Gotcha.*

I laughed and handed his device back to him.

"No, but you may if you were lying supine."

I thought about making a flirtatious comment along the lines of he was welcome to observe my sleeping, but not in a lab, but I couldn't bring myself to do it. But I didn't automatically deny the possibility, either.

"So, what's the next instruction?" I asked.

"Get out of the car and walk into the woods about two hundred yards."

"Isn't this how horror movies start?" But I got out of the car, and we found the path behind the crumbling red brick building.

Once we'd lost sight of the parking lot and could no longer hear the highway, Sir Raleigh, who'd trotted along behind us, raised his hackles and growled. A second later, Lawrence stuck his arm out.

"Stop," he said. "I smell wolf."

I opened my senses and felt the presence of a lycanthrope. "That may be him."

A rustling in the underbrush behind us made us both turn, and Lawrence's skin took on a gray tone as his eyes went from slate gray to black.

"Don't shift," I murmured. "I don't feel in danger, and you're not fully healed yet."

He took a few deep breaths, and his pallor faded back to its usual tan, but his eyes stayed dark. "I'm going to protect you whether you like it or not."

"Oh, stop it with the alpha crap. Even here I have more power than you." Which might or might not have been true, but I couldn't heal him again if his shift went wrong. Plus, I didn't drive cars, so I didn't know how I could get him out of there if he did lose consciousness.

He nodded and crossed his arms. Good.

A man stepped out from a thicket of mountain laurel. His wrinkled and red clay-stained clothing looked like it had been sitting outside for a couple of weeks, and dark circles emphasized the bright green of his eyes. Even in his disheveled state, he had a certain attractiveness that said he'd probably, at one point, eaten female interns and younger colleagues for lunch.

"Robert Cannon, I presume?" I asked.

"Yes, Doctor Gordon and Doctor River?" His voice came out raspy, and he coughed. "Forgive me, I haven't spoken to anyone in months."

I couldn't sense any familiarity between him and Lawrence. When Robert and I shook hands, his curiosity and wariness came through, but also relief. Could he be ready to spill the beans and assuage a guilty conscience?

"How did Lawrence get in touch with you?" I asked.

"My wife. She sent me a message."

"So, you don't talk to her regularly?"

"I doubt we're here to talk about my marital situation," he said. "She mentioned you have questions about my role in the CLS vector?"

"Yes," Lawrence said. "You were the primary researcher on its spread, correct?"

"Yes."

All right, a man of few words.

"But you also were the liaison between the laboratory that created it and your company?" I asked.

"I'm not admitting to anything," he told us.

"Then why did you agree to meet with us?" Lawrence's eyes had returned to gray.

"She said a CLS researcher may be in danger." He rubbed his temples. "Sorry, headache."

Lawrence looked at me, and I shrugged. Then he inclined his head and gestured at Robert, who'd closed his eyes.

"Oh, right," I mouthed. I took the opportunity to give Robert a mental nudge to open up to us. Nothing too blatant.

"What if they are?" I asked and channeled my best television detective bluffing skills. "You know the government is closing in on the origin of the vector. It's only a matter of time."

"And what does a Scottish Fae care?" Robert shot back. "What's your motive for helping out?"

"I'm here as a physician associated with the Institute for Lycanthropic Reversal," I said and pushed a nudge more. "I'm trying to help the victims. If we know who created it and who leaked it, we can come up with a less dangerous cure."

"Oh, you're the one who trained the physicians there in safe"—air quotes around *safe*—"blood magic. But at what cost? Believe me, I know your kind, and there are always layers. Be careful, Doctor Gordon."

"If you're not going to tell us what you know, we can't help you in your situation," I added gently. "It can't be fun living in the woods, even as a wolf, for months on end."

"Who do you think I'm hiding from?" he spat. "If I told you what I knew, she would find out where I am and come after me."

"She?" I asked. I added a layer of *innocent and trustworthy* to my aura.

"Yes, *she*. Fine, there's something. Your surprised look says it all. She's clever."

"So who are you concerned about?" Lawrence asked. "At the very least, let us help her."

Another slight push, and Robert rubbed his temples again. "More information, huh? Fine. Her name is Latonya Francis. She's a behavioral epidemiologist. I trained her, and she put me in contact with...the person you're looking for. But she doesn't know what she did, what her role was. If she did, she'd never forgive herself."

I stumbled where I stood, and Lawrence caught my elbow. A mental check revealed I'd drained myself to forty percent. Hades, how could I do anything useful if this was what would happen? I extracted my influence from Robert as gently as I could and allowed the glamour I'd added to myself fade. My heart raced, and I forced myself to swallow through my dry throat.

"Thank you," I croaked out. "We'll do what we can to protect her."

Robert gave me a too-long look. Too drained to do anything to appear other than what I was, I looked back. I clutched my talisman in my pocket, but it had gone cold. No comfort there.

Finally, Robert said, "You're welcome, I suppose." Then, to Lawrence, "As I said, be careful with this one. She's been withholding information from you the entire time."

"Do you have any proof?" Lawrence, ever the scientist, asked.

"No, but that's what her kind does."

Then Robert stepped back into the bushes. Another rustling preceded a wave of wolf smell, and then I knew he'd gone.

Sir Raleigh rubbed against my ankles, and tendrils of strength twined up my legs. I reached down to pet him and ended up plopping on my ass. Dampness from the leaf mulch soaked through my jeans, but I couldn't get up.

"More powerful than me?" Lawrence asked. His eyes had

gone dark again.

"Oh, gods, don't change here. We may never get back. Just help me to the car."

I'm not a light Fae, being the height and build of a slender, medium-sized human woman, but he picked me up as though I weighed nothing. I thought about protesting, but I laid my head against his shoulder. Sir Raleigh appeared on my stomach, and I held him to me.

I went in and out of consciousness until we got to the car, and Lawrence placed me in the passenger seat.

Just before I passed out, I heard him make a phone call.

"Corey, hey. Yeah. Interesting stuff. Grab Doctor Rial and let's do a picnic at Stone Mountain. I need to charge my Fae."

His Fae? I managed to pry my eyelids apart just long enough to give him a good side-eye, but I also couldn't stop my lips from twitching into an almost-smile.

ALTHOUGH THE EQUINOX ritual had long been over, the granite hill still hummed with the energy. Once we reached the top courtesy of the cable car again, I found the secluded clearing with the exposed rock where I'd spoken to my mother. No trace of the doorway remained, but that didn't matter. I placed my hands on the granite and closed my eyes. My palms and fingers warmed, and the sensation of a thrumming golden glow filled my body.

Words came into my head—*"You need to be more careful, Sister."*

"Thank you, Sister," I replied to the spirit of the mountain. *"I didn't realize I was at such a disadvantage."*

"Something else is draining you. Be aware..." Then her presence faded.

Great. What could that be? Another puzzle on top of the too

many I already had.

Corey and Selene soon appeared, carrying white plastic bags of food. Corey had a red-and-white striped picnic blanket rolled up under one arm. Soon we were all seated on the ground, and Selene passed the food around—salads for everyone. I didn't say anything about the plastic containers or utensils, at least not out loud.

Selene and Corey looked at each other, and then Selene leaned forward and said in a hushed tone, "We found a secret room."

"The one Latonya was talking about?" I asked. "Where she said it would be?"

"Not exactly," she said. "I would never have found it if it hadn't been for Corey's sharp eyes and nose."

"Aw, shucks, ma'am." Corey said and assumed a bashful look. "I was just doin' my job."

"That Southern thing doesn't work for you," Lawrence teased even though he'd played that card, at least as far as I knew.

"But the secret room," I prompted.

"Right," Selene said. "It's behind the storage area, basically between that and the file room. So, opposite where she told us. What if there's another one?"

"It's possible," I murmured. "By the way, she may not be as innocent as she seems." Lawrence and I related what we'd found out from Robert Cannon.

Selene sighed and pulled her sweater around herself. "We should go before we said we'd meet her. What if she's somehow involved and it's a trap?"

"Are you up for it?" Lawrence asked me. "It seems like you should rest."

"You as well." But again, I didn't know about gargoyle anatomy. Dammit, why hadn't I studied other paranormal creatures as much as humans and Fae?

Because I hadn't considered them worthy of my notice. It was a common enough Fae attitude. We accepted we needed cooperation from the humans, although we'd never let on to them how dependent we were on them to make space for us in their world. But shifters, especially gargoyles? They were there to serve us. Same for most other paranormal creatures. We had our hierarchy. That was how things worked. How it would all work better.

Wasn't it?

I shook my head. This was no time to ponder nuances, especially since it cast a shadow over Faerie, which I, of course, still desperately wanted to return to. There would be no questions there. No challenge. No handsome gargoyles that drove me to distraction with their attitudes...and pecs and abs. No matter how hard I tried, I couldn't get the picture of gargoyle-Lawrence out of my head. He'd activated my lust drive, and I couldn't reconcile his condescension with his words... *"We used to guard you."*

How long had it been since I hadn't had to guard myself?

"Are you sure?" he challenged. "It looks like you just had a nice mental wander."

I wanted to argue with him, but I guessed he had watched me, so I couldn't say anything.

"We don't need as much sleep as everyone else," I finally told him. Corey turned his head, and his shoulders shook, and Selene adopted her neutral shrink face, so I could only surmise one thing—they were amused.

Good for them. We had a job to do, and the sooner we could accomplish it, the sooner I could return to Faerie and not have to deal with all this ridiculousness.

Just when I thought we'd managed to avoid any unnecessary drama, I heard an angry young female voice behind me.

"What are you doing back here? And why are you having a *picnic*?"

23

"Kestrel!" Corey stood. "What are you doing here? I thought you had class today."

"It's Equinox, idiot. School holiday." She pointedly looked from him to Selene. "You certainly seem to be enjoying it."

Selene stood. "Miss Graves, it's good to see you again. I was just telling Corey about my fiancé, Gabriel."

Of course, she hadn't been, but...

"No, you weren't." Ouch. "You were talking about sneaking into the lab. For what?"

I held up a hand. "Kestrel, you're right, and Selene shouldn't have lied. You may be able to help us."

"How?" Her expression shifted from annoyed to interested.

I knew I shouldn't reveal what we'd discovered outside our foursome, but Kestrel would be a good ally.

"What are you doing?" Lawrence asked via secret conversation.

"Using our resources. Think about it—she's practically invisible at the lab. They've become so accustomed to her being there. She's

probably overheard something useful, although she may not recognize it as important. We can at least ask her."

"Waiting," Kestrel said.

"We've found out that the vector leak is a female," I told her. "You've hung around the lab enough to know people pretty well there. You may have noticed or overheard something that could help us."

She sat cross-legged on the blanket between Corey and Selene and touched her knee to Corey's. I stifled a laugh.

"So, you think the person is still there?" she asked.

"Good question," Lawrence said. "I can't think of anyone high up enough or involved who would have left. In fact, we haven't had any turnover of female staff since the leak that I'm aware of."

"Right. Me, neither." She frowned. "So, if we're talking about people who were involved with the project, that leaves Doctor Francis, Leah, my dad's tech..." She wrinkled her nose. Did she suspect something going on between Leah and her father? "Andi the lab manager, and Tricia Yu the genetics tech."

"And your mother," Selene pointed out.

"There's no way. My mom's not a mastermind type."

"We can't rule anyone out," I said. "Or you."

"Me?" Kestrel looked at me, then laughed. "I can barely manage my school and externship schedule, much less some grand scheme. Plus, Corey can tell you I'm honest, even if I'm an underachiever."

"You're not an underachiever," Corey said. "It's not your fault that your witchy powers haven't settled yet."

"Right. Tell that to my parents." She followed that with a classic young adult eye roll. "I'll think about it, though, and let you know if I come up with anything. But if you're sneaking into the lab, you need me. I can take you in through the service duct entrance."

"The what?" Corey and Lawrence asked.

"There are tunnels all under campus in the case of a nuclear or bioterrorism attack. I found one that leads into the CPDC. It opens into Uncle Lawrence's animal lab."

"And you didn't tell me this, why?" Lawrence asked.

"I was waiting for the right time. But that way even if there are people still upstairs, you can still get in without them noticing and wait for them to leave."

Corey put an arm around her and hugged her to him. The expression on her face—bliss—until he said, "It's too dangerous."

"No, it's not. And if you don't let me come along..." She gave him a significant look.

"All right," he said. "If everyone else is okay with it."

"Definitely," Selene said.

Lawrence frowned, but grumbled, "Yes, with hesitation."

"Yes," I said. "So, it's agreed? Let's meet at our hotel rooms around seven."

BEFORE WE LEFT, I whispered thanks to the granite hill and got a response.

"You are quite welcome, sister. Don't forget to seek that which may be draining you."

"Thank you for the warning. I will seek it." I hated to think it may be Sir Raleigh, and I doubted it, considering he gave me comfort and strength, albeit the latter in small doses. What would his capacity be when he was full-grown? I wish I knew more about grimalkins, but in my grandmother's court, only spies knew about such creatures.

Once we returned to the hotel, I collapsed onto my bed on top of the covers. Sir Raleigh curled up next to me, but I couldn't sleep. My mind kept jumping to suspects to scenarios to...

After half an hour of my tossing and turning, Lawrence came in from his room. He wore black wire frame glasses and must have been running his hand through his hair because it was tousled. Gods, he looked sexy.

"If you don't stop with the sighing, I'm going to have to check your oxygen levels," he teased.

"I..." I had to start over. Dark curly hair, glasses, and a half-grin? *Fates kill me now.* I'd always had a weakness for the geeky ones. "I can't get comfortable."

"Yeah, a lot has happened." He sat on the edge of the bed. "Roll over, away from me."

"What are you going to do?"

"Reine..." Now he let out an exasperated sigh. "Just trust me."

Easier said than done, but I complied. I startled when his large hand touched my back.

"It's all right," he said.

Sir Raleigh, who had given up with all my tossing around, jumped back on the bed and curled against my hip. Between his purring and Lawrence rubbing soothing circles on my back, I drifted into sleep.

When I woke, the sun had set, and I felt remarkably refreshed and awake. My hand went to my pocket, where my talisman normally was, and panic jolted me upright when I found it gone. Sir Raleigh, who lay in the same place he'd been when I fell asleep, scrambled out of the way. I turned on the light, and a sparkle on the floor told me what had likely happened—it had fallen out of my pocket and become a cat toy. I picked it up and placed it on the nightstand.

"Not a kitty toy," I told Sir Raleigh, but he blinked sleepily at me. Okay, so maybe he wasn't the culprit. As much as I hated to be separated from the only key I had to Faerie, I decided to leave it in the hotel room safe so I wouldn't lose it.

The door between my and Lawrence's rooms had been

closed, and I didn't want to disturb him in case he was resting, too. If we ran into any trouble tonight, he'd likely shift, so he needed to be in the best shape possible to do so.

I changed into all-black clothing and put my hair under a black cap. There was nothing to be done for the luminescence of my skin, but I'd dampen it with a glamour as best I could.

The time read six-fifty, so I knocked on the door to Lawrence's room. I wondered again who had poisoned him and when. Someone at the vampire club? Or someone closer? Any of the women in the lab could have had an accomplice. A mastermind never worked alone. They always had minions, often in high places. Again, Dr. Cimex popped into my head. There had been something shifty about him from the beginning, and not in the changing forms way.

"Ready?" I asked when Lawrence opened the door. His black turtleneck hugged the planes of his pecs and accentuated his flat abs. He'd hidden his curls under a black cap, and now he looked the opposite of the straitlaced gargoyle scientist I'd first met. Damn, Clark Kent and a dangerous criminal type all in one?

"Are you?" Huskiness dropped his voice an octave, and his gaze turned dark, but not in an about-to-wing-out kind of way, when he took in my form-fitting attire.

"Yes," I whispered, homing in on his lips. "Well, as soon as Selene gets here."

She arrived just as I'd finished talking about her, keeping me from doing anything stupid. We set off for the lab with Corey driving his almost-sensible black pickup truck. At least it had an extended cab so we could all fit.

"Is it legally required for young men in this part of the country to drive these things?" I asked.

"Not always, but it's encouraged, and we like to stay on the right side of the law," he replied with a wink.

We pulled up to the lab a little after seven-thirty. Corey

drove by the building and parked in the deep shadows of a nearby parking lot. I couldn't see any other cars or sense any other beings except for one whom I presumed was a security guard about a quarter of a mile away and Kestrel, who'd been waiting for us.

"Now, everyone be quiet," Corey said, somewhat unnecessarily, I thought. Kestrel took the lead, then Corey, and I fell in behind him. That close, I heard him humming something.

"What are you singing?" I whispered.

"Oh, you could hear that?"

"Yes, we Fae have good ears."

"Um, well, it was the 'Dance of the Sugarplum Fairies' from the Nutcracker," he replied, somewhat sheepishly.

"Are you Fae-ing kidding me?"

"It always sounded like they were up to something," he murmured. I whacked him on the arm.

"Shhh," Lawrence hissed from behind me.

Kestrel led us to a small utility building, where she unlocked the door. I could practically feel the questions bubbling up in my colleagues' brains—how did she get the key? Who'd showed her the secret entrance? Who else knew? But they remained silent. We walked inside, and she shut the door behind us. Several large tanks and gages lined the walls, and the air felt humid. Kestrel led us to one of the tanks, turned a dial, and a section of wall opened behind it.

"Careful," she said. "There's a ladder. We'll go down it and then across."

"How did you find this?" Corey asked. "I didn't even know about it."

She grinned. "I had a short flare of passage-finding and unlocking power. It was useful while it lasted. Well, except..." She shook her head. "Never mind. Follow me."

We arrived at the lab without any other conversation—or offensive humming. Kestrel let us into the broom closet that serviced the veterinary laboratory. It felt like ages since Sir Raleigh and I had been there.

We took the stairs up to the main level, and we stuck to the shadows in the hallway. When we walked into the section of the lab where Selene and Corey had discovered the secret room, we found someone had beaten us to it. A section of the wall was open, and inside at a metal table, surrounded by files, was John Graves.

"I knew it," I murmured.

24

J ohn looked up and pulled his glasses from his face. "Kestrel? What are y'all doing here?" he asked. His hair stood up in gray-black spikes, and he sported red rims around his eyes and bags under them.

"I could ask the same," Lawrence said and moved to the front of our group. He crossed his arms and frowned. Hmmm, not what I expected. But what did I think he'd do? The two of them had been up to something, and I still didn't know what.

John appeared unfazed. "Why? I'm here working late, and you're all here dressed like cat-burglars. No offense, Corey."

"None taken," Corey replied. "But seriously, what are you doing here?"

John gestured to the files around him. "I've recently been made aware of a secret project our group has been involved in." He sighed. "Don't ask me how I know, I just do."

Lawrence seemed genuinely nonplussed. "What sort of project? Animal or human?"

"A little of both." John motioned for us to come closer. The rest did, and I hung back, looking for the trap. When it appeared that no cage would fall from the ceiling—not that there was one up there—or a spell would be triggered, I gingerly moved to join the others by the desk.

The "secret room" had unfinished cinder block walls and the same dark, gray, cement floor as the rest of the lab, but shinier. File cabinets lined the walls in the cramped space, and unlike the uniform black ones in the main lab, they were various shades of dark and dented. They looked like they'd been squirreled in from the surplus department and other places they might not be missed. So did the desk, which had obviously seen better days, according to its scratched finish. Whoever had set this up had wanted to stay under the proverbial radar.

"How did you find this?" I asked.

John glanced up from the file he was showing Lawrence. "Got a tip," he said. "Someone texted me, but the number was listed as anonymous. They told me how to unlock it and get in." Something rang false about his words, but I didn't press in case he'd clam up.

"This is fascinating," Lawrence said. "Doctor River, come see."

I moved to stand beside him and tried not to be aware of his warmth and strength next to me. Damn, something had been triggered in my psyche by him going gargoyle in my hotel room. Even Sir Raleigh, who'd been draped around my shoulders, purred softly.

The papers in the folder made almost all of my distracting thoughts about Lawrence flee. I looked over the charts and figures—it was some sort of trial, and it had numbers for the CLS vector, which I'd expected. But there were others. One vampire chart. One cat shifter one. And one for witches. The one for Fae was blank, but a handwritten note said, "subject's arrival imminent."

Suddenly cold, I looked at the top of the chart and saw that particular page was dated a week previously, which matched up to when the invitation had been sent to Gabriel and Lonna.

Selene, who had moved to the other side of Lawrence, apparently had the same thought. She and I locked gazes, and it was evident we shared the sudden suspicion that we had been set up. Sir Raleigh's purr faded into a low growl. She and I both stepped backward out of the small room and into the main lab.

"What is it?" John asked. "Doctors, is something wrong?"

Selene and I didn't wait. We broke into a run and darted as fast as we could through the lab.

"What the...?" Corey said. "Lawrence, come on!"

A wave of shifter energy propelled me forward. Oh, Hades, they were coming after us. We'd almost reached the door to the outside when Sir Raleigh dug in with his claws. Instead of holding on, he leaped off my shoulder backward, landing behind me. I skidded to a stop.

"Raleigh!" I yelled and grabbed for him, but my hands passed through him.

Selene reached the outer door and yanked it open.

"Reine, come *on!*"

"I can't leave him." I didn't know what he was doing, but he'd folded into a ball of dark energy that glowed purple and white around the edge, like I'd always imagined a black hole doing. And like a black hole, he seemed to have incredible mass because I couldn't move.

LAWRENCE COULD BARELY MAKE it through the hall in his gargoyle form. His half-folded wings scraped the walls, leaving scratches with the claws at the ends of his wing bones, but he wasn't the one who worried me the most. No, it was Corey, a mountain lion, who rounded the corner, his lips drawn back in a snarl to show his sharp teeth.

And, like in nightmares, I couldn't move.

The ball of energy that had been Sir Raleigh expanded to fill the width of the hall, and both the pursuing shifters halted on the other side of it. The dark sphere coalesced into a panther-like creature with bat-like wings and one white paw, and its snarl made the walls rumble.

Well, damn. My kitten had a major intimidation factor.

"Reine, please," Lawrence said. "I need to explain."

I arched an eyebrow. "You have an interesting way of showing it." But Hades, he was sexy. He'd come out of his turtleneck, the shreds of which still ringed his neck, wrists, and waist, and his dark jeans strained over his muscles and, er, yeah. Apparently changing was a turn-on for gargoyles.

Sir Raleigh and I backed up, and I resisted the urge to touch his soft gray fur to make sure he was, indeed, the sweet little cat who had somehow come to me from...well, I didn't know where. But now I had more proof that he had been sent to protect me, and the thought that someone, somewhere was watching out for me made an unfamiliar warmth come to my chest. And fear—what would they want in return for this gift? That's how things worked in Faerie, among all Fae—nothing came free. It's how we protected ourselves from going soft. Going human.

"I'm listening," I said, although I really wasn't.

"We knew someone in our company had betrayed us," Lawrence said. "But we didn't—*don't*—know who. We need you to help us flush them out since they obviously need a sample of your DNA."

"No way, Jose," I said. "I'm not here to be a trap." And I definitely didn't want to give them any of my genetic material, even as part of a trap. That would go counter to my Fae mission.

Corey tried to sneak around, but Sir Raleigh blocked him,

and with a snarl, sent him flying backward, claw marks across his chest.

"I'm serious," I said. "I'm not going to cooperate and I sure as Hades won't be forced."

"Please," Lawrence said. "Can we sit down and discuss this rationally? Call off your pet?"

"Nope."

I had reached the door and had almost made it through when Selene came running back in.

"What is it?" I asked.

"The soul-eater is out there," she said and steadied herself against the wall, breathless.

I grabbed her by her shoulders and looked into her eyes, inhaling her energy and scent. Satisfied it was truly her, I let her go.

"How do you know?"

"The security guard..." She gulped back a sob. "There was something odd about him, and he kept asking for you. He shouldn't have known about you."

I turned to see a dark shape at the door. The translucent glass may have made him look bigger than he was, but I didn't want to find out.

"I'm glad he didn't hurt you," I said, "but I'm not sure what to do."

The door opened inward with a bang, and the security guard came in, his pistol—they issued those to security guards? —raised. He started firing, and I grabbed Selene and pulled her into a doorway. The unlocked door gave way, and we tumbled into a custodial office.

THE SOUNDS OF GUNFIRE, snarling, and growling resonated through every cell of my being, and I cursed in every language I knew as Selene and I took cover behind a desk. Not that it would give us much help if a gun-crazy soul-eater were to come in, but at least it was something.

Then everything went quiet. Like, deathly, press-on-your-ears absence of noise that in itself made its own racket and faded into silence.

Tomb silence.

"Shit," Selene whispered, barely audible.

I nodded. "Wait a few minutes."

The sound of scampering footsteps heralded the arrival of Sir Raleigh, who looked like he had blood around his mouth and on his white paw. He stopped in front of us and proceeded to clean himself. I couldn't watch him—he seemed to be relishing the grisly task. He was indeed a grimalkin, which meant he'd been sent by a dark or gray Fae. But who? And what would my debt be?

We waited ten minutes, and I crept into the hallway. The lights were out, even the emergency ones, and my eyesight, although good, could only make out dark shapes. The one in front of me groaned, and I found it was Lawrence. Part of me was relieved he still had his throat intact.

"Lawrence," I whispered in his ear.

He rolled over, and my hand met his shoulder. He had returned to human.

"Reine?" he asked.

"Yes, come on." I brought him into the office, which, for some reason, I could see better in. "Where's Corey?"

"He was battling that thing that came in." He shook his head. His voice sounded thick. Had he been injured internally? "They knocked me over, and I blacked out."

"Great," I said. "Soul-eater's still on the loose." Not good news.

"How did it get in?" Selene asked. "This building is supposed to be warded."

"It must have gathered enough energy from the security guard, who I presume is welcome to patrol in here," I said. "Hades, that means it's getting stronger. I'm guessing the real guard is knocked out or dead somewhere outside."

"This is going to be a mess," Lawrence groaned.

"Way to have sympathy there, gargoyle," Selene told him.

"I do feel bad for him. His name is—was?—Oscar. He was a nice guy. It's going to be a mess because he protected us from the rest of security getting too nosy."

"Oh." Selene didn't say anything else.

"What now?" Lawrence asked. I realized he was looking to me to be the leader.

"Can you, uh, shift again?" I asked. "I hate to burden you since you're probably weak from earlier, but I'm hoping that you can protect us better if you're in your gargoyle form."

"I can't." He grabbed me, his hand cold, and something pressed in on me, making me feel like my spirit was being compressed.

"Oh, shit." It was the soul-eater. I hadn't checked.

SIR RALEIGH JUMPED ON NOT-LAWRENCE'S head and wreathed him in black smoke. The creature disappeared with a howl, and the air around us seemed to lighten. I almost choked on my heartbeat, it was so strong, but I ran into the hallway. There I found real Lawrence, still in gargoyle form, lying unconscious and barely breathing. I took a deep breath and probed his energy to make sure it was him. He smelled of sweat and shampoo and the earthy, stony odor of marble after a rain. I'd never found gargoyles to smell good before, but this one did. Damn.

"Come on," I said. "Selene, can you help me?"

"Yes," she told me and knelt on his other side. "What do you need?"

"Can you do chest compressions? Wait." I touched her and confirmed she was her. Sir Raleigh trotted out to join us, and somehow he relayed the message to me that the bad creature had disappeared into the ether, which I took to mean whatever dimension it traveled through. Hopefully it had been knocked outside of the wards and wouldn't be able to get back in.

"Right, chest compressions. What about you?"

I took a deep breath. "I'm going to breathe life back into a gargoyle."

She started with the compressions and hummed the "Stayin' Alive" song. I tilted his head back, which opened his mouth slightly. When I pressed my lips to his, a jolt went through me, like two puzzle pieces clicking together.

Perhaps there was something to his tale of gargoyles protecting Fae, after all. It wasn't unheard of for princesses to mate with their guards. It figured that prejudice would cause certain details to be left out of the old tales.

I closed my eyes and reached for the energy surrounding me, of which there wasn't much. The wards blocked what I could get from the trees outside, and the cinderblock walls around me had long had the life ground out of them. But that didn't mean I couldn't pull a Fae trick, although it might drain me. I placed my hands on either side of Lawrence's head and felt through the linoleum, concrete, and various plumbing and sub-structures to the red clay earth below. Metaphysical roots grew from my hands into the space beneath, and I pulled the energy from the earth to heal the stone man whose lips lay slack under mine. I breathed healing and light into him, a life force generated by the growth of the roots and wriggling crea-tures underneath.

With each breath I blew into him, his body inflated, and Selene continued to count. I was almost ready to give up in despair when he lurched up and took a deep, rasping breath. We backed off, in my case with a wrenching feeling as I released the roots I'd made into the earth below, leaving two holes in the floor. I rubbed my palms together, then held them over his chest and allowed the last of the healing energy to seep into his chest.

He continued to breathe, and each inhale and exhale went smoother. Finally, he opened his eyes.

"What happened?" he asked, his gargoyle voice again deep and resonant.

"The soul-eater got you," I said. "It stole your energy and impersonated you. The only way you're not dead right now is because you're in your strong shifter form."

He rubbed a hand over his chest. "I tingle. What did you do to me?"

"Selene did CPR on you. I breathed for you until you could do so on your own." I didn't want to explain more than that— for it to become another data point about the Fae in his never-ending study of me. Hopefully no one would notice the tiny holes in the floor. Probably not since bullet marks now riddled the hallway.

He didn't look like he believed me, but he didn't press. Selene and I helped him to stand, and we limped further into the building, followed by Sir Raleigh. We found the lab in disarray and the door to the secret office closed. It lay flush against the cinder-block, so it was no wonder we hadn't noticed it. Now that I knew it was there, I would hopefully be able to open it.

"John? Corey?" Lawrence asked. No answer. They weren't anywhere else in the lab, so where else could they be?

"Can you open it?" Selene asked.

"I can't," Lawrence said. He looked at his clawed hands. "I could perhaps force it, but it's designed to make that impossible."

"Let me try," I said. I placed my hands on the walls and again felt inside them. The cinder blocks felt like stone sponges, dead and hollow, but the metal of a locking mechanism beckoned to me. I followed its signal and coaxed the tumblers to open. Luckily, I'd done some training with an unlocking witch, so I knew what to do.

The wall swung inward to reveal Corey and John standing behind the desk, each of them pointing a gun at us. Kestrel stood between them looking miserable.

25

My nostrils flared to take in the smells and energies again, but a pain traveled through my right nostril and into my eye socket. I clutched at my face with a groan. I must have used all of my strength rescuing Lawrence. As if to agree, my stomach growled.

"I can't tell," I gritted out, "if it's the soul-eater." But I hoped it had exhausted itself as well. What was I to do? It seemed to grow in strength while I remained the same or weakened.

"It's all right," Lawrence said. "They're them. I can tell."

It pained me to say it, but I told him, "I trust you. And Doctor Graves and Corey, we don't mean to harm you."

Both men lowered their weapons but kept wary eyes on us.

"What was that thing?" Corey asked. He was shirtless, and scratches showed on his broad chest. Damn, did all these men have impressive physiques?

"Sorry about that." I pointed to his chest. "Sir Raleigh is protective of me."

"Not him," Corey smiled fondly at the kitten, who had resumed his place on my shoulder. "He's a good kitty, protecting you. No, what was that thing that came in? It looked like Oscar, but not."

"That was the soul-eater we encountered earlier." The weight of the words made my tone grim. "It's getting stronger and better at impersonating energy. It fooled me for a few minutes just now. Are you all right?"

"Yes," Corey said. "I fought it off and came back in here to protect the lab and John."

"Thanks," John said, although he didn't look happy to be rescued. Must be a man thing. "Why did you two run earlier?"

Selene cleared her throat before I could reply. "Come on," she said and put her hands on her hips. "You showed us a file indicating that Reine was the object of someone's intense scientific curiosity. In every book, movie, and television show, that's when the trap gets sprung."

"Perhaps it was," I said. "But by the soul-eater. Doctor Graves, the situation is getting more dire by the second. Who was this anonymous tip from?" I air-quoted 'anonymous.'

He sank into the chair and rubbed his eyes. "Would you believe Kestrel?"

He couldn't see Corey's reaction, but I could. A guilty look flashed across his face.

"How would Kestrel know anything about this?" I asked. But I had already answered my question that afternoon—she was a clever girl and noticed things.

"Cimex sometimes lets her use his office for homework when she comes to visit us here and observe. She has clearance through her school, and Beverly and I may have pulled some strings to have some of her field observation be here."

"You're overprotective of her," Selene said. "You worry that since she's not come into her complete witch powers, she's vulnerable as part of the PBI."

"It's more her mother than me," John said, perhaps too quickly. "I know she's a strong and capable young woman." He glanced over his shoulder at Corey. "And I know Corey keeps an eye on her."

Corey nodded, and his facial expression looked too stony. I felt for him. It must be hard for him and Kestrel to hide their feelings for each other from everyone, especially her helicopter parents.

"So, she found these in Cimex's office?" I asked. "What's the point of having a secret laboratory, if that's the case?"

"She didn't find the files. She discovered the presence of the office. There's a door between here and his office. One of the file cabinets moves outward. She had a flare of unlocking power, which allowed her to discover how to release the security mechanism. Thankfully it went better this time than during her last flare."

"That must have been when the top-security storage lock got broken," I said. "And why it hasn't been repaired—you don't want her to lose her clearance by letting someone outside the lab know." Yet more than one person did know.

"Right," he said with a sigh. "So now what? You report me? You figure out what Cimex is up to?"

"Nope." I assumed my best drawing room detective pose, which might have made me look like a little teapot with one hand on my hip and the other gesturing to Graves and Lawrence. "I think the bigger question is what you two were up to. I found the notes."

"What notes?" John asked at the same time Lawrence exclaimed, "What?"

This time John wasn't lying, and Lawrence looked pissed. Whoops.

"Um, never mind," I said. I gathered up the last of my dignity. "I was trying to bluff. Didn't work. Sorry."

John shrugged and laughed. "Well, I hope you found out what you needed. I'm innocent of whatever you were going to accuse me of."

He might be, but Lawrence glowered at me.

"Would you mind if I had a private word with Doctor River?" he asked.

I'd never been called to the principal's office, but I had the feeling I was about to experience something like it.

"WHAT THE HELL WERE YOU THINKING?" Lawrence asked once we got down to his lab. Human angry Lawrence looked even more frightening than angry gargoyle Lawrence, if that was possible. And it didn't help that his turtleneck hung around his torso in shreds, reminding me of his potential rage.

"Um, when?" I asked. I tried to muster some sort of indignation—I was a Fae princess and not subject to the interrogation of a gargoyle. But I'd made a pretty big mistake, so, also, I needed to own up to it.

"Oh, I don't know," he said. "When you looked through my files? When you decided to accuse John Graves of something you had scant evidence for? When you kissed me?" His mouth worked for a second. I guessed he hadn't meant for that last one to come out.

"I knew something was up, that someone wasn't telling me something, so that was self-preservation. Two, I thought for sure you and John were up to something, so I've now established his innocence." And all fingers pointed to Cimex plus a female accomplice—maybe Leah? But something didn't feel quite right about that, either. "And three, I wasn't kissing you, I was giving you mouth-to-mouth."

He shook his head. "Do you want to know what it was about? We were trying to figure out a media strategy for when the CLS leak went public, as we knew it would."

"So, the materials you were talking about..."

"Was a press release we were going to give to Ted. Damage control."

"Oh." Relief and ridiculousness fought for dominance in my chest.

"As for the kiss, you were giving me mouth-to-mouth," he said. "Right, that's all it was."

Had he, in his unconscious state, had the sensation of two puzzle pieces locking together, too? I didn't dare ask. I'd already made too many incorrect assumptions.

Sir Raleigh hopped down from my shoulder and slid under the desk. Smart kitty, although what did he sense coming? Or maybe he felt as done with the day as I was.

"I'm leaving," I said, again stepping back from the precipice I felt us both heading to. "You're obviously in no shape to engage in logical discourse. Considering you almost died twice in the last twenty-four hours."

"And you saved me."

"And I saved you. Damn straight." I crossed my arms and attempted to look stern, but he smiled.

"Damn straight," he said and placed one hand behind my head. "Thank you."

I looked into his dark gray eyes, which had lost some of their hard inquisitiveness. Now he seemed to ponder what my behavior would be if he were to—

He brought my face closer to his, and I didn't pull back. I had my own experiment to perform. Could I tolerate kissing a gargoyle? Just kissing, I told myself. Just for the sake of knowledge.

When our lips met, that sensation happened again, but this time with the level of satisfaction of putting the final piece into a puzzle I didn't know I'd so desperately wanted to finish. Our bodies fit together perfectly, and sensations I hadn't experienced in centuries raced along my limbs and to my core. I braced myself against him, and the threads of his shirt against his hard, warm chest made the situation more sensual.

All too soon, he pulled away.

"Thank you," he said again.

"You're...welcome?"

"Thank you for saving my life. And for showing it was just mouth-to-mouth. Now I know the difference." With a wink, he turned and went into his office, closing the door behind him.

Someone raced down the stairs, and the door burst open.

Kestrel stood there, tears running down her cheeks, and her chest heaving. "Where's Uncle Lawrence? My mom is here, and my parents are having an awful fight."

LAWRENCE CAME out of his office, having changed into one of his ubiquitous buttoned-down shirts. "Where are they?"

"In the lab. Doctors Cimex and Francis are up there, too. They're all having a terrible argument."

Corey and Selene came down the stairs, their expressions grim.

"What happened?" Lawrence asked.

"Apparently there was some sort of laboratory gathering this evening, and someone put something in the wine," Corey said.

"They're all up there accusing each other of being the vector leak," Selene added. "Whatever they ingested, it's reducing their inhibitions."

"What do we do?" I asked.

"We have to separate and calm them," Selene said. "But there aren't that many of us."

"Or counter the spell," I told her and the others. "Something brought Beverly and Cimex back here."

"Could Latonya have planned all this?" Lawrence asked. "It's almost when we were supposed to meet her."

I called Sir Raleigh out from under the desk, where he'd been curled up. "Can you go upstairs and find out who's driving the magic? Let me hear what they're saying?"

I had a suspicion, but I needed to check. Now that I knew Lawrence and John were innocent, that left one person with a motive, someone I'd avoided accusing in my mind—Beverly Graves. I didn't want it to be her, but she'd been working on a shifter disrupter, as Corey and Lawrence had talked about when I'd discovered Sir Raleigh's talent at eavesdropping. Plus, she desperately wanted her daughter to develop some sort of magical talent, and she'd demonstrated she was willing to do almost anything to accomplish it, including making a bargain with a Fae.

I held up my hand as Sir Raleigh related to me what he was hearing.

"I told you to bring them to the prison room," Beverly was saying.

"They aren't here," Latonya replied. "I've done all I can. Do I look like I can make them materialize out of thin air?"

"No, call them or something."

"Fine. Wait, what is that cat doing here? Ow!"

The voices stopped, and a dark streak came down the stairs. Sir Raleigh twined around my calves, and I rubbed his head.

"Good thing we came early," I said. "It would have been a trap."

"Set by...?" Selene asked.

"Let's go up and see."

Before I took a step, the sound of a gunshot echoed through the mostly brick-and-stone building.

"Not again," I groaned.

26

My favorite part of a good English mystery is the drawing room reveal scene, where the detective shows his cleverness in outing the murderer, putting together all the clues in a way that indicates there can't be any other solution. I loved how everything got wrapped up in a neat little bow, often with a confession. And then Hercule Poirot would have his matched eggs, or Lord Peter Wimsey would allow the murderer to take the gentleman's way out...

That wasn't going to happen here.

First, we'd had to sneak in, then duck for cover. Second, instead of a drawing room, we had the main lab, where equipment lay strewn about, and I could still hear the tinkling of glass and the dripping of some liquid that could have led to a level three contamination lockdown, but no one cared anymore.

The level of chaos exceeded that of most English mysteries. Cimex stood, wide eyed, his gun leveled at anything that moved. Lawrence and I crouched behind an overturned metal table, and I doubted it would be thick enough to stop a bullet should one end up coming our way. Selene and Corey peeked out from the secure storage lab. Good, no one had seen them, at least not that I could tell.

John had grabbed Kestrel the second we walked in and ushered her into the hallway.

Latoya Francis and Beverly Graves huddled behind another table, their location evident by their continued whispered arguing.

"Give it up, Beverly," I called, softly. "I know what you did. What you're doing."

"I don't know what you're talking about." Anger laced her words.

"Lucius, can you please put the gun down?" Lawrence asked. "It's not going to do anyone any good if you shoot us."

Finally, Cimex lowered the weapon, but he didn't release it. We all stood, slowly with hands up. A hush descended over the room.

"Beverly, you're the one who leaked the vector," I said. "You knew the lock to the storage unit was broken. John told you. And you're the only one who had reason. The Shadow Project."

She flinched when I named it. "Please, not here. Not now," she begged and glanced at her daughter, who peeked around the door.

"Mom?" Kestrel's face crumpled in confusion. "Mom, what does she mean?"

"I did it for you," she said. "I did it so you could find your powers, find what you were supposed to be, and have more besides."

"What?" Kestrel started to come in. John stopped her motion but not her words. "I thought you said it didn't matter, that you were happy for me to be mundane, if that was all right with me. And it is. I'm happy without having to deal with the pressures that you and Da—" Her voice cracked on the syllable. She took a deep breath. "That you and Dad had to deal with, being such a powerful witch and wizard."

"I am fine with whoever you wanted to be. But I wanted you to have a choice." Beverly took a deep, shuddering breath.

"But did you?" I asked. "We found the protocol, Beverly. We found what you wanted to try on your own daughter."

"What protocol?" Kestrel asked. "Oh, god, the shots. It was the shots you wanted me to take, wasn't it? It wasn't about my allergies at all. And the vitamins you've had me on for years."

Her voice rose in pitch, and Cimex brought the weapon up.

"Please stay calm, all of you," Lawrence said. "It's not safe here." He inclined his head toward Cimex, who blinked, confused. What had happened to him?

Oh, gods, the soul-eater? No, that creature would be weakened. I did my best to read Cimex and found deep disappointment in what had happened. And...a deep, unrequited crush on Beverly. Oh, Hades.

"Yes, Beverly, what was the protocol?" I asked, to keep someone talking. "What exactly were you going to do with all those samples, with the essence of so many paranormals?"

"I was going to create an angel," she said, and now a strange glint came into her eyes. If Cimex had lost his mind in the moment, Beverly had been hiding a deep, warped sense of reality for years. She continued, "A being that has the speed of a were, the cunning of a vampire, and the magic of a Fae, all wrapped up in the cleverness of a witch. My witch. My Kestrel. And I wasn't alone. I had the help of—"

A shot split the air, and we all ducked. Beverly clutched her stomach, and horror crossed her features. The glint left her eyes, and she looked down.

"What... What happened to me?" She crumpled to the ground, and John and Kestrel rushed to kneel beside her.

Corey managed to get the gun away from Cimex, and I knelt on the other side of Beverly along with John.

"Reine, please, you have to help her," Kestrel begged. "You can heal her, can't you?"

I placed my hands on top of Beverly's. Sir Raleigh hopped down from my shoulder and sniffed, then looked up at me, his little face somber.

"I'm afraid not. The bullet has done too much damage."

Beverly shook her head. "I promise I wouldn't have done anything without your consent, Sweetheart. But I need to come clean. I did steal the sample. I did bring it to my contact at Cabal, hoping they could turn it into something useful."

Cabal. Robert Cannon. I'd have some words for him the next time we met.

Beverly coughed, and blood coated her tongue.

"Reine, please!" Kestrel clutched my arm, wide-eyed. "Please, I'll give you anything. My firstborn, anything."

I remembered others looking at me like she did, pleading with desperation for the lives of their loved ones. My coven co-leader, devastated over the imminent loss of her child. My brother, faced with a life of exile because I couldn't heal his cheek. Countless others who thought a powerful creature like me could do anything... I couldn't save them, and I couldn't save her.

"I'm sorry," I said. "I truly am, but I cannot extend the thread of life that the Fates have already cut short. Spend your last moments with her truly being with her. It's the last gift you can give your mother."

"Are you sure?" Selene asked when I joined her on the other side of the room. We walked out of the lab and into the hallway. I leaned against the brick wall, seeking solace from the blocks that had once been living riverbed clay.

I nodded. "I can't heal a mortal wound. Never have been able to. If I could, do you think I would have bothered to study medicine?"

"Good point. What about him?" She indicated Cimex, who walked from the lab in front of Corey, who guided him. "And the soul-eater."

"We know it's getting scary strong. I need to find out more about it before I can determine how to defeat it. Which means..."

Lawrence came up to us. "Beverly's gone," he said. His red-rimmed eyes told the story of his sorrow, but I didn't know how to comfort him. I'd accused him of betraying his colleagues, after all, and I knew betrayal took a long time to recover from. But he took me into his arms and laid his cheek on the top of my head.

"I'm so sorry," I said. "For all of it. For everything."

He stroked my hair, and his tears warmed my scalp. A healing or benediction? Perhaps both.

"I understand, and I forgive you," he said.

Something loosened in me at that moment. I'd been waiting to hear those words for centuries, although I didn't know from whom. And maybe they wouldn't be enough when I really thought about it. But they were enough for now.

Sir Raleigh appeared in between us, and we both caught him, making a kitty sling out of our arms. He purred, offering the soothing rumble to ease both our hearts. Another mystery I'd yet to solve—where had he come from? Who had sent him? And worse—once he'd accomplished what he'd been sent to do, would he leave me?

Those were questions for another time.

WHEN WE RETURNED to our hotel room, Lawrence and I spent the night holding each other close. It had been an intense evening, and I felt his sorrow. Nothing sexual happened, though, which was for the best. Men who took Fae lovers often ended up pining for them after it was all over. Once dawn began to touch the sky, I left him to his slumber. I had an appointment to keep.

I removed the talisman from the safe, and now that I'd been apart from it for so long, I noticed how it felt to be reunited with it—not good. I'd managed to use some of my limited powers the previous evening without my energy draining as quickly. Now the crystal and jewel wand felt heavy in my pocket, my steps sluggish as I crossed the lobby and caught the waiting car.

When my mother's form shimmered into view in the clearing atop Stone Mountain, I crossed my arms.

"I'm not amused," I said.

"By what, Daughter?"

"Why is this talisman draining my power? It should hook me to Faerie, the source of my strength."

"Perhaps you've spent too long in the human world, have become more human than Fae."

Her words chilled me.

"Not possible."

"Why did you call me here?" she asked. "You know how it pains me to travel this far."

"I'm making a report. I found out who leaked the vector, and I managed to keep our secrets." Even from a handsome and inquisitive gargoyle. It hurt to think of leaving him, of the potential for us, but I needed to return home. I could always come back to him later, a full Fae, not the half-magical being I felt I'd become.

"Yes, you did, but there are loose ends, Daughter. Remember, that was part of the deal—no loose ends."

"I am also here to make a petition. The creature grows more powerful by the day, and I need to be at my full capacity to defeat it. If I were to return to Faerie for even a day, I feel I would be replenished enough to have a fighting chance."

I watched to see if she would budge, but her expression didn't waver a millimeter. "I'm sorry, but no. That's not possible until you fulfill your end of the bargain. That was our agreement."

I now understood humans' frustration with us. "Can you offer me any help?"

"No. You will either succeed in defeating the creature or you will not." She shrugged. "You disappoint me, Daughter."

I sighed. "As per usual. And you disappoint me as well." The anguished faces of Beverly and Kestrel Graves flashed through my mind and released a flare of anger I hadn't been aware of holding back. Even so, when I spoke, I only allowed sadness to color my words. "Some mothers would do anything for their children." With that, I turned and walked away.

"Reine! I have not dismissed you. Where are you going?"

I kept walking, refusing to look back.

"Fine, you ungrateful brat," she snapped, "I'll send someone, but you may not consider them helpful."

I declined to ask whether that was a promise or a threat. The air shimmered as I left the area of the doorway. When I reached an appropriate spot, I took the talisman from my pocket and looked at it. How had I ever thought such a cold object could be beautiful? Before it could steal any more of my magic, I threw it as hard as I could over the side of the mountain into an area humans weren't allowed to enter. The sound of its crash both broke and started to heal my heart.

As the sun peeked over the horizon, Sir Raleigh appeared on my shoulder, and I coaxed him into my arms. We watched the sunrise, and in spite of my difficult situation, I felt peace.

"Let her send her worst," I told the cat. "I'm ready."

Then, when I turned, I spotted Lawrence making a note on his phone. "I didn't realize Fae needed sunrise strength after a trauma," he said.

I laughed and walked over to him, hooking my arm through his. "Sure, let's go with that."

We'd just started down the path when I spotted the tall,

lanky form of the last person I wanted to see—my brother Rhys. He looked up and gave me his signature grin, crooked due to the scar on his cheek.

"'Ello, Sis. I heard you could use some help?"

Oh, Hades.

THANK you for reading *The Shadow Project*! Reine's adventures continue in Book Two, *Shadows of the Heart.* Grab it from your favorite retailer or order it from your local bookstore through Ingram Spark using the ISBN 978-1-945074-63-9

FROM THE AUTHOR

Thank you for reading *The Shadow Project*! I hope you enjoyed it.

I know you probably see this kind of request at the end of just about every book, but it really does mean a lot for authors to get reviews. It helps your fellow readers to see what you liked and didn't like and helps them to find new authors and books to love...or avoid.

I prefer to focus on the positive and think reviews help others find a new-to-them author who can help them escape the world and be someone and somewhere else for a while.

So, that said, will you please leave a review at the site where you bought the book or on Goodreads or Bookbub and help another reader? We could all probably use a little more Fae sass right now.

Thanks!
   - Cecilia

THE ADVENTURE CONTINUES...

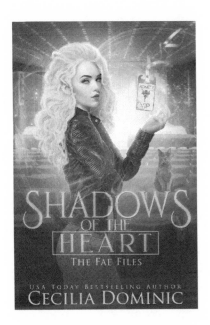

Fae Files Book Two: *Shadows of the Heart*

She has one "simple" task to complete to earn her way back home. Too bad the monster she needs to capture is hunting her, too.

Nobody said Fae life was easy...

Reine has one minor loose end to tie up before she'll be allowed to return to Faerie — an invisible soul-eating creature is on the loose at a major fantasy convention, and the hotel manager doesn't believe in the paranormal.

As if living in a horror movie isn't bad enough, Reine's brother Rhys and the gargoyle she's becoming too attracted to have some sort of history between them.

Instead of a "loose end," Reine is dealing with the unraveling of her life. Can she embrace a side of herself she's afraid to acknowledge and defeat the soul-eater in time to meet the conditions of her bargain to return to Faerie? Or will her life – as well as those of the convention-goers – be sacrificed for greed, ambition, and a good performance review?

Or worst of all, will love tempt her to stay on Earth?

In this second installment of the Fae Files, Reine has to balance her desire to return home with the humanity she doesn't want to admit she has and the need for a love she can't accept. If you like snarky, con?icted heroines, slow-burn romance subplots, and lots of drama, then Shadows of the Heart is the book for you.

Order Shadows of the Heart to immerse yourself in a strange yet familiar new world today! Available through your favorite online retailer or from your local bookstore, which can order it for you from Ingram with the ISBN 978-1-945074-63-9

Please enjoy this excerpt from Chapter One:

"'Ello, sis," the scarred Fae prince greeted me.

"Oh, no. It's my brother," I murmured to Lawrence before forcing a smile and exclaiming, "Rhys!"

Sir Raleigh's weight disappeared from my shoulder. I knew the cat would be back, so I didn't think anything of it and instead turned my attention to my not-so-long-lost brother. If this was my mother's idea of help, I had to question whose side she was on.

Rhys moved up the hill toward us, his actions lithe and precise. He'd still not learned to move like a human. It was like watching the difference between a domesticated dog and a coyote. I made a mental note to mention that to him—he'd need to blend in.

Oh, Hades, this was a mess. But it wasn't like I could send him back.

The ground under our feet rumbled, and a shock of electric energy went through me. "*Welcome, sister and brother,*" the spirit of the hill said, more clearly than I had heard it previously. "*I am honored to host two royal Fae.*"

Interesting. Even exiles deserved honor, I guessed.

Rhys and I both bowed, which meant I had a confused gargoyle by my side. In fact, as soon as Rhys had greeted me, Lawrence's brows had drawn together and his lips had tightened in a perplexed frown. I'd have to tease him about his stoneface later. If he would accept teasing.

I'd left things in a mess earlier. He didn't know I'd been about to head back to Faerie without saying goodbye.

"How did you get here?" I asked Rhys.

Instead of answering, he raised his eyebrows and inclined his head toward Lawrence. "Who's your friend?" His nostrils flared, which I knew was for show. Rhys could tell what kind of paranormal creature someone was by reading their energy, like I could. "Your *gargoyle* friend?"

Lawrence tensed, and I squeezed his arm. "This is Doctor Lawrence Gordon. He's part of the Center for Paranormal Disease Control and Prevention. Lawrence, this is my brother Rhys."

Rhys narrowed his eyes. "You look familiar, mate. Have we met?"

"Not that I'm aware of," Lawrence replied, his voice low and tense.

Neither of them moved to shake hands. The air between them held the repellent tension of two magnets turned toward each other with the same pole.

"Well, then, we'll have to catch up later," I said to Rhys. "We have a problem."

"So I hear."

Rhys fell into step on my other side from Lawrence as we descended the mountain. I decided to skip the gondolas. It seemed a bad idea to have the two men in the same enclosed space. We'd deal with the hotel elevators later. Plus, at least at this early time of the morning, with the rising sun still making long shadows on the path, we were alone. I couldn't sense anyone else, human or paranormal. Even the ghosts had cleared out. Or maybe they'd gone dormant. Every creature, living and dead, had its own rhythm, and even a Fae wouldn't know all of them.

Or... Rhys' energy had a certain wildness to it, as he hadn't embraced life in the human realm as I had. I'd had it easier, but what had I lost touch with?

"You're lost in your thoughts, Sis," Rhys teased. "You going to tell me what we're up against?"

Before I could respond, Lawrence stopped, and I skidded to a halt beside him.

"You two go ahead," he said. "I'm not feeling up for this right now. I'll take the gondola down. Meet you at the bottom?"

"I have a car," Rhys said. "I'll take her back to the hotel since you're too weak. Go on ahead and take a nap."

Lawrence advanced, his right hand clenched into a fist, and I put a hand on his chest.

I looked over my shoulder at my brother as I held Lawrence back. "Gods, Rhys, you can't help yourself, can you? In the past few days, Lawrence has been poisoned and then attacked by the soul-eater. If he's not at his full strength, he's got reasons."

"Soul-eater, eh?" Rhys shrugged. "Fine. I take it back. Well, except for the part about bringing my sister back to the hotel." The glare he gave Lawrence would have made for a comical, *"I'm defending my sister's honor,"* moment in any other circumstances. I bit my tongue—literally—before I could tell Rhys that Lawrence and I had spent the night together. True, nothing had happened, but he didn't need to know that. He didn't need to know anything, really. In fact, the less he knew about my current life, the better.

At that moment, Sir Raleigh, my kitten-shaped grimalkin, reappeared. He had an aura of cold around him, and his fur chilled my neck as he draped himself over my shoulders.

"And where have you been, wee lad?" I asked. He didn't typically go away for so long when he disappeared. I'd have to ponder that later.

"Are you all right with this plan, Reine?" Lawrence asked. Poor guy, he did have dark circles under his eyes. He put a hand on my upper arm, and I sensed his reluctance to leave me and concern I'd disappear again.

Yeah, that had been a dick move on my part, sneaking out of his bed. Even if I didn't have a dick, I could act like one sometimes. Like my brother.

"I am. I'll see you back at the hotel. I promise."

"Right, be careful."

Half-hoping he'd reappear and ask me to come with him, I watched until he disappeared around a bend in the wooded path.

Rhys didn't wait even a minute before he asked, "A gargoyle? Really, Reine? You know—"

"Yes, I know. Traditional enemy. One helped maim you. Blah blah blah." I put my hands on my hips. "But this one is a good one."

"No such thing." He shrugged and started walking down the mountain again.

I followed him. "I guess we'll have to agree to disagree on this one." *Like most everything else.*

What was my mother up to? Most obvious explanation— this was a way to get my brother in on my chance to return home so my grandmother would make an exception to the "perfect Fae only" rule and allow him with his scarred cheek back into Faerie. Mother had always liked him better.

But then, wasn't there always another layer with the Fae? We didn't just do subplots and subterfuge—we wove in hidden motivations, loopholes, and a good measure of deception.

Whatever her motivation, I had no doubt Rhys would only get in my way.

What is Rhys up to? Order Shadows of the Heart *to continue reading today through your favorite online retailer or from your local bookstore. They can look it up with the ISBN* 978-1-945074-63-9

ABOUT THE AUTHOR

By day, clinical psychologist Cecilia Dominic helps people cure their insomnia. By night, this USA Today bestselling urban fantasy and steampunk author writes fiction that keeps her readers turning pages past bedtime. She prefers the term "versatile" to "conflicted" and has published both short story and novel-length fiction. She lives in Atlanta, Georgia, with her husband and the world's cutest cat.

ceciliadominic.com

Sign up for Cecilia's newsletter and get a free story, perhaps more than one, at the following link:

https://www.subscribepage.com/CeciliaDominicbackofbook

I hate spam and promise to keep your email safe!

ABOUT THE WOLF'S SHADOW

The Fae Files can be read on their own, but if you'd like to see where the story began, check out *The Lycanthropy Files* starting with The Wolf's Shadow.

Life as she knew it is over. At the next full moon, the real trouble begins...

Epidemiologist Joanie Fisher can't catch a break. After her lab burns to the ground, her boss simultaneously fires her and ends their affair. And though she's inherited her grandfather's multimillion-dollar estate, Joanie's shocked to discover the property comes infested with werewolves.

Confronted by a ruggedly handsome shifter who begs her to continue her cutting edge research into the wolves' physical changes, Joanie unearths a sinister conspiracy that puts her own life in danger. And as she pushes hard to find the cure, shadowy figures will do anything to make sure she never develops a treatment... including resorting to murder.

Can Joanie end the wolfish disease before she's next on a killer's list?

The Wolf's Shadow is the first book in the pulse-pounding Lycanthropy Files urban fantasy series. If you like strong female characters, insidious cabals, and medical thriller-style storytelling, then you'll love Cecilia Dominic's hair-raising genre mashup.

Order *The Wolf's Shadow* to claw your way to the truth today. Available online or from Ingram through your favorite local bookstore with the ISBN 978-1-945074-64-6

Made in the USA
Las Vegas, NV
02 October 2021

31541752R00148